Katey Lovell grew up in South Wales and now lives in Sheffield with her husband David, son Zachary and their friendly moggie Clarence. If she's not writing, she'll most likely be found with her nose in a book or reviewing on her blog *Books with Bunny*.

 @katey5678
www.facebook.com/kateylovell
www.kateylovell.blogspot.co.uk

Also by Katey Lovell

The Singalong Society for Singletons
The Café in Fir Tree Park

Short Stories
The Boy at the Beach
The Boy at the Bakery
The Boy Under the Mistletoe
The Boy with the Boxes
The Boy on the Bus
The Boy at the BBQ
The Boy with the Board
The Boy and the Bridesmaid
Three Men and a Maybe

Joe & Clara's Christmas Countdown

KATEY LOVELL

A division of HarperCollins*Publishers*
www.harpercollins.co.uk

HarperImpulse an imprint of
HarperCollinsPublishers
The News Building
1 London Bridge Street
London SE1 9GF

www.harpercollins.co.uk

This paperback edition 2017

First published in Great Britain in ebook
format by HarperCollinsPublishers 2017

A catalogue record for this book
is available from the British Library

ISBN: 9780008260644

Set in Birka by Palimpsest Book Production Limited,
Falkirk, Stirlingshire

Printed and bound in Great Britain

For Zachary. Thank you for brightening my world.

Prologue

Clara

The beauty of a signature scent is also its danger. Everyone associates it with you. And Bella's overbearing perfume had clung to Dean's clothes the way a baby being left for the first time clings desperately to its mother.

Clara had been suspicious for months, but her stomach still churned as she told the tale. It felt like history repeating itself. 'When I confronted him about it he didn't lie. I don't know if that's a good thing or not. No one wants to be lied to, but no one wants to feel replaceable either, do they?'

'He's a scumbag,' Deirdre replied. 'A complete and utter scumbag. Cheating on you with his masseuse? It's such a cliché. Especially after you introduced them.' She shook her head disapprovingly. 'I said it all along, he's got no

3

class, that one.'

'Physio,' Clara corrected absentmindedly, before finding herself adding, 'He's not a bad person'. Why she was defending Dean to her boss when she'd spent the previous night alternating between hurling abuse at him and crying for the relationship they'd once had, she couldn't say. Things hadn't been perfect for a long time – Dean had seemed distant, and Clara herself had been exhausted, carrying the pressures of work home with her – but why Bella? Clara couldn't see the attraction.

'He sure as hell isn't a good one. He told you he was having a sports massage when all the time he was having a shag! It's shameless. You should sell your story to the press. I can see the headline now, "Rovers player in Physio Romp". I'm sure there'd be some money in it for you,' she added, with a worldly-wise nod of her head.

If it wasn't so tragic, Clara would have laughed. 'I don't think so. A former Man United youth teamer, who now plays semi-professionally for the local team? There's no story in that.'

Deirdre was having none of it. 'There's always the women's magazines. They'd be all over this. There was a double-page spread in one about a woman who wanted to marry her cat. Her cat! Your story busts that crap right out of the water.'

'Why did you read it if it was crap?' Clara asked, tongue firmly in her cheek. She knew full well how much Deirdre loved the weekly women's magazines. She had a stash of them secretly shoved in her desk drawer.

'I was at the hairdresser's this morning,' she replied haughtily, patting her softly permed locks to plump up the fresh waves. 'It was practically thrust into my hands as I was sat under the lamps.'

'Your hair looks good,' Clara observed, noticing her boss's hair had also turned a soft shade of ash blonde rather than its usual salt-and-pepper flecks.

'It does, doesn't it?' Deirdre smiled with pride. 'Hey, maybe you should go for a new look too. Reinvent yourself. It might help you get over Dean.'

'It'll take more than a new hairdo to do that. I'm beginning to think humans aren't cut out for monogamy. I should have learned from Mum's mistakes.'

'Not all men are dirty dogs.'

'Dean is, though. And my dad was too.' An acrid taste filled Clara's mouth.

'I still can't believe Dean actually thought he'd get away with cheating on you right under your nose.'

'The worst part is knowing I'm going to have to see her again. She helps our next-door neighbour with the exercises for her arthritis. Her and her perfume will be getting right up my nose.'

Deirdre laughed. 'Good one. Nice to see you've not lost your sense of humour.'

'If I didn't laugh, I'd cry.'

'And you're sure you'll be up to speaking in front of everyone tonight?'

Clara hoped so – the kids at the youth club had been talking about the talent show for weeks. They'd been diligently practising their dance routines and comedy sketches. One ambitious twelve-year-old had been keen to juggle knives whilst riding his unicycle until Deirdre had put a stop to it on health and safety grounds. He was reluctantly settling for using bean bags instead of blades.

'Yep, I've set the chairs out for the audience and the microphone's rigged up. I've taken the iPod dock through for any acts that need music and prepared a welcome speech for the parents. Oh, and I've got a bucket ready for collecting donations. Hopefully it'll get people putting their hands in their pockets.'

'As long as they take them out again with a fistful of notes,' Deirdre said with a sigh. 'The waiting list keeps on growing. What annoys me the most is that we've got the space, but can't take any more kids on unless we employ more staff. Fat chance of that, looking at the finances.'

'It's tough times for everyone,' Clara pointed out.

'Even the big charities are struggling. But things will work out in the end. They always do.'

'Are you talking about the staffing issue or are you back to talking about relationships?'

'Staff,' Clara said firmly.

Deirdre tutted. 'It's such a shame. A lovely girl like you shouldn't be sat on the shelf.'

'I'm twenty-seven and split up with my fiancé yesterday. That's hardly on the shelf.'

'Still, you don't want to be on your own too long,' Deirdre replied. 'I'm sure we can find you a nice young man who treats you well and keeps his pants on around other women.'

'Deirdre!'

A cheeky glint sparkled in the older woman's eyes. 'Who knows, maybe there'll be someone at the talent show to put a spring in your step.'

'Don't start,' Clara warned. 'I don't need a man.'

'Oh, I know you don't *need* one,' Deirdre replied. 'But everyone enjoys a good seeing to once in a while, don't they?'

Clara wasn't sure how to reply to that. Instead, she nodded, smiled and made her way to the youth club's main hall. She'd fiddle with the speakers again, double check they were set up properly. She'd go and unblock the sink in the boy's loos that was forever emitting an eggy odour. Anything rather than stay here, because she sure to goodness didn't want to listen to her boss discussing the ins and outs, quite literally, of her sex life.

* * *

Clara peeped from behind the red velvet curtain that flanked the stage.

There was quite a crowd gathering in the hall. The additional emergency chairs that were usually stacked high in the broom cupboard and only brought out on rare occasions had been filled, and it looked as though it was standing room only at the back.

Her stomach fluttered at the prospect of welcoming the parents. Despite her apparent confident demeanour, Clara had never been a natural when it came to public speaking. She put it down to the time she fluffed her line in the nativity play at infant school. Her mum had tried to assure her that no one had noticed, but Clara hadn't believed her then and she certainly didn't believe her now. She'd been dressed head to toe in white, with cotton-wool balls sewn over the t-shirt to make it obvious to everyone she was a sheep, yet when it reached her turn to take centre stage, Clara had panicked. The only thing she'd managed to say was 'moo'. A mooing sheep. No wonder everyone had laughed.

But there'd be no mistakes like that tonight; Clara had come prepared. She'd written notes on crisp white index cards to ensure she remained sharp and to the point.

Gulping down her nerves, she smoothed her hands over the rough fabric of her denim mini dress and stepped out onto the stage.

'Good evening everyone, and welcome to The Club on the Corner's annual talent show. This never fails to be anything other than a brilliant evening, where we get the opportunity to celebrate the talents of our wonderful members, so please whoop, holler, clap and cheer to show them your support.' Clara paused as she looked out into the sea of faces, before quickly refocusing on her cards. She didn't want to be thrown off her stride. 'However, as many of you know, this is one of our main fundraising events of the year. We are committed to keeping our subs at the lowest possible level to ensure as many children and young people as possible can access all that we offer. However, demand is currently so high that although we have the space to accommodate new members, we don't have the staff to supervise them. Our hope is that your donations will make a real difference, to both the club and the community as a whole, by enabling us to employ an additional member of staff. We've always made it our mission to work closely with other local groups, particularly the food bank and the hospital, as well as supporting local events such as the church summer fete and Christmas lantern march. Please dig deep so that the club you know and love can continue to thrive.'

A lump lodged in Clara's throat. This place meant so much to so many, not least Deirdre. The club was her boss's baby, the children who attended the closest she had to a family of her own. And not only the children – she was like a second mother to Clara too, never anything less than protective, supporting and mildly embarrassing.

'But now, without further ado, I'd like to introduce our first act. Tonight Cally, Tiffany, Phoebe and Simone are The Club on the Corner's cheerleading squad. Let's give them a big round of applause!'

Clara initiated the clapping as the girls bounded on to the stage, waving fluffy red and white pompoms high over their heads. They looked full of pep and vim, and the audience clapped along to the rhythm of the cheesy music, encouraged by the energetic teens.

The temperamental sound system was working. That was a weight off Clara's shoulders.

The night continued with a varied programme of acts. There were some fabulous dance routines show-cased, some less than hilarious comedy acts and a surprisingly brilliant solo rendition of 'Amazing Grace' by a normally gobby girl called Shannon. There hadn't been a dry eye in the house.

But it was Ted's beautiful acoustic guitar-playing that ended up winning fair and square. The concentration etched on his face as he moved his fingers into the correct chord positions on the fretboard was endearing, and his delight when he made it to the end of the performance earned him the loudest cheer of all.

'Nights like this make it worthwhile.' Deirdre shook her collection bucket loudly as the crowds dispersed, making sure everyone was clear that a donation was expected. The families she knew best didn't dare throw in loose change, instead pulling crinkled notes out of their wallets and back pockets. They knew that to give any less would be to face Deirdre's wrath. It wasn't worth the hassle. Far easier to cough up their hard-earned cash instead. 'People want the club to succeed.'

'We've got something special,' Clara agreed. 'There's not enough in here to get close to what we'd need to employ a new member of staff, though, even in the short-term,' she added glumly, looking at the smattering of money in the bottom of her bucket.

'There's got to be another way,' Deirdre said. 'It's a shame Lynsey isn't able to help out as often since she had the baby. An extra pair of hands made all the difference. Maybe we could ask about volunteers again? Some of the parents might help out if we can get a rota going.'

'We didn't get any interest last time,' Clara reminded her. She was aware of coming across as the queen of doom and gloom, but it was true. 'Part of the reason they like the kids coming here is so they get a bit of peace and quiet. They're not likely to want to give up their time to spend it somewhere as loud and crazy as this.'

'You never know,' Deirdre said optimistically, as a generous grandfather dropped a twenty-pound note into her collection bucket. 'We might fall lucky and find someone willing to give up a few hours for the cause.'

Simone, one of the enthusiastic cheerleading troupe who also happened to be the smiliest sixteen-year-old Clara had ever seen, appeared as though from nowhere, her tight, dark curls bobbing in bunches either side of her head.

'Thank you for organising the talent show,' she gushed. 'It was fun, even though we didn't win.'

'Yeah, thanks Deirdre. Thanks Clara,' added Tiffany, before chewing on her gum and blowing a large pink bubble. She was always chewing and popping, chewing and popping. Clara was amazed she'd gone without gum long enough to complete the cheerleading routine.

Tiff could have been subtly chewing the whole time, she supposed, even though she most definitely hadn't been popping. She wouldn't mention that possibility to Deirdre, though. She was, quite rightly, big on following health and safety regulations to the letter.

'You're welcome,' Deirdre said. 'And I loved that routine. Those high kicks were brilliant, and when you ended with the splits it took me right back to my youth.'

'You used to be able to do the splits?' Tiff gawped, then chewed, then popped.

'I was quite the gymnast back in the day,' Deirdre said, a wistful smile passing over her face. 'Splits, cartwheels, backflips – I could do the lot. I'd have given Olga Korbut a run for her money.'

The girls looked back at her in disbelief. Deirdre looked about as far from a gymnast as you could get, with her bulky build and the crutch she used whenever she had to stand for any length of time propping her up. Her dodgy knee had been giving her gip recently. Probably all those years of acrobatics finally catching up with her, Clara thought with a smile.

'I've not always been this old, you know,' Deirdre added.

'And here was I thinking you were born old,' Clara teased.

'Ha-ha,' Deirdre replied with a roll of her eyes. 'Very

funny.' She turned her attention back to Simone. 'Are your parents still here?'

'They're in the kitchen, washing the pots,' Simone explained. 'We thought it'd save you two a job.'

'Oh, that's so kind!' Clara exclaimed. She didn't add she was pleased that she might get home in time to watch the season finale of the drama she'd been glued to for the past month. It started at ten, and with a bit of luck, and the help of the families chipping in, she'd be back, showered and in her pyjamas by then. 'I'll grab a tea towel and start drying, if you're alright hanging around here, Deirdre? You're better at asking people for money than I am.'

She peered into Deirdre's bucket, which held a healthy layer of notes with a shimmer of pound coins twinkling through the gaps. Clara's bucket contained mainly copper and silver, where people had felt obliged to give something – anything – so pulled out whatever was lurking in their coat pockets. The fluff balls and sticky sweet wrappers mingled in with the coins attested to that.

'You go and give them a hand,' Deirdre said. 'I'll finish off here, and if Tiffany and Simone help me stack the chairs we'll all get home sooner. It takes me a bit longer these days,' she added, gesturing to the crutch. 'Is that alright with you, girls?'

Simone set straight to it, putting one brown chair on top of the other and moving them to the corner of the room when they were stacked five high. Tiff was less enthusiastic, but begrudgingly assisted her friend.

'Thanks, girls,' Clara called from the kitchen as she grabbed a striped tea towel from the towel rail and started drying the mugs. They hadn't been rinsed properly – bubbly suds clouding their glossy surfaces – but Clara was so grateful for the help that she didn't feel she could complain. Simone's family hadn't wasted any time. The washing up was all but done.

'Thanks, everyone,' Clara said, passing the dried mugs to Simone's mum to put away in the cupboard. 'It makes things much easier for me and Deirdre if people lend a hand now and again.'

'I'll bet,' Simone's dad replied. He was the local vicar and a familiar face in the community. The strip-lighting was reflected off his shaved head as he grinned the same infectious grin as his daughter. 'Don't think the hard work you two put into this place goes unnoticed. We're very grateful for everything you do for these kids.'

'It's worth it to see everyone enjoying themselves.' Clara truly believed that, and loved being able to boost the confidence of the club members. There was a special atmosphere to the old place on showcase night, an almost palpable buzz of joy thronging through the building. 'Plus, the kids are great, and it's them we do it for.'

'When I used to come here there was nowhere else for teenagers to go at this end of town,' Simone's brother added. 'At least now there's the indoor skate park, and the ice rink's not bad since it's been refurbished.'

'They're expensive, though,' Clara pointed out. She'd been shocked at the cost of the tickets on a recent cinema trip with Deirdre, and that was before she'd splashed out on popcorn (sweet, naturally) and a large diet coke. By the time she was done she'd spent almost a day's wages. 'Not all the families around here can afford it. At least here they only have to find the money for subs once a term. Plus, some of the kids just want somewhere to hang around away from their parents.'

'I suppose that's what I did when I was a member. Me and my mates used to spend all our money in the tuck shop and then talk about music for a few hours in between stuffing our faces with strawberry laces.'

'Strawberry laces. Good choice.'

'We'd have competitions to see who could cram the most into their mouths,' he laughed. 'I managed forty-eight once.'

'Wow. You must have a really big mouth.' Clara clamped her lips together in embarrassment as she realised how insulting that sounded. 'I didn't mean any offence ...'

'None taken,' he said with a shrug as he plunged the last mug into the soapy water and rubbed it with a battered scourer. 'There,' he proclaimed, placing the mug on the draining board. Suds slithered down its side. 'We're done.'

'Thank you,' Clara said genuinely. 'You've been a great help, all of you. I'll finish off here, though, if you want to get home. It's getting late.'

The clock read half-past nine. She'd have to get a wiggle on if she was going to make it back home in time for her programme.

'If you're sure?' Simone's mum replied, reaching for her large straw sunhat. She was well presented, as though dressed for an event. Mind you, she always looked smart. Part of the role of being a vicar's wife, Clara supposed.

'Absolutely. There's not much to do now, you've done most of it already. You go,' she smiled. 'And thanks again.'

'It was a brilliant evening,' the vicar added. 'A real celebration of everyone's talents. I'm glad I came.'

'It was fun,' Simone's brother said. 'I thought the girl who did *Riverdance* should have won, though. She was amazing.'

'She was great, wasn't she? She's got dreams of dancing on the stage one day. She'll probably make it too, she's a hard worker.'

'You are too, by the look of it,' he said, sliding into his leather jacket.

'Well, there's no point doing anything half-heartedly. My work's important to me.'

'It shows. It's nice to finally meet you, Clara. Simone talks about you all the time at home. And Deirdre too, of course.'

'Nice to meet you too ...'

Clara paused, realising she didn't know his name.

'Joe,' he said, extending his hand to invite a handshake. 'Joe Smith.'

The Countdown

Clara

Clara had always loved everything about Christmas, and although Advent hadn't yet started she was fully prepared for the season. She'd retrieved her collection of knitted Christmas jumpers from the back of her wardrobe (they were now hanging prominently from the picture rail in her bedroom so she could admire them in all their hideously gaudy beauty), and already done the majority of her shopping. Her cards were written and stamped, ready to go into the post box at the end of the road on the first day of December. And now she was trying to persuade Deirdre to let her decorate the youth club with spangly decorations galore.

'There's no way you're putting them up today, Clara. Not a chance. It's still November!' Deirdre shook her head with such vigour that her monstrous clip-on

21

earrings threatened to fly off. 'The ones at home don't go up until at least the middle of the month. If they were up any earlier I'd get bored. I'm gagging to take them down by Boxing Day as it is.'

'Spoilsport,' Clara pouted.

'You're not going to change my mind. It's November. It's too early.'

Clara sighed, ready to admit defeat. It was the same every year – she'd be itching to get the club covered in tinsel and glitter whilst Deirdre would be putting the Christmas dampeners on.

'I've been patient. The supermarkets have had their decorations up since the day after Hallowe'en.'

'Bully for the supermarkets!' Deirdre blustered. 'Go and work for them if you're so desperate to have your bloody baubles up!'

Clara laughed. 'You don't mean that. We're struggling enough as it is with the two of us running this place. You'd have no chance if you were doing it single-handedly.'

'Ah, but that's where you're wrong,' Deirdre replied, a cryptic smirk curling at the corners of her lips. 'I wouldn't be doing it alone. My new volunteer would be able to help me out.'

Clara's ears pricked up. 'New volunteer? You mean someone's actually been daft enough to sign up to spend their free time in this madhouse?'

'Yes, and, what's more, I think he'll be great with the kids.'

'He?'

'Yes, he. He's young and enthusiastic and it'll be good for the boys to have a male role model. I know it's all about equality these days, but I switch off the minute Jordan starts talking about football. What do I know about whether United would be better moving their right back into central defence or whatever it was he was rambling on about last night? This way he can chew someone else's ear off about it rather than mine. Someone who might be able to make a more incisive comment than "Hmm, I don't know".'

'Are you going to tell me who this saviour is or are you going to sit there teasing me all night?'

Deirdre jokingly tapped the side of her nose with her index finger. 'I could tell you, but it's far more fun to keep you guessing.'

'You're so mean!' Clara hated being left in the dark over anything, especially when it came to the youth club. Deirdre might be the manager, but Clara had taken on more and more responsibility over the years until they were pretty much equals. Everything was a team effort, from budgeting, to choosing which fundraising events to run and which local groups to work in partnership with. Clara couldn't remember the last time Deirdre had made a decision without consulting her first. 'So you're not even going to give me a clue?'

Deirdre shook her head once more. 'Nope. This one's for me to know and you to find out.'

'Meanie.'

'You love me really. And you'll love me even more when you find out who our new volunteer is. I've got a good feeling about the two of you.'

Clara's face dropped. Deirdre and her meddling.

'If I've told you once, I've told you a thousand times. I'm not looking for a man. They're smelly and lazy and slob about on the settee with their hands shoved down their pants.' Clara remembered the time she'd called Dean out on that, because she'd been sick of the sight of him with his hands in his trousers. He'd insisted he wasn't playing with himself but she'd had her doubts. The excuse that his hands were cold didn't wash with her. Hadn't he heard of pockets? 'Not to mention they have a habit of sleeping around.'

Bitterness filled her mouth. She'd got past the sadness of their relationship ending, but she couldn't get past the anger at being lied to and cheated on. It took a lot for her to trust someone. Watching her mum's confidence dwindle away to nothing after her dad's infidelity had been painful. Dean screwing around behind her back had only reaffirmed her distrust.

'Not all of them, and not this one. This one's a good one.'

'I thought Dean was a good one, once upon a time,' Clara grumbled in retort. 'If there are good ones out there, why have you never got married, eh? Answer me that.'

'I'm married to this place, remember. The club, the kids – they're all the family I need.'

'Well, maybe that's enough for me, too,' she answered defiantly. 'Maybe I'll be married to this place.'

Deirdre waggled her finger in front of her face, wearing a stern expression no one in their right mind would argue with. 'I don't think so, Clara. I think you need to trust me for once.'

'I always trust you. Except when it comes to your decisions of when to put the Christmas decorations up, because when it comes to that you're just downright wrong.'

'The decorations can go up tomorrow. December the first. Which is still too early, but at least it'll tie in nicely with the lantern parade. Plus Joe will be around then, so you can do it together.'

'Joe? Simone's brother Joe?'

Deirdre smacked the heel of her hand into her forehead. 'I can't believe I let that one slip. Me and my big mouth! But yes, he's our new volunteer. Be nice to him, Clara. I've known Joe since he was eleven years old and he had lines shaved into his eyebrows like he was some sort of gangster. He was trying to be tough, but he's was a softie then and he's a softie now.'

She looked dreamy, and Clara suspected her boss was imagining Clara in a puffy meringue-like dress and Joe in a jet-black top hat and tails. Typical Deirdre, never one to let reality get in the way of a good story.

'Don't go getting any ideas, Deirdre. I barely know the guy.'

'But you'll get to know him,' Deirdre reasoned. 'Don't rule anything out yet, that's all I'm asking.'

Clara didn't have the energy to argue. In ten minutes' time they'd be opening the doors and the stream of excitable kids would flood into the hall ready to spend the next two hours wreaking havoc.

'If I can't have fairy lights, I'm going to need caffeine,' she grumbled, heading towards the kitchenette.

'Clara?' Deirdre called after her.

'Yeah?'

'If you believe in the magic of Christmas, you can surely believe in the magic of love too.'

Clara rolled her eyes. Christmas was one thing. Love was something else altogether.

Joe

Joe's stomach fizzed as The Club on the Corner came into view. He couldn't recall the last time he'd felt this excited.

He'd been at a low ebb for such a long time. Not officially depressed – nothing that a doctor would prescribe medication for – but weighed down by a lethargy that had taken away his usual bounce. 'It's a perfectly normal part of the grieving process' the GP had said when Joe had finally given in to his mum's desperate pleas to seek help. 'Survivor guilt.' It was supposed to be reassuring, but he'd left the surgery more defeated and deflated than ever.

Joe had tried to keep moving forward and not to dwell on events of the past, but sometimes everything was so damn overwhelming. When guilt-induced anxiety had reduced him to tears at work last Christmas as he'd unpacked a delivery of poinsettias, he'd taken it as a sign and halved his hours at the hardware store. When spring brought longer and lighter days he'd felt a little stronger, but by then he'd decided the freedom of part-time hours suited him. He had money saved, and it wasn't as though he'd been a big spender to start with. He had plenty of clothes. He didn't smoke and although he enjoyed a beer, he didn't often drink to excess. Socialising took place mainly at his flat or at the home of his friends, usually Billy and Emma's, since the arrival of baby Roman earlier in the year. Other than rent, bills and food, Joe didn't have any regular outgoings, and the only real extravagance – annual trips to Jamaica to see his maternal grandparents – were paid for by his parents. He lived a simple life, and it worked for him.

But after taking a step back for the best part of a year, Joe was excited at the prospect of volunteering. He had a soft spot for The Club on the Corner, where he'd spent so much time during his most formative years.

If those walls could talk they could tell a story or two about Joe Smith. They'd seen his first kiss, a clumsy snog with a petite girl with a penchant for heavy eyeliner. They'd watched on as he'd broken his arm when he was fooling about breakdancing with Billy and a guy called Simon who he hadn't seen in years. He wondered if the graffiti Billy had dared him to scrawl one reckless Friday night was still on the wall in the games room. He'd been petrified of getting caught, because no one wanted to get on the wrong side of Deirdre; so although he'd accepted the challenge he'd written his name in the tiniest writing he could, discreetly hidden in a gap between a plug socket and a skirting board. That room had also been where he'd first met Michelle, her skills at eight-ball pool enough to make every boy in the place fall for her. When she'd chosen Joe from the many admirers he'd been unable to believe his luck. The Club on the Corner ... it had actually changed his life.

From the outside the building looked much the same as ever. Two big wooden doors painted in a vile pea-green shade detracted from the grandeur of the Victorian architecture. The paint was tired and peeling away near the hinges, and Joe vowed to make time to give it a sanding down and a fresh coat if Deirdre would allow him. It wouldn't take much to tart it up and make it look more inviting.

The lead window panes were beautiful, very much of the era, and the arch above the doorway stated 'Vestry Hall', a nod to the building's original use as a more general meeting place. The green-and-cream sign advertising the youth club was attached to the terracotta brickwork, along with a handwritten laminated notice stating 'Waiting List Now in Operation'. Joe hoped his volunteering would give a few more kids the opportunity to join up.

The smell in the large entrance hallway transported him back in time. It was dusty, like an antiques showroom. Although Deirdre had always kept the place spick and span, the air was heavy with history and secrets.

'Joe!' Deirdre exclaimed, wrapping her arms so tightly around him that he caught his breath. 'It's good to see you.' Her eyes twinkled mischievously. 'I wasn't sure if you'd turn up. Thought you might have chickened out.'

'Ah, it can't be that bad. I know what it's like, remember? I spent many a happy night here.'

Deirdre shook her head. 'It's all different these days, Joe. The kids grow up so fast. And the technology they've got! It was bad enough when you and Billy got that camera phone, remember? You were taking pictures of everyone and everything, but the photos were all grainy. Now they film each other and put it online for the world to see. They've got the Internet at their fingertips. It's all gone too far, if you ask me.'

'It's a different age,' Joe agreed. 'The iPhone Simone's got is better than mine. But all her friends have got them. They don't know any different.'

'We had none of this new-fangled stuff back in my day,' Deirdre poo-pooed. 'And we all turned out alright.'

A glint appeared in Joe's eyes as he took the bait. 'That's debatable.'

'You cheeky so-and-so! It's a good job I like you. I wouldn't let any Tom, Dick or Harry get away with that.'

Clara appeared from the kitchen, carrying a mug in each hand.

'Oh, I'm sorry,' she said. 'I'd have made you a drink if I'd known you were here. I didn't hear the door go. I can always brew up if you want one, there's water in the kettle still, freshly boiled.'

'Clara.' Deirdre gave a stern look over the top of her steel-rimmed glasses. 'You've met Joe before, haven't you? Simone's brother. He used to be a member here so I know him well. He's a good lad, but you'll have to keep your eye on him. He used to be one for the ladies when he was a teenager.'

Joe held his hands up in defence. 'I could have you for slander, Deirdre Whitehall. I only had two girlfriends in the whole seven years I was a member at The Club on the Corner.'

'You must have got serious young,' Clara interjected. 'I've only had one relationship I'd class as serious.'

'And the less said about that the better,' Deirdre added pointedly, before turning to Joe with a grimace. 'Stupid bugger was sleeping with his masseuse, can you believe?'

'He must have been an idiot,' Joe replied, rubbing the heel of his hand against the chocolate- brown skin of his forehead. He could feel the start of a stress head-ache coming on. Probably from nerves. He really hoped it wouldn't develop into a full-blown migraine.

'He was,' Clara replied shortly. 'Didn't realise it at the time, though, obviously.'

'You had a lucky escape,' Deirdre said. 'Imagine if you'd married him!'

Clara shuddered, then pulled her thick black woollen cardigan more tightly across her chest. 'It doesn't bear thinking about.'

'They were engaged, you know,' Deirdre continued, wrinkling her nose in obvious distaste. 'But I always had a bad feeling about him. He thought he was better than Clara, because he was a local star. I told him on more than one occasion that Clara's the star around here. I must have had an angel watching over me the day she came for her interview.'

Clara tutted and her cheeks flushed pink. It made her appear vulnerable.

'I don't know about that,' she replied modestly, before visibly perking up. Her shoulders sprang back, her eyes brightened. 'But ... it's December the first today, and you know what that means.'

Deirdre rolled her eyes theatrically, while Joe watched on with interest.

'Hand over the keys to the store cupboard. It's time to unleash the decorations.' Clara waggled her eyebrows excitedly before doing a dance of delight on the spot. 'You can't put it off any longer, it's well and truly time to count down to Christmas.' She grinned enthusiastically in Joe's direction and Joe forced an uncomfortable smile. So Clara was a Christmas junkie. 'Don't you just love Christmas!' she enthused, clapping her hands together.

Joe didn't have the guts to tell the truth – that one of the reasons he'd volunteered at the youth club in the first place was to *avoid* all the preparations. He'd hoped to lose himself in endless games of table tennis and conversations about which teams had a chance in the FA Cup this season. Anything, so long as it didn't involve Christmas. Since Michelle's death, the festive season had never been the same.

'Here you go,' said Deirdre, handing Clara a long silver key attached to a small red key fob. 'But don't go overboard,' she warned. 'Leave Santa's grotto to the Trafford Centre.'

'Don't worry, Deirdre. You can rely on me.'

'When it comes to Christmas, she doesn't know when to stop,' she said with a laugh. 'You're not an elf in disguise, are you Joe?'

'Far from it.' He was aware his voice was short – clipped – so in a vain attempt to lighten the mood he added, 'Green's never been my colour.'

Clara laughed. 'I'll get you in the Christmas spirit soon enough. Come on, let's get that box down. If we work fast we'll have the whole place dressed before the kids arrive.'

She turned on her heels, beckoning for Joe to follow on.

Deirdre gave a little wave before saying, 'You'd better get a move on. Christmas is a serious business to Clara. Oh, and good luck!'

Joe smiled weakly as he followed Clara, who was enthusiastically humming 'Jingle Bells', all the while silently thinking he might need all the luck he could get.

* * *

By the time the majority of the main hall had been decorated, plastic pine needles from the artificial tree that stood proudly on the stage were coating the well-trodden parquet flooring and Joe had clumps of silver glitter clinging to the tips of his fingers. Long metallic decorations were strung from the beams overhead, reminding him of the ones his parents had had in his childhood, and thick swaths of scarlet tinsel curled around the creamy-white pillars, so they resembled barber's poles.

'Just the lights to test now,' Clara said, crossing her fingers in front of her. 'They should be fine, they were new last year.' Then she frowned and added, 'But have you got a torch feature on your phone?'

Joe nodded. 'Yeah, I think so.'

'Good. Get it out and set up ready, just in case.'

'In case what?'

'In case the lights trip the electrics. That's what happened last year. The whole place went black and I could hear Deirdre shouting but couldn't see where she was. It was like something from a film.'

'And Deirdre doesn't like to relinquish control of anything,' Joe smiled.

'Tell me about it,' Clara replied, unravelling the tangled wires. 'She's not always the easiest person to be around.'

'But you like working here? I mean, I suppose you must or you'd have got a different job.'

'I love it,' she said, her eyes bright. 'It's the kids that make it special, but the whole place has a positive vibe that makes it so much easier to come to work. I joke about Deirdre, but she's a friend as well as a boss. I never understand when people complain about their job, because I've always loved coming here. I guess I'm lucky.'

'Sounds better than my job.' Joe thought of how he'd spent the morning stock-taking. He'd had one customer, a pensioner looking for polyfilla. That had been the extent of his social contact – one customer in a four-hour shift. And although he'd like to think he'd made a difference, Joe couldn't, hand on heart, say he had.

'What's it you do?'

'I work at a hardware shop at the far end of the Northern Quarter. It's pretty dull, most of the time.' He shrugged his diffidence. 'I'm only there part time these days, though. Hard to believe I used to do forty hours a week. Most of the time I was twiddling my thumbs.'

'Fancied a change of scene?' she smiled, and Joe's stomach twisted. It was an innocent enough question, but he didn't want to talk about the reasons behind the changes in his lifestyle.

'Something like that.'

'Well, there's not much time for thumb-twiddling here,' she warned, plugging in the lights. 'We'll be glad of the extra body. In the past we've tried to get people to help out but no one's volunteered.'

'I know what a difference this place makes to the kids,' Joe said, 'and I've got the time to give, so it makes sense to help out.'

'Well, we really appreciate it. Now ... the moment of truth.'

Clara flicked the switch and the lights pinged on, the multi-coloured bulbs twinkling perfectly against the hardwood flooring.

'At least they didn't trip this year,' Joe said.

'It's a relief,' Clara agreed. 'Now we need to get them around the tree before we open the door. In five minutes' time it'll be bedlam in here.'

Joe pushed himself up off the floor, scooping up the string of lights. 'Let's get cracking, then.'

'Thank you so much for helping.' An enormous beam of gratitude took over Clara's face. 'Don't you just love Christmas?'

'I used to,' he muttered under his breath.

Clara didn't reply and Joe was unsure whether she'd heard him or not. He suspected he'd been drowned out by strains of Wham's 'Last Christmas', which was playing over the sound system.

And although he wouldn't admit it out loud, Clara's enthusiasm was infectious. Joe *was* beginning to feel just a little bit of the festive spirit.

*   *   *

'Calm down,' Deirdre warned, holding out her crutch to funnel the rush of kids spilling out of the building onto the street. 'There's no need to run.'

'Oh, I think you'll find there is,' Clara replied. 'Don't you know that Christmas is coming?'

'In three and a half weeks!' Deirdre said in an exasperated tone.

'Ah, come on. It's the night of the lantern parade and light switch-on, they're bound to be excited.' Clara grinned. 'I'm pretty excited myself.'

'Really?' Joe said. 'I'd never have guessed you liked Christmas ...'

'Everyone likes Christmas, though, don't they? Except for Mrs Scrooge over there,' she added as an afterthought. 'There are so many happy memories tied up with the season. It's not only the lights and the presents and overdosing on rich foods; it reminds me of happy times with my mum and grandparents. We lived with them for a while, and they always made a big deal out of Christmas. All the rules would go out of the window for December, and no one minded. I'd laze around in new pyjamas watching films with my gran, then we'd settle down together around the open fire and play board games way past my bedtime. Happy times.'

Joe braved a smile, despite Christmas bringing very different memories to his mind than it brought to

Clara's. There had been happy times, and lots of them, but they were now tainted by the special person he'd shared them with being so cruelly snatched away.

'Do you still do that?'

'Spend the day in my pyjamas?' Clara laughed. 'Mostly, if I can get away with it.'

'I meant, do you still spend Christmas with your grandparents?'

Her face hardened. 'Not any more.'

'Oh,' he said awkwardly, feeling terrible. He, of all people, knew that losing someone cut deep. He should never have pried, it wasn't his place. 'I'm sorry. I'm really lucky to still have all four of my grandparents ...'

'They haven't died!' Deirdre replied, guffawing, as though the suggestion was absurd.

'They sold up when they retired,' Clara explained, throwing a withering look in Deirdre's direction. The older lady's shoulders were still shaking through laughing so violently. 'They wanted to have more adventures while they're still fit enough, so they put everything in storage and have been travelling ever since. They're in South America at the moment. They climbed Machu Picchu last month.'

'Wow.' Joe was seriously impressed. 'Whereas my Grandma Smith thinks her summer coach trip to Chester is a big adventure.'

Clara shrugged. 'Anything can be an adventure, depending on how you look at it.'

Joe mulled the words of wisdom over as everyone ground to a halt outside the church hall, where a make-shift stage bedecked with fairy lights and something Joe assumed was an approximation of Santa's sleigh was lit up by a spotlight. In reality it was little more than a mess of scarlet crêpe paper and cotton-wool rolls, and Joe dreaded to think what'd happen if it rained. It'd be a disaster. Crêpe paper and cotton-wool carnage.

The effect of so many lanterns en masse was nothing short of spectacular, the flickering flames (or in the cases of the youth-club kids battery-operated tea lights – Deirdre had made it clear she and Clara were taking no chances when it came to naked flames) giving the evening sky a warm amber glow. There was a nip in the air, which was to be expected now they were in December, and Joe was glad of his warm scarf and beanie hat. The hat in particular – a shaved head might suit the shape of his angular face, but it wasn't doing any favours now the temperature was dipping to arctic levels.

There was a moment of hush as the local MP stood to address the crowd. She was a small lady, her petite frame drowning underneath a long, beige raincoat, which couldn't have been doing much to conserve her body heat, but her voice was loud. She completely bypassed the waiting microphone, instead opting to increase her natural volume.

'Good evening everyone, and welcome to our annual lantern parade and Christmas light switch-on. It's fantastic that so many of you have braved the cold to come and support us in what has become a bit of a tradition in these parts.' She rubbed her hands together. Joe couldn't tell if it was with excitement or for warmth. 'I'm delighted to have a very special guest turn on the lights for us this year, and what's more, the council have invested in some new decorations to complement those from previous displays.'

'Maybe more than half of them will actually work,' Deirdre said, in a voice probably meant to be conspiratorial but which earned her a few glares from loyal locals. 'What?' she fired back. 'It's the truth. Last year they were a mess.'

'I'm more interested in the special guest,' Joe said, keen to change the subject.

'Oh, it'll be Santa flicking the switch,' Clara replied. Her cheeks were rosy, a combination of the biting cold and the flattering half-light. 'He does it every year.'

Joe couldn't hide his disappointment. 'That's a letdown. I was expecting Hollywood royalty the way she was going on.'

'It's hardly the Blackpool Illuminations. No big-name celebrity would turn up here and do it for nothing. The only media coverage they'd get would be via the free paper.'

As though on cue, an eager photographer pointed a lens in Clara's direction.

'And you,' he said, physically pushing Joe closer to Clara in a bid to fit them both in the frame. 'That's a good one,' he said dully as he took the photograph. 'Look out for it on Thursday when the new edition comes out.'

'We will,' Joe said politely, as Clara rose onto her tiptoes to try and get a better view of the stage.

The politician was building up to a climax now as she encouraged everyone to join in with a rendition of Mariah Carey's 'All I Want for Christmas is You'. Her cringey dancing involved stepping from side to side like a particularly uncoordinated uncle at a wedding, and she didn't seem to realise that people were laughing at her on-stage antics rather than singing along to the tinny backing track.

As the music came to a close everyone cheered (and jeered) as she motioned for quiet. 'And now, without further ado, it's time to welcome our special guest. Here he is ...'

'It's "Santa",' Clara whispered, making air quotes with

her fingers. 'I'll put money on it.'

'... Rovers star striker, Dean Harford!'

Dean strolled onto the stage with a swagger – well, as much swagger as anyone could manage wearing an enormous puffa jacket. He pumped his hands over his head in a 'raise the roof' motion and the predominantly teenage crowd whooped their approval.

Joe lifted his hands above his head and joined in with the clapping, swept away on the wave of excitement. Dean might not be a major star, but on the local circuit this was quite the coup.

It was only as he saw Deirdre frantically shaking her head that he slowed, noticing Clara had lowered her lantern to the floor and turned her back on the stage.

'What?' he asked, puzzled. 'What's up?

'I'm going to shoot off,' Clara replied. Her voice cracked as she spoke. 'The kids are getting picked up from here anyway and it's nearly over. I'll see you tomorrow, right?'

Deirdre sympathetically rubbed Clara's shoulder. 'Fine by me, love. I'll see you tomorrow at the club.'

'That was a bit sudden,' he said, as he watched Clara disappear into the crowds.

Deirdre leaned in. 'It's Dean,' she explained, spitting his name like an insult. 'He's the ex-fiancé. She's avoided him so far, so I think him being here was too much for her to take.'

'And everyone acting like he's some sort of hero. No wonder she wanted to get away.'

His eyes followed Clara, who was slinking away down a gennel. Joe couldn't repress the urge to go with her. More than anything, he wanted to let her know he understood how it felt to be sad, afraid and alone. His experience was different, but the resulting emotion was much the same.

'Am I alright to go now, too?'

His eyes flickered back towards Clara and he caught a final glimpse of the tail of her coat as she turned a corner.

'Go,' Deirdre replied with a knowing smile. 'I can finish off here.'

'See you tomorrow,' Joe called, already breaking into a jog as he made his way towards the gennel.

He'd definitely lost fitness. By the time Clara was back in view he was panting.

'Clara!' he called breathlessly.

She turned quickly, a look of startled surprise on her face.

'Joe.'

Now he was closer he could see she'd been crying. Even in the semi-darkness her eyes looked red and small.

She laughed. 'You must think I'm stupid, letting myself get in such a state over him.' She dragged her hand under her nose and sniffed. It was noisy and ungainly. 'We were together a long time and even though I know he's a bastard, I can't forget the past. We did have some good times along the way.'

'I take it you didn't know he was doing the light switch-on?'

She shook her head, the pompom on her bobble hat bobbing like a rabbit's tail. 'Not a clue. It's always Santa, every year. They probably thought Dean was an upgrade.' She laughed again. 'I can just imagine how he revelled in being asked. He always liked to think he was some big-wig celeb. In his mind he was the next David Beckham.'

'He's well known around here. Especially since the cup run last year.'

The look Clara gave was scathing.

'Whatever you do, don't mention the cup run. It was all he ever spoke about.' She tutted. 'I went to that game, you know. Third round, versus Rochdale. Me and all the other "wags". It was bloody freezing. It snowed all second half.'

'I remember. I went to that match. A year ago this weekend.'

'Really?' She looked interested. 'I've not been to a

match since we split up. That's one thing I don't miss, standing out on the touchline come rain or shine.'

'I'll bet.' He smiled softly. 'Are you sure you're alright? It must have shaken you up, seeing him unexpectedly like that.'

'It's made me realise what a lucky escape I had,' she replied, although Joe could tell from the tremor in her voice she was masking her hurt. 'Did you see him in that ridiculous puffa jacket? He looked like the flaming Michelin man.'

'He did, too,' Joe said with a laugh. 'I bet if he'd fallen over he'd have never been able to get back up again. That coat could double up as one of those sumo-suits they have for corporate away-day bonding sessions.'

'I wish he had fallen over, and that the photographer had captured it for good measure. And that it had made the front page of the paper. Am I a bad person for saying that?'

'Nah. Anyone would think the same, given the circumstances.'

'It's not even about Dean, really,' she admitted. 'The whole situation made me doubt my judgement. I thought I knew him inside and out, but it turned out I never really knew him at all. That's one hell of an eye-opener.'

'Not all men are like him.'

'That's what Deirdre says, but with his actions, and what happened with my dad ...' Her voice trailed off. 'I've been asked out a few times since me and Dean split up, but I'm not ready to put my heart on the line again.'

'Not all men are like him,' Joe repeated. 'And if you let me take you out somewhere, I'll prove it.'

He could have sworn her eyes brightened, but when she spoke there was a hesitance in her voice. 'Are you asking me on a date?'

'No!' Joe replied, a fraction too quickly. He forced himself to swallow down his embarrassment. 'I don't really do dates. I meant as friends. If we're going to be working together, we might as well get to know each other.'

'I can't decide whether that's really gentlemanly or if I'm a bit insulted.'

'Well, I was trying to be gentlemanly ...'

'In that case, I'll go out with you,' she said, glancing up through her long, dark lashes. 'On one condition.'

'Go on ...'

'I can tell you're not a fan of Christmas from the way you've acted tonight.' Joe went to talk, but Clara raised mitten-clad hands to stop him. 'You joined in, but the joy wasn't shining out of you. Christmas is the most magical time of the year to me. So, I'm going to make a suggestion. You can take me out and show me that not all men are grade-A losers, if you'll let me share exactly why I love the festive season so much with you.'

Joe sighed. Clara had piqued his curiosity. 'What are you suggesting?'

'We'll be seeing a lot of each other anyway, what with you helping out at the youth club every other night, so, as a thank you for volunteering I'd like to give you some festive gifts.'

'Presents? I don't think anyone in their right mind would argue with presents.'

'On the nights you're at the club I'll bring you something to remind you why Christmas is so amazing. And on the nights you're not volunteering, you can pick me up and take me out.'

Joe raised an eyebrow. 'That escalated quickly. So we've gone from one date to multiple dates?' He wasn't sure how he felt about that, but he was aware of his heart beating faster than normal, and the sensation wasn't entirely unpleasant.

Clara waggled what Joe thought was probably a finger, although it was hard to tell through the silhouette of her pink and blue striped mittens. 'Not dates, remember? But a chance for you to prove there are still some chivalrous men out there that aren't either married or gay.'

'Challenge accepted.'

'But there's one more condition.'

'Name it.'

'Wherever you take me on these non-dates has to be Christmassy. I don't care where, but it's December. I want to feel festive.'

Joe wasn't sure he was ready to embrace eggnog and carol singing and all the memories that were tangled up with the run-up to Christmas. The tree-decorating and lantern parade had been more than enough festivity for him. But because he already liked Clara he found himself saying, 'Okay. You've got a deal.'

'Fantastic,' Clara replied. 'I've got high expectations.' She smiled before adding, 'I'll have your first gift ready for you tomorrow, if one night with the kids hasn't put you off helping out.'

'Not at all. I'll be there with bells on.'

'See, you're already getting into the festive mood,' she laughed as she started walking away. 'Until tomorrow,' she called.

'Until tomorrow,' Joe echoed, pulling down his beanie to cover the chilly tips of his ears.

As he headed back towards the now-glitzy lights twinkling above the square, Joe was pleasantly surprised there was a new-found spring in his step.

Clara

Saturday, December 2nd 2017

Clara couldn't wait for Joe to arrive at The Club on the Corner that day so she could give him the first of his gifts. She'd been slogging away all afternoon, sorting out the seemingly endless amount of paperwork that was required to keep a youth club up and running in the twenty-first century, and was ready for some festive frivolity. Admittedly, she'd already managed to distract herself by attaching two new strands of thick golden tinsel to the edge of her desk. She'd seen them in the market that morning and hadn't been able to resist. It was Christmas, after all.

'Afternoon,' Deirdre called cheerily, as she popped her head around the office door. 'How are the accounts going, busy bee?'

'Ah, you know. Not the most positive reading.' Clara

pulled a face. No matter how hard she looked at the numbers on the spreadsheets, there was no way she could make them add up. 'Then again, it's no worse than normal. We'll keep ticking over. We always do.'

'That we will.' There was a pause, and Clara had a suspicion she knew where Deirdre's conversation was about to head. She had that look in her eye that suggested she was ready to start digging. 'So,' she began, 'what's going on with you and Joe?'

'Nothing,' Clara replied. 'I don't know what you mean.'

It was a half-truth, but Clara pushed away the guilt rising in her chest by assuring herself that Deirdre was only concerned with romance, and there was none of that between her and Joe. A hint of harmless flirting and a countdown to Christmas, but no full-blown love affair like her boss was craving.

Deirdre peered over the upper rim of her glasses like a TV detective scrutinising the evidence.

'Nothing?' she frowned. 'Are you sure?'

'Absolutely.'

'Because the way he came charging after you at the lantern parade ... well, it didn't seem like nothing to me. In fact, I'd go as far as to say it looked like the act of someone trying to get into your good books,' she pressed, with a suggestive jiggle of her eyebrows. The implied meaning was clear. Deirdre's voice might be saying 'good books', but her eyebrows were saying 'bed'.

'You said it yourself, Joe's a nice guy. He could tell I was shaken after seeing Dean and wanted to make sure I was okay. That's all there is to it.'

The mention of Dean was all it took to set Deirdre off. Dean-bashing had become one of her favourite hobbies over the past few months.

'Didn't he look ridiculous in that massive coat?' Deirdre said. 'And what the hell was that dancing all about? What a cock.'

'Deirdre!' Clara exclaimed. 'That's harsh.'

'Not harsh enough. I speak as I find.'

Deirdre gingerly lowered herself onto the sofa that backed against the far wall of the office. Her face strained with the effort.

'Oooof, that's better,' she said, sticking her right leg straight out in front of her. 'My knee's been giving me gip all day.'

'You're doing too much,' Clara chided. 'The aches and pains are your body telling you to take things more easily.'

'Stop giving me orders. You're not a nurse.'

'No, I'm not,' Clara replied, biting her tongue, 'but I've been working with you long enough to know when you're overdoing it.'

Deirdre's face softened as she spied the tin of chocolates on Clara's desk. 'I'd feel better if I could have one of those orange creams ...'

Clara froze rigid. The chocolates were her first festive gift for Joe, but she knew that if she tried to explain the countdown to Deirdre she'd only end up reading more into it than there was. It was easier to say nothing.

Reluctantly, she handed the chocolates over. 'Knock yourself out,' she said with a smile she hoped didn't look forced.

Deirdre was practically salivating as she clamoured to pull back the seal. 'A brand-new tin, what a treat. Means nobody's hogged the best ones already.'

'Like I said, knock yourself out.'

As Deirdre rummaged noisily through the confectionery, seeking the distinctive amber wrapper of her most coveted chocolate, Clara hoped there'd be more than a tin of empty foils to give Joe when he arrived for his shift at six o'clock. Although, she reasoned, it wouldn't be the end of the world if that was all that remained. Not much says Christmas quite as well as a half-eaten tin of Quality Street.

* * *

By the time they were shutting the heavy doors after

the last group of kids had left for the night, Joe looked beat. He leant against the door and let out a long, slow sigh.

'I don't know how you do this and look so young. I'm convinced I've aged twenty years in one night,' he said, rubbing his fingertips against his cheeks.

'Lightweight. One night and you're ready to throw in the towel?' Clara clucked her tongue sarcastically. 'I expected you to have more staying power.'

'I didn't say anything about giving up,' he clarified. 'Just that I feel like I've been mauled by a pack of wolves, and my shoulder's killing me.'

He massaged the joint, before rolling his shoulder in a circular motion.

'You should never have told them you could break-dance. You should have known they weren't going to stop badgering until you demonstrated your windmill,' Clara teased.

The group of awestruck pre-teens had watched on in amazement as Joe showed off his flips and tricks with apparent ease, and Clara herself had been impressed. These were the kind of moves Diversity would be proud of and, she'd realised, Joe had a look of Ashley Banjo about him. Part of it was the height and rich skin, although Joe's was darker than the break-dance king's, but it was more the open face and wide, friendly smile. Clara had to admit, Joe was handsome, and, from what she knew, kind and unassuming too. The total opposite of blonde, show-off Dean in every possible way.

It had been Clara leading the applause when Joe had stood, arms folded across his chest and an unbelievable mean look on his face as he finished his routine, but she wasn't his only fan. She'd noticed a group of girls whispering, and recognised their giggling ways as a sure-fire sign of a crush on someone older and unobtainable. She'd had a similar infatuation herself when she was twelve, with her maths teacher Mr Miles. He'd been the one thing that had held her interest in trigonometry and quadratic equations.

'I've learned my lesson,' he said. 'I'm sure it's swelling up.'

'Come on,' Clara said, nodding to the stairwell. 'There's all sorts of stuff in the first-aid cupboard in the office. I'm sure we can find something to make it more bearable.'

She started up the stairs, her fingers tickling the strands of tinsel that were wrapped around the banister.

'Ouch,' Joe said, as he slowly followed in Clara's footsteps. 'I think I've strained a muscle in my thigh too. I've not pulled off those moves for the best part of ten years.'

'Well, you've still got it.' Clara was glad Joe couldn't see her face, which was half smug grin and half flushed cheeks. 'Right,' she said, pulling open a tall cupboard and whipping out a green bag marked with a white cross, 'let's see what's in here.'

She unloaded bandages and plasters (always near the top, as they were the most frequently used) until she found a tube of Deep Heat. She tossed it to Joe, who caught it with one hand and a wince, before checking the use-by date.

'These aren't standard first-aid kit supplies,' Joe noted.

'This is the staff first-aid kit.' Clara held up some of the other contents, which included a box of Alka Seltzer and a family-sized box of Rennies. 'The Deep Heat is Deirdre's, for when her leg's playing up. She says the warmth helps her bones.'

Joe smiled. 'And the Alka Seltzer?'

'Mine,' Clara admitted, shamefaced. 'I had a couple of big nights out when I split up with Dean. I never came to work drunk,' she added hastily, 'but there were a couple of occasions where I was a bit ... let's say "worse for wear".'

'Ah,' Joe said, raising a knowing eyebrow. 'They work wonders, don't they?'

He squirted a generous dollop of the smelly cream onto the palm of his hand before rubbing it into his shoulder, and Clara watched as he closed his eyes with blessed relief and exhaled.

'That's taken the edge off,' he said finally.

'I've got something else that might cheer you up.' Clara walked to the desk and picked up the now half-empty tub. 'This was supposed to be your first gift.'

His eyes lit up at the sight of the trademark purple packaging. 'Chocolate. That's exactly what I need right now.'

'Don't get too excited. Deirdre got to them before I had chance to hide them away.'

His lips curled up into a knowing smile. 'So my first gift is a half-eaten tin of chocolates?'

'Yep,' Clara replied with a chuckle, relieved Joe could see the funny side of the situation. 'I'm a chocoholic, but Deirdre is something else. As soon as she saw them she pounced. I'll have to up my game next time I bring anything sweet for you.'

She handed him the tin and he prised off the lid. It popped as it loosened. 'At least all the good ones are left,' he said, taking in the golden wrappers of the toffees.

'That's because Deirdre can only have the soft centres. The chewy ones play havoc with her false teeth.'

Joe pulled at either end of the wrapper of a slender toffee finger, the sweet twisting as he unravelled it from its shimmering casing. He moaned as he popped it into his mouth.

'So my first gift was a good choice, then?'

'Mmm,' Joe replied with a nod, still chewing on his toffee. 'The Deep Heat works, but this is the best medicine.'

He swallowed it down, then offered the tin to Clara, who shook her head.

'I'll admit it, I had a few earlier too. What's left are all yours.'

'I admire your honesty.'

'So food works as a gift for you?'

'Food's always a good choice,' he said, selecting a second chocolate.

'That's useful to know.'

'And what about you? I'm supposed to be taking you out on a non-date tomorrow,' he reminded her. 'And the place I was thinking of probably involves half your daily calorie intake. You're not one of these women who doesn't eat, are you?'

Clara swallowed down the laugh that was rising in her throat, thinking of how much she loved her food. If it wasn't for her constant nervous energy about the future of The Club on the Corner she'd probably be a good few dress sizes larger than she was.

'It's safe to say food's always good with me, too,' she confirmed. 'I'm looking forward to it.'

And she realised with a jolt that she was. She really, really was.

Joe

Clara tilted her head back as she inhaled the super-sweet aroma that lingered in the air. Sugared almonds and cinnamon. Whiskey and mulled wine. Balsam and fir trees.

'This place smells amazing.'

Joe grinned. 'I know, right? The food here is incredible too. We'll have to make sure we sample as much as we can.'

The Christmas market was thronging with people, all wrapped up against the elements with their thick coats, bobble-topped hats and woolly scarves. Wind-chapped cheeks and noses bright enough to rival Rudolph himself were all that was on show other than their eyes, sparkling with festive joy as they took in the array of wooden cabins selling everything from tree decorations to squidgy pastel cubes of fresh Turkish delight.

For tonight Manchester's Albert Square was the heart of the city, alive with cheer. It was full of life and energy and the overwhelming sense of togetherness that the city had become known for after the horrific terrorist attack earlier in the year. Manchester was resilient, and Joe felt he had a lot he could learn from his home city.

'Look at that!' Clara squealed, pointing to a wooden hut selling squishy ring doughnuts by the dozen. They were piled high, dusted in a fine layer of speckled sugar that looked like morning frost. 'Oh, I bet they taste amazing. And the stall next to it is selling Gluhwein. I could do with something spicy and alcoholic after the day I've had.'

'We'll drink later,' Joe promised, 'but let's get something to eat first.'

'Doughnuts?' Clara sounded hopeful.

'I was thinking something a bit more substantial,' Joe laughed. He'd purposely not eaten all day, saving himself for the delicious fare on offer.

Clara pouted. 'Spoilsport.'

'You'll enjoy your doughnut even more after a hot dog, I promise. Especially from the stand over there.'

He waved his hand in the direction of the town hall, where an enormous orange-faced Santa proudly watched over proceedings from his lofty vantage point high up above the entrance of the neo-gothic building. Joe couldn't tell if it was meant to resemble Zippy from *Rainbow* or not, but it did. He found the Santa bizarre, and slightly sinister, so rather than dwell on it he grabbed Clara's hand and began to weave his way through the crowds.

It was busier than he'd anticipated. He'd thought people might be having a quiet night in front of the telly before all the Christmas madness and mayhem really kicked off in the next week or so, but no … it seemed everyone in Manchester had decided tonight was the night to head to the town centre and splash the cash on gourmet food and overpriced Christmas 'necessities'.

He'd been to one of the big European markets on Billy's stag do. They'd wanted to go to Oktoberfest, but Billy's brother hadn't been able to get holiday from work at the start of the academic year. He was a chemistry lecturer, based at Manchester Met, and September and October were no-no's for time off, unless he wanted to make enemies with the course leaders before he'd really started; so everyone else had fitted in around his plans instead. It wasn't like he was the groom, nor even the best man (that honour had gone to Joe, and he'd been exceptionally proud of being picked for the job), but

Billy had compromised on the stag do in a magnanimous act of brotherly love.

The group of ten had booked a dirt-cheap flight that set off from Manchester Airport at an ungodly hour and a 'bargain' hotel that had turned out to be a filthy hovel well out of Munich city centre. They'd had to get an underground train to access anything more than a corner shop or the ladies of the night that had lurked opposite the hotel's main entrance, and Joe had accessed neither, nor had he wanted to. Some of the other lads had, though, which had repulsed Joe. He'd never had so much as a one-night stand and prostitutes were way beyond his moral compass.

On the last night, when he was steaming drunk after too many tankards of beer to count, he'd given a handful of euros to one of the girls. She couldn't have been much older than Simone was now, her thick red lipstick clown-like and gaudy, her black dress short, tight and low- cut. There had been a sadness to her face, and her eyes darted around the shadows of the surrounding alleyways as she took the money. At the time Joe had thought she was afraid he was going to attack her, but with hindsight he thought the girl was scared in case her pimp saw her taking money from a potential client without earning it. He'd wished he could speak German, but as it was he could only say 'Danke' as he gave her the money, which he later realised meant 'thank you' rather than 'please'. It weighed heavy on his mind and heart that he'd never know her fate.

He was snapped out of his thoughts as Clara shouted, 'Don't you just love it here?' Even at full volume her voice could barely be heard above the blend of laughter and chatter and the mellow Christmas panpipe music blaring out over the speakers.

Joe didn't love the crowds, but the way Clara's face was shining perked him up enough to smile; that and the sight of the bratwurst sausage logo coming into view.

'We made it,' Joe said breathlessly as they joined a queue of people waiting for hot dogs. 'And I promise they're worth the fuss. I reluctantly came with Simone last week because she wanted to start her Christmas shopping and we ended up eating two of these beauties each.'

'Two? But they're enormous!'

Joe looked to the ground, guilty as charged. 'I know. But honestly, when you've tasted it you'll see why one wasn't enough. They're incredible. And we had to make the most of it, because once the markets are gone for another year there won't be the opportunity to have them again until next November or December.'

'Ah, so you're making the most of the opportunity

by aiming to eat your annual quota of hot dogs in a month.'

'Exactly.'

The round-faced man in the hut was wearing a gigantic furry hat with earflaps that hung down like spaniels' ears. It was at odds with the professional-looking apron he was wearing, the combination giving him the air of an eccentric elf. He beamed as he rubbed his palms together. 'Good evening!'

'Good evening,' Joe echoed. 'Can we have two of your finest hot dogs, please?'

The man nodded as he pressed the meat into a bread roll. The sausage was too long, poking out at both ends, and Joe was already salivating at the thought.

'Onions?' the man asked.

'Yes, please,' Clara replied quickly. 'And lots of them.'

Joe pulled a face and shook his head. 'No thanks.'

Clara looked on in disbelief. 'A hot dog without onions? What are you, some kind of maverick? Next you'll be saying you don't have red sauce.'

'I don't.'

The look of sheer horror that passed over Clara's face at that revelation made Joe snort with laughter.

'I can't believe I'm willingly spending time with someone who has such terrible taste in hot dogs. I bet you're one of those weirdoes who has mustard too, aren't you?' The man offered the hot dog to Clara, loaded high with the soft, curled onions. She reached straight for the bottle of red sauce and drew two thick lines of ketchup along the top of the sausage. 'Red sauce is the only way forward when it comes to hot dogs.'

Joe accepted a hot dog from the man and handed him a note in payment. When Clara reached for her purse, Joe stopped her. 'My treat,' he said, as she gratefully withdrew her hand from her bag and bit into her food.

'Mmmm,' she said, her eyes closing as she chewed the hot dog. 'This is amazing.'

Joe couldn't hide his pride, as though he'd made it himself from scratch. 'I know, right? And I think it tastes better because we're out in the cold and there's all the smells. It tricks your senses into thinking it'll taste a certain way and then it doesn't at all. It's a million times better.'

'I couldn't eat it like that, though,' Clara said, nodding her head towards Joe's plain hot dog.

'I like it naked.' As soon as Joe realised what he'd said he waited for Clara to pounce as she undoubtedly would.

'If that's not too much information then I don't know what is,' she said, with a salacious giggle.

Joe glanced coyly at the floor before meeting her eyes.

'Oh, stop acting all innocent and virtuous, you don't have to get embarrassed,' she said. 'We're only having a laugh.'

She wrapped her mouth around the hot dog sausage and although he knew it wasn't meant to be sexual – she was only eating, after all – Joe was aware of his cheeks getting warm. All the innuendo was making him hot under the collar.

'I'm a vicar's son, remember? I *am* innocent and virtuous.'

As though to prove the point he fluttered his eyelashes, and Clara laughed. It was a beautiful laugh, Joe thought, full on and loud and brimming over with positivity. Being around Clara was certainly a tonic. The heaviness that weighed down his heart lessened in her presence.

'Yeah, right. I bet you're not as innocent as you make out. No one is.'

'That sounds like an invite for me to ask about your deepest, darkest secrets.'

'Uh huh.' She shook her head. 'No way. This is about you, not me! Come on. Share something that'll surprise me.'

Joe thought for a moment as he chewed on the sausage. The herbs and spice exploded on his tongue, fizzing like fireworks against the roof of his mouth.

What could he share? Nothing about Michelle, not yet, and nothing about his ambivalence towards many aspects of life, either. He wracked his brains for something witty and light-hearted. There were plenty of minor exploits from his youth, but nothing shockworthy. The time Billy dared him to go into the ladies' toilets at The Club on the Corner and Deirdre had been lurking outside waiting for him because one of the girls had snitched on him. He'd got into a lot of trouble over that. Or when he'd downed the best part of a bottle of White Lightning behind the bus shelter, again a dare from Billy. Billy was almost always involved when he got in trouble, now he thought about it.

'I kissed a boy once.' The words were out of his mouth before he could think about what he was revealing.

'Really?' She looked surprised. 'Even if I'd had a hundred guesses, I wouldn't have predicted you were going to say that.'

'Sometimes there's more to people than meets the eye.'

'You can't say something like that and just leave it there,' she said, looking forlornly at the now-empty napkin. All that was left of her hot dog were a few stray crumbs and a smear of red sauce. 'Come on. Spill the beans.'

'There's not much to spill. It was during my first month at uni. The guy I lived next to in halls had a friend come to stay.' He could picture him clearly in his mind's eye, even now – the slicked-back blonde hair, the sharp, pale features, the all-black clothes. 'He looked like the actor who played Draco Malfoy in the Harry Potter films.'

Clara nodded her approval. 'Not bad.'

'We all went out to a club, everyone from our floor, and when we got back someone suggested we played spin the bottle. There were maybe ten of us still up, all steaming drunk. And when he spun the bottle, it landed on me. I thought he'd kiss the girl I was sat next to instead because he'd been flirting with her all night, but he didn't. He walked straight across the middle of the circle and lowered down onto his haunches, placed his hands on my cheeks and kissed me.'

Clara fanned her hand in front of her face. 'Sounds hot.'

'It wasn't. Not for me, anyway.'

Michelle had been there, sat on the other side of the circle, watching in amusement, not remotely threatened by someone else kissing him. If roles had been reversed he'd have been squirming with jealousy, but then Michelle had always been easy-going, a free spirit. She'd teased him mercifully about it forever more. At least, as forever more as they'd been granted, which hadn't been long enough.

'Were there tongues?'

Joe pressed his lips firmly together, wondering what had made him willingly share something so personal with Clara, who he barely knew. He'd not breathed a word of this to anyone who hadn't been there, not even Billy.

'Yeah.'

'You're a dark horse, Joe Smith. Snogging men after a drunken night out. I wouldn't have had you down as the type.'

'It was a game,' he shrugged. 'And it wasn't for me. Anyway, why is it me revealing all this stuff? Make it fair, come on. Tell me more about you.'

'I might go down in your estimation if I tell you too much.'

'Not a chance.'

'When I was fourteen I let Darren Wilder touch my boobs at the school disco.'

Joe laughed. 'That's not shocking, that's just teenagers being teenagers.'

'I graffiti-ed the toilets in the Imperial War Museum once on a school trip.'

'What did you write?'

'Clara was here,' she laughed.

'Stealthy,' he nodded. 'I like it. But it doesn't shock me.'

'I once climbed out of my window to go to an Avril Lavigne concert at the Apollo because I knew my mum wouldn't let me go if I asked.'

'Now that's shameful. Avril Lavigne? Really?'

'She had some classic tunes, I'll have you know.'

Joe snorted. 'Whatever you say.'

'She did!' Clara laughed, playfully slapping his arm. 'I bet even you liked Sk8er Boi.' She proceeded to sing it theatrically, and Joe found himself joining in. He hadn't realised he still knew the lyrics after all these years.

'Ha! I knew you were a closet fan.'

'Simone liked her.'

'She did not, you liar. She's not the right age.'

'It's only that one song. It's a catchy tune.'

'It's immense,' Clara agreed. 'But enough talk about Avril. Are you ready to hit the stalls? Because I noticed one back there that I'd like to have a look at.'

'The one with the alpaca-wool hats?' he grinned. The stall had stood out for Joe, the brightly coloured garments catching his eye. There had been shawls and ponchos hanging on a rack and one of those twizzly stands covered in hats with earflaps, like the one the sausage-seller had been sporting. Then there had been

72

knee-high socks, thick and striped, and pairs of mittens that looked warm and snuggly, similar to the ones Clara had been wearing the evening of the light switch-on, but in an array of garish clashing colours.

'Haha,' she said, poking out her tongue. 'That wasn't the one I had in my sights, actually. There was a stall with wooden ornaments that I thought would make nice gifts. My mum is as nuts about Christmas as I am, so I always get her a new decoration as part of her Christmas present.'

'Cool,' Joe replied, before looking through the crowds to try and locate the stall. There were so many, and every hut looked alike. He hoped Clara could remember where it was because otherwise it could take a while to find. 'Any idea which direction we need to head in?'

Clara wafted her hands around. 'Somewhere towards the middle.'

Joe couldn't help but smile at her vagueness. 'We'd better get searching then, hadn't we?'

And they amiably linked arms and headed off in search of the perfect gift for Clara's mum.

* * *

'Aren't they gorgeous?' Clara said, as she ran her fingers gently over the smooth curves of a carved reindeer. The wood was varnished, yet the colour remained delicate and pale.

Joe wasn't usually won over by ornaments, but even he had to admit they were beautifully made. The attention to detail was phenomenal and the intricate nativity scenes had particularly caught his eye.

'Handcrafted in Scandinavia,' said a ruddy-faced blonde in a fisherman's sweater. 'And all individual. You won't find two the same.'

'That's what I like about them,' Clara enthused. 'That they're all unique.' She picked up a small reindeer, not much bigger than her thumb. 'I think something like this would be best. Our place isn't really big enough for one like that,' she laughed, nodding towards the largest of the reindeers. It came up to Joe's waist, and he wondered who would ever buy a decoration that big. He supposed they appealed to people who had mansions, or those families who turned their gardens into a winter wonderland for a month so it became a bizarre local attraction.

Clara handed the miniature reindeer to the stall-holder with a decisive nod. 'I'll take this one.'

As she handed over the money in exchange for the wooden trinket, now wrapped in shimmering silver tissue paper, she beamed.

'My mum'll love it. Thank you,' she added, waving

to the man as they moved on to the next stall, where a wild-haired lady was waxing lyrical about her home-made scented candles.

'I've tried to conjure up some more *unusual* scents,' she said, every word deliberate and pronounced. 'Everyone likes vanilla, but I wanted to give them more of a Miranda vibe.' Sensing Clara's bemusement and mistaking it for confusion, she added, 'I'm Miranda.'

'Right,' Clara said, stifling a giggle.

Joe elbowed her in the ribs, hoping it would encourage her to keep a straight face, but it only caused Clara to pull her hand to her face and clamp it over her mouth to hide her glee.

Something about Miranda's manner was comical. She was intense, and Joe picked up on how the way she spoke, as though she was thinking about every word that came out of her mouth, was so at odds with how Clara blurted anything that came into her head the moment she thought it.

'I create original blends that add the traditional Christmas aromas to the most popular scents.'

Clara moved closer and examined the labels, plain white with an embossed gold script. 'Vanilla Berry, Cinnamon Rose, Sea Breeze and Balsam ... Interesting combinations.'

'Have a smell,' urged Miranda, shoving a candle

under Clara's nose with such force that she jumped back in surprise. 'This is Sunrise and Snowflakes. It's a combination of summer mornings and winter nights.'

'Wow,' Joe said, swallowing down a laugh that was bubbling in his throat. 'There really is something for everyone.'

Clara wrinkled her nose as she inhaled. 'This smells a bit gingery,' she said. 'And maybe bergamot too?'

'You've got a good nose for scents.' Miranda's bob of the head suggested she was impressed by Clara's ability to pick out the key ingredients in her bespoke candles. 'I bet you're a woman who uses her senses to their full potential.'

She gazed intently at Clara, which Joe found unsettling, so he could only imagine how it must feel for Clara being in the spotlight like that. And what was she rambling on about, Clara using her senses to their full potential? Joe was beginning to feel both trapped and weirded out by Miranda and her scented candles, and was keen to escape. Not least because he didn't fancy being coerced into buying a candle he'd never light.

'Oh Clara, look!'

He started to wave frantically at a group of young people eating churros a few feet away. Never mind that he'd not seen the youths before in his life, if it got him and Clara away from Miranda and her candles, he didn't really care.

Her eyes darted to where he was looking, just as a girl with bright-green hair gave an awkward smile and waved back.

'We really should go and say hello,' Joe said pointedly. 'It's a long time since I last saw ... erm ...' he wracked his brain for a name that he could pretend belonged to the girl, '... Erin.'

'We must,' said Clara, a flicker of recognition in her eyes. Joe was relieved she'd understood what he was trying to do and that she was willing to play along. 'Nice to meet you, Miranda. I hope you have a successful evening.'

'Don't waste that nose of yours!' Miranda called after them as they walked away as quickly as they could.

'Thank you,' Clara gushed when the pair were safely out of Miranda's earshot. 'I was beginning to wonder what she was going to say next. Talking about using my senses to my full potential and all the other mumbo jumbo,' she laughed.

'It might not be mumbo jumbo,' Joe reasoned. 'I was thinking we might put our sense of taste to good use again in a minute. That doughnut stall is just over there,' he said, nodding towards a crowd of people queuing for the sugary delights.

'And the Gluhwein. You did promise,' Clara reminded him.

'You're right, I did.'

Clara linked her arm through Joe's once more. 'Now you're talking. Tasting that is the kind of sense I don't mind using to my full potential,' she said. 'Let's go.'

Clara

Monday, December 4th 2017

The gloomy grey clouds hadn't lifted all day, and the darkness they cast around the office at The Club on the Corner wasn't encouraging Clara to work. The paperwork she'd been staring at was also tedious and depressing, so much so that she'd almost caved and opened the stollen she'd bought for Joe. The sweet bread-like texture dissolving in her mouth would have been an antidote to the charity submissions she'd been working on all day, first at home and then at the office. If the cake hadn't taken so bloody long to wrap the previous evening she'd have opened it first thing; all that would've been left of it would be a Hansel and Gretel trail of crumbs leading from her house to the club. Or halfway to the club, more likely. It would never have lasted her all the way to work.

Stollen was another of the traditional Christmas foods that she couldn't resist, and the brand she'd bought from a European supermarket on Ayres Road was her absolute favourite. It was packed with so much dried fruit that it wasn't far off being a Christmas cake, and the icing sugar dusted on top was thick and generous. Most importantly was the marzipan rope woven through the centre of the dough, the sharp almond tang the perfect finishing touch. Her grandparents' next-door neighbours were Austrian and gifted her family one of the cakes each year, and the sight of the distinctive wrapper alone was enough to set Clara's mouth watering.

At the Christmas market Joe had mentioned in passing that he'd never tried stollen and she'd immediately known it was the next gift she'd get him. She only hoped he liked it as much as she did, because she'd gone for the biggest they'd had in stock.

Clara looked at the clock, noting it was later than she'd thought. She really should start setting up for the session, especially as it was doubling as a much-needed fundraising event. Deirdre had decided a bake sale was a relatively easy way to bring more money into the club, but Clara wasn't in the mood for swarms of adults descending on the place. She loved being with the youngsters, finding them much easier to talk to than their older counterparts. They were more straightforward, less prone to game-playing. If they had an issue with you it'd come firing out in a hormone-fuelled rage.

Picking up her bag, along with her mum's spotty cake tin, she headed downstairs, hoping people wouldn't laugh her misshapen Smartie cookies out of town. Clara never professed to be a baker and didn't aspire to be one either, and she'd only brought something along to the event to show her support. If no one wanted to buy them, she'd throw a tenner into the margarine tub they used for collecting money and take them back home herself.

* * *

Deirdre was flapping. She often got like this when there was an event, keen to show the club in its best light. Plus, of course, there was the near desperation, the need to make as much money as possible from this bake sale to keep the club open and available to as many young people as possible. Clara understood all that, but the tension in the kitchen rubbed off on her as soon as she walked through the door.

'Oh, Clara. Thank goodness! I thought you were never going to come down.' Deirdre peeled back the lid of a Tupperware container and examined the contents –

mince slices – before adding the box to a pile. 'I've got a system,' she said, her voice hurried and flustered. 'Buns and cupcakes near the kettle, biscuits next to the microwave and big cakes and Christmassy goods here on the table.'

Clara cast her eyes over the offerings. There seemed to be an awful lot of buns, plus an abundance of Cornflake Crispy bites, which were Deirdre's speciality. She made them for every event, every time.

'I've brought some biscuits,' Clara said, putting her tin near the microwave with a tray full of beautifully iced gingerbread men. 'They don't look that appealing, though, I'm afraid.'

'They'll be fine,' Deirdre said, 'people buy anything at these bake sales. They're not fussy.'

Clara didn't rise. Much like the chocolate cake in the corner hadn't. It was as flat as a pancake.

'Who brought that in?' Clara asked, pointing at the paper-thin cake.

'Oh, that was Joe,' Deirdre said with a laugh. 'I don't think he's much of a baker. Bless him for trying, though, eh?'

'It's not so bad,' Clara said, surprised at how quickly she jumped to defend Joe's efforts. The cake was thin, but the chocolate buttercream smothering it still looked tasty and tempting. 'And, like you said, people aren't fussy. They'd buy anything if they thought it'd support the youth club.'

'I hope you're right, because if we don't raise some money fast we'll have to cancel the Christmas disco.'

'We'll find the money somehow,' Clara said optimistically. 'There's been a Christmas disco every year since the club opened. We're not going to start letting the kids down now.'

'You're right,' Deirdre agreed, as she opened a tin. The tempting waft of chocolate brownie flooded out and Clara's mouth started to water in response. 'Where there's a will, there's a way.'

Clara rummaged in her bag for her purse. It was buried at the bottom, beneath a pile of crumpled receipts, an empty chocolate-bar wrapper and a couple of emergency tampons. Wasn't that always the way? She took her rubbish and posted it in the bin, and removed the present for Joe, placing it on the work surface until she found the purse. Unzipping it, she took out a newly-minted coin.

'Well, for starters, can you bag me up a piece of that brownie? And make it a large one. It looks amazing.' She placed the pound coin in the margarine tub, the two-tone disc mingling in with the float of silvers and coppers.

'Brianna Moore's mum made it, so you know it's

going to be good.'

'Ah, that explains why it smells amazing,' Clara replied, inhaling deeply to get another hit from the sweet aroma. Mrs Moore had started up a small bakery on the same row as The Club on the Corner, and apparently the orders had been flooding in. She'd been especially busy over the summer with wedding cakes, and Clara imagined she'd be in demand over the Christmas period too, for those who had neither the time nor skills to cobble together a Christmas cake.

'I'm going to buy the ginger loaf she contributed,' Deirdre said with a wry smile. 'And she's donated a voucher for a celebration cake too as a raffle prize. I was going to ask if you'd stand on the door as people arrive to encourage them to buy a strip or two.'

Clara snorted. 'Encourage? Bully them into it, more like.'

'It's a fantastic prize. Everyone likes cake. We could take a lot of money on that raffle, if we're lucky.' She picked up a bag and peered into it, looking most dissatisfied by the contents. 'French Fancies,' she said, with a disparaging shake of her head. 'Shop-bought.'

'Mr Kipling's?'

Clara licked her lips. She loved French Fancies. They reminded her of childhood birthday parties, the bright icing drizzled with purest white zig-zagged lines brought back happy memories.

Deirdre shook her head. 'Own brand.'

'Oh.'

Clara was momentarily disappointed, until Joe strode into the room, a woven jute bag in each hand.

He held them up proudly. 'More supplies!' he announced.

Deirdre smiled half-heartedly. 'You been busy doing more baking, Joe? You shouldn't have.'

'Oh no,' Joe laughed. 'It took me hours to make that chocolate monstrosity, there was no chance I was going to do any more baking. I got Mum to make something instead. She hadn't realised the cake sale was tonight until I told her – she'd written it in the wrong space on the calendar.'

'Oh, she's a star finding time to bake like that.'

'She appreciates the work the club does so she'll always make time to support it as best she can. Plus, she's the vicar's wife. Baking's what she does best,' he joked.

'I'd better go and look for that book of raffle tickets,' Clara said, picking up her handbag. She didn't fancy her chances of finding them, though. The stationery cupboard was a disaster area. 'Are they where they were left after the summer fun day?'

'In the box with the receipt book,' Deirdre confirmed.

'And make sure people buy plenty,' she added. 'Don't let anyone get away with single tickets, make them buy a strip. Channel your inner sales girl.'

'I don't have an inner sales girl,' Clara shouted over her shoulder. 'I only lasted a day at the one shop job I had.'

'Well, find your selling mojo somehow,' Deirdre said sternly. 'You've got a important job today with those raffle tickets. It's a big day for all of us. Let's make some decent money to give these kids what they deserve.'

*   *   *

'Thanks for supporting The Club on the Corner,' Clara said for the umpteenth time, smiling at the family heading home. It was a forced smile now, admittedly, after freezing in the doorway for an hour ushering people in and out of the club.

They were leaving happy, though, and laden down with baked goods, just the way Deirdre had planned. She'd be happy with the proceeds of the raffle too. Clara's calculations suggested they'd made more than enough to fund the DJ coming to set up his flashing lights and glitter ball and play some of that noise the kids these days class as music. The cakes looked to have gone down well too.

'Thanks for coming,' Clara said, as Tariq's parents left cradling the in-demand raffle prize. Tariq followed, a few steps behind, as though he didn't want to associate with them. Why is it that teenagers are so embarrassed to be seen with their parents?

'Merry Christmas,' she said cheerily as Joe's parents left for the night, Simone in tow. 'We hope you've enjoyed the bake sale.'

'Have we ever!' laughed Mrs. Smith. She held aloft a bag, which Clara presumed was full of cakes. 'I've bought more than enough for the Knit and Natter group. They meet on a Tuesday and all love a cake. They'll be delighted with the selection I've picked up tonight,' she said happily.

'We aim to please,' Clara smiled, 'and thank you for your contributions too. Everyone's been so supportive.'

'It's a tough time for charities right now, with so many worthy causes competing for the funding out there,' said Reverend Smith. 'But I've been talking to Deirdre. Every year the church chooses a local group to benefit from our church community fund. Other local groups are putting themselves forward too, but, I have to say, the parishioners have a real soft spot for the youth club. We're voting for our 2018 charity of the year next week, and the lucky one will be announced at the nativity service on Christmas Eve.' He smiled. It was reassuring.

'It would be worth you making an application.'

Clara was stunned. 'Really? The church might be able to help us financially?'

He nodded. 'A significant amount of church funds are set aside to assist local groups that impact positively on the local community. In my humble opinion, The Club on the Corner is a perfect candidate.'

Clara hoped he was right. External funding coming in would lighten the load, maybe even contributing towards paying for another much-needed staff member.

Reverend Smith looked so like Joe, so warm and friendly and trustworthy, and Clara could see why people came to him to offload their troubles. He was the kind of man who would make even the darkest situation seem okay, and when Clara thought about it, she realised that a large part of his job must involve helping people through some of the most challenging periods of their lives.

'Where can I get an application form?' Clara asked, hoping beyond hope that they'd be the lucky group to benefit. 'I can get straight on with it. I'm becoming a dab hand at them with all the funding pots we've been applying for lately.'

'There is a form,' he said, 'but you'd also need to make a presentation to the church committee, saying how the funding would benefit you. The meeting's next

Monday, though, so it wouldn't give you long to get prepared.'

Clara gasped. She had faith in her abilities, but a week wasn't long, especially not at this time of year with all the club's other commitments. 'I'll be there,' she said, defiantly, despite the ripple of doubt washing over her.

'I'm glad to hear it. We did advertise the funding and were surprised The Club on the Corner hadn't applied.'

Clara vaguely remembered a flyer that she'd promised to look at later, buried somewhere on the office desk. That had been weeks ago now. She'd been so busy she'd not had chance to get around to it.

'I'll look forward to your application and keep you in my prayers,' he said.

When nearly everybody else had left, Clara made her way to the kitchen, where she found Joe and Deirdre clearing away the last remaining cakes. Clara had to hide a smile as she noticed Joe's chocolate cake, untouched, on the cake plate he'd brought in. It was hardly surprising. It hadn't compared to the other temptations on offer.

'Your dad is one of my favourite people right now,' Clara said, holding up her hand for Joe to high-five. 'He thinks The Club on the Corner is a possible candidate for the church's charity of the year.'

A grin took over her face as his palm met hers.

Deirdre's eyes welled up with tears. 'Just imagine! Think how much of a difference that money would make.'

'We've got to put together a presentation, though, to prove we're worthy candidates,' Clara grimaced at the thought of all the extra work that would entail. 'And the meeting's a week today.'

'Easy peasy,' Deirdre scoffed. 'You're great at all the organisational stuff.'

'And I'll help,' Joe offered. 'My happiest memories are tied to this place, there's no way I'm going to let it fade away without a fight. Simone and her friends deserve a place like this to come to, and they couldn't have better youth workers than the two of you. I'm sure the other charities are worthy, but this place is magical.'

Clara had to resist the urge to throw her arms around him in gratitude. 'Thank you. Thank you so much.' Her brain was already whirring as she tried to process the information she'd need to present. Joe's help would be gladly received and she knew he was more tech-savvy than she was. Mind you, that wasn't hard.

'Whatever I can do for this club, I will.'

They quietly set about tidying away, hope hanging in the air. It was only as Clara was spraying the work surface with disinfectant, moving her mittens and wallet out of the way to make sure she didn't miss a spot, that she realised she couldn't see her present for Joe.

'Have you seen a parcel?' she asked Deirdre, her brow furrowing into a frown. 'I left it here.'

'No, not seen a present. Why? What was it?'

'A stollen? Wrapped in a red ribbon?' Clara prompted. She couldn't bear to think of the stollen going missing before she'd given it to Joe, especially after the debacle with the Quality Street.

'Oh, you mean the fruit loaf? The one with the icing sugar sprinkled all over the top?'

Clara could have cried with relief. 'Yes! For one awful moment I thought you were going to say it had been sold.'

'Oh, Clara,' Deirdre replied, her mouth twitching apologetically. 'I'm afraid it has. I thought it was one of the donations for the bake sale.'

Clara's heart sank. After all her efforts and her special trip to buy something she was sure Joe would love, she was still failing miserably. 'No. That was a gift for someone.'

She looked over at Joe, catching his eye and mouthing the word 'sorry'.

'It was there on the side with everything else. I just assumed it was for sale. It went for a good price, though, I think someone paid a fiver for it!'

It had cost almost double that, and taken Clara's

ever-decreasing bank balance deeper into her overdraft, but that wasn't what was making her heart weigh heavy in her chest. More than anything she'd wanted to share something she loved with Joe.

'I'm sure whoever you bought it for would be glad that it raised money for the youth club,' Joe said. His steady voice calmed Clara, just the way his father's words had earlier. 'Somewhere that gives hope to so many kids from all different backgrounds. That's a pretty special present to give.'

And as he smiled, Clara smiled back. Because while she was mourning the gift she was unable to give, she knew he was right. The mishap had given Joe something he'd appreciate just as much as the stollen, if not more.

Joe

'Wow.' Clara's eyes were as big as dinner plates, let alone saucers, as she took in the enormous mug of hot chocolate that Joe had placed before her. The extravagant swirl of whipped cream on top resembled a '99 ice cream, something that was only accentuated by the milk chocolate flake poking out at an angle. Crumbled chocolate was sprinkled on, along with a mountain of cheeky pink and white marshmallows. 'This looks calorific.'

Joe grinned. 'When it comes to food, there's no point doing anything by halves.'

He gave a nod to the young waitress, who scuttled across with a plate of mince pies and a pot of clotted cream. She placed them in the centre of the table before giving Clara and Joe a side plate and fork each.

'These can't all be for us!' Clara squealed, taking in the quintessentially Christmassy treat.

'Oh, they can. And they are.' He picked up a mince pie and placed it on his plate, flinching ever so slightly as the fresh-from-the-oven pastry casing sizzled against his fingertips. 'Dig in. They're best when they're piping hot.'

Clara gingerly placed a mince pie on her plate, before piercing it with her fork. The filling oozed out, dark and rich and smelling divine.

'Ohhhh,' she breathed. 'This looks amazing.'

'The best mince pies in Manchester, bar none.' Joe took a forkful into his mouth, before letting out a moan of pure pleasure. 'My mum's are good, but there's something about these. The pastry is so buttery.'

'And they smell like Christmas.'

'Help yourself to cream. You'll be blown away by how delicious they are when they're loaded up.'

Clara added a delicate dollop of cream to the side of her plate, before offering the pot to Joe. He was far less restrained, putting a large spoonful on top of what remained of his first mince pie.

'Now do you see why I ordered so many? One is never enough.'

'They're incredible.' Clara dabbed the corner of her mouth with a napkin. It came away marked with the sticky residue of mincemeat. 'How did you find this place, anyway? It's well off the beaten track.'

Joe had driven them towards the centre of Manchester after picking Clara up from The Club on the Corner and, despite her questioning, hadn't told her where they were heading, instead telling her she'd find out when they got there.

They'd arrived at the wooden-fronted café situated towards the far end of the city's popular Northern Quarter when most people were already well into their night out. The bars around the surrounding streets were abuzz with life, full of young professionals letting their hair down with a few pints of craft beer after a hard day at work. The café seemed quiet in comparison, the warm glow of the table lights homely and inviting. There were a few groups sitting at the wooden tables enjoying their enormous hot chocolates, but Joe knew from experience that the café was busier by day. Then the queues were winding out of the door as people waited for their take-out drinks, or crossed their fingers and hoped lady luck would save them a table. By night-fall it was a different place altogether, somewhere book groups met to dissect their latest read or where friends would come to catch up on each other's news.

'I work near here,' Joe said. 'The guy who owns this place came in one day with a bunch of flyers to leave on the counter at the hardware store. They had a twenty-per-cent-off coupon on the bottom so I found myself coming in on my lunch break. I've always been a sucker for a bargain.' He stopped to take a sip from his mug, the rich hot chocolate sliding down his throat like silk. It was pure bliss. 'Anyway, by the time all the flyers had been used up I was totally addicted to the hot chocolate. They don't do mince pies all year round, obviously, but the muffins are excellent too, especially the double choc chip. I've been a regular here for a long while.'

'I can see why. Although I'm glad we don't have a café like this near the youth club. I'd end up spending half my wages on food.'

Joe smiled, thinking of Linda's, the café across the road from The Club on the Corner. The lace voiles that hung in the window were a dirty yellow from years of exposure to grease and the laminated menus looked as though they hadn't been given a wipe clean since the last millennium. 'Yeah, it kinds of eclipses Linda's burnt toast and stewed brews.'

'Just a bit. At least the cake shop's on hand for the days when I can't survive without a sugar rush.'

They sat quietly, savouring their drinks and each tucking into a second mince pie. They watched the people on the street passing by through the haze of the steamed-up window, bundled-up bodies rushing past as quickly as they could to get to somewhere – anywhere – where the biting wind wouldn't sting their cheeks. The silence was comfortable.

'How are you enjoying it at the youth club?' Clara finally asked, placing her fork on her plate. It made a tinkling sound, reminiscent of Christmas bells. 'I know the kids are a bit crazy, but they've got good hearts beneath the tantrums and teen angst.'

'I remember my teenage years,' Joe said, with a shudder. 'Pretty horrific. And although Simone isn't the sort of girl to get into any bother, even she has her moments.'

Clara nodded a knowing reply. 'They all do. I was a right little madam when I was her age. I remember the newsagents ringing my mum when they'd caught me stealing.'

Joe's mouth formed a questioning 'o'. 'I didn't realise I was liaising with a common thief. If I had I might have thought twice before bringing her to the best café in Manchester.'

Clara cocked her head and winked.

'That's me, Manchester's answer to the Artful Dodger, pinching things all over the city,' she grinned. 'Not really, obviously. I was caught taking a lipstick that was free with a magazine. I'd probably have got away with it as well if it wasn't for Mrs Long's eagle eyes spotting the rip on the cover where I'd pulled the Sellotape too hard. She always did notice every little wrinkle in her precious stock. Hated anyone looking at the magazines before they bought them.'

'What happened?'

Clara grinned. 'I had a flash of genius. As she was shouting at me I put the lipstick on. I knew she'd never ask for it back once it had been near my lips.'

'Crafty.' Joe was both shocked and impressed by teenage Clara's brazen behaviour. 'Thinking on your feet. That probably prepared you for the work you do now.'

'Oh yeah, I'm sure it did,' Clara replied. 'Everything they do I did myself.'

'Sounds like I've still got a lot to learn, both about you and about youth work.'

Clara eyed up another mince pie and reached out to take one before withdrawing her hand and letting out a sigh.

'Go on, have another,' Joe encouraged. 'I'm going to. And best do it quick before they go cold. The burn on your tongue is half the fun.'

'You've twisted my arm,' Clara said, taking the largest of the remaining mince pies and adding it to her plate. 'Although when you have to roll me along the road like a snowball because I've eaten too much, you'll be regretting telling me to go for it.'

'I'll probably need rolling myself, but it'll be worth it.'

The waitress came by, asking if they wanted another mug of hot chocolate. Clara clutched at her stomach, making out as though she couldn't manage another drop of the thick chocolatey drink, but Joe ordered two more regardless.

'No flake with mine this time, please,' Clara called after the girl, showing a modicum of control. 'I've already had to undo the top button of my jeans,' she whispered conspiratorially.

Joe could feel his cheeks heating up at the thought. Clara was a striking woman, with her edgy haircut and the small diamond stud in her nose. Now he was getting to know her better he'd noticed how she tried to hide her vulnerabilities. He recognised the bravado for what it was, though. He'd been painting on a brave face for long enough. In the half-light of the café, and loosened up by the super-sweet liquid chocolate, Joe felt more attracted to Clara than he had to any woman for a long time. It left him wracked with guilt.

'You dodged my question,' she said afterwards. 'How are you finding it volunteering? It's a bit different from working in a shop.'

'Some of it's the same. Chatting to people, trying to

help them out. It's just that most of my customers are at the other end of the age spectrum to the kids. And I've never had one of them tell me to piss off, like Jordan did last night.'

Clara put her face in her hands. 'Deirdre told me about that. He's got a bit of a chip on his shoulder, but he's a nice lad underneath it all. He's a young carer for his mum,' she revealed. 'She's got multiple sclerosis and needs a lot of looking after. On a bad day she can't make it out of bed without someone to help her.'

'That's tough for anyone to go through, let alone a young lad like Jordan. No wonder he lashes out from time to time.'

'He's not got an easy life. He'd have every right to be a misery on two legs juggling what he does at home along with keeping on top of his schoolwork, but most of the time he's a decent kid. That's one of the things I love about being at the club, though, it gives kids like him a place to get respite. Jordan's only real escape is the club. No wonder he values the freedom from his responsibilities and the chance to talk about football until the cows come home.'

'That's why I volunteered in the first place. It benefits everyone if there are places like the club. It's good for the young people to feel part of the community too, and to give them a chance to make a difference. I've never forgotten the way Deirdre forced us to get involved in the summer carnival. It was embarrassing as anything dressing up like an Oompa Loompa for the float, especially as a fourteen-year-old trying to pretend to have some street cred, but we made loads of money shaking buckets at all the bystanders who'd come along to laugh in our round, orange faces. We donated it to the hospital.'

Joe hoped he didn't sound as if he was bragging about volunteering – he'd hate to come across as holier than thou – but having parents who worked for the church made a difference too he supposed. 'Love thy neighbour' was an action his parents both encouraged and lived by, not just an empty platitude, and he and Simone had been brought up to donate their time to worthy causes.

'Deirdre was right when she said you had a good heart.'

'Has she been talking about me again?' he said with a modest smile. 'She's terrible.'

'All positive, though,' Clara replied. 'Kept saying you were good boyfriend material.'

Joe spluttered, shocked by Deirdre's audacity. What was she playing at talking about him in those terms when she knew he was still struggling to deal with Michelle's death? He'd had to be honest with her. When

101

he'd offered to help he'd told her part of the reason was facing the past, including the memories linked to Michelle and the club, head on.

Clara looked at him as she sipped at her hot chocolate. All of a sudden he felt flustered.

'Dean's made me very cautious about relationships, sadly. I want to fall in love again, one day, but only if it'll be straightforward.'

Joe smiled. 'Sadly I don't think there are any guarantees when it comes to love.'

'That sounds like the voice of experience,' Clara replied with an empathetic smile. 'Have you ever had your heart broken? And I mean *really* broken, where you don't think you'll ever give it to anyone again because it's damaged beyond repair?'

Joe thought before he replied. 'I've not had many serious girlfriends, to be honest, despite what Deirdre said the other day.'

Clara shifted her eyes so she was focused on the drink in front of her.

'I've only been in love once,' he continued, 'and although I don't think either of us went into it thinking it'd last forever, the more time went on, the more I realised how much better my life was for having her in it.'

Joe swallowed, uncomfortable.

'Did she cheat?' Clara asked, sympathetically clucking her tongue before carrying on without waiting for a reply. Joe had the feeling that once she got onto the subject of lovers' betrayal Clara could go on for days. 'It's the worst. I wish Dean had told me straight out that he'd been sleeping with someone else, because deep down I knew. He'd been carrying on with her for weeks and all the time I'd been driving him to the clinic pretending everything was fine. Talk about a mug. I might as well have had it written on my head in permanent marker,' she babbled, shaking her head. 'I've learned from it, though. I won't give anyone the chance to treat me like that again.'

'She didn't cheat on me.'

Joe closed his eyes, concentrating on breathing. He still found it hard to talk about Michelle. When he opened them Clara was watching with confused wonder.

'I met her at The Club on the Corner, the day after her fifteenth birthday,' he said, his heart beating furiously in his chest; and Joe thought, not for the first time, that if he'd spoken about it more often he'd have a speech down pat by now. As it was, most of the conversations he'd had about Michelle since her death had been with himself, either talking to the mirror like a crazy man or going round and round in circles in his head. 'It was Hallowe'en and she was dressed as Morticia Addams, head to toe in black.' He smiled at the memory, at how her perfect feline eyes had been circled with eyeliner the colour of midnight. He'd loved her eyes, especially her irises, which had been a brilliant purplish-blue like Parma Violets. She hadn't realised how beautiful they were, but he had. No one else had eyes like Michelle's. No one. 'I found out after that she hadn't need a wig, she had long straight hair that trailed right down her back anyway.'

Clara listened, but didn't speak.

'We'd been together for six weeks when I first told her I loved her.' A cynical laugh escaped him. 'Looking back, fifteen seems so young, but it was pretty intense, you know. We spent all our spare time together. We were a package deal. When it came to time to apply to universities, we applied to all the same ones, and were so happy to both get accepted at Durham. We were even placed in the same halls of residence. It was as though it was meant to be. We moved into a shared house in our second year and on her twentieth birthday I asked her to marry me. Everything was perfect. We rented a tiny flat together in our third year, just us two. We thought we were so grown up. But she died.' His mouth was dry, the words sitting heavy on his tongue. 'In a car crash.'

'That's terrible, Joe. Horrific. I don't know what to say.'

Clara's hand was clamped tightly over her mouth as Joe's words hit home.

'I still miss her every day.'

'Of course you do,' Clara said, reaching out and touching his hand. Joe instinctively pulled back, memories of Michelle raw and painful. 'You loved her.'

'Love wasn't enough to keep her alive.'

Joe took a sip of his hot chocolate so he wouldn't have to talk any more. It was cold now, and the milk had formed an ugly layer of skin on the surface.

'So when you asked if my heart's ever been broken, I guess it has. I feel cheated, mainly. Cheated out of finishing my degree because there was no way I was staying in Durham after that, with memories of Michelle on every corner. I thought coming home would help, but I soon discovered memories haunted me here, too. Cheated out of a relationship that could have gone the distance, if it had had the chance. Cheated out of Christmas, too. She always loved it, just like you do, but she died in December.'

'It makes sense now, why you don't like Christmas.' The pity etched on Clara's face made Joe feel worse. 'I should never have asked in the first place, it was too personal a question. You didn't have to tell me.'

Joe shook his head. 'I wanted to tell you, but it's not something I talk about often. It's not the easiest thing to bring up, a dead fiancée.'

'I guess not.'

'You'd have loved her,' he said, his voice a whisper. 'Everyone did.'

Joe looked out of the window, at a couple walking past. The young woman had a bobble hat pulled down tightly over her baby-pink hair, her hands pushed in the pockets of her heavy woollen coat. The man had an arm draped around the woman's waist, his fingers gripping against the coarse-looking fabric.

'Sorry for putting a downer on the night.'

'You haven't put a downer on anything. I'm glad you felt you could be honest with me. I just wish you hadn't had to go through it in the first place. It must have been dreadful.'

'It still is,' he admitted. 'It's eight years since it happened, but some days it feels like it happened yesterday. It's like a cut. It starts to heal, but all it takes is one knock for the scab to fall off and it hurts more than it did in the first place.'

'I can't imagine what it must be like. You were so young yourself. You must have been really mature.'

Joe laughed. 'I didn't feel mature at the time. I dropped out of uni with just one semester to go before graduation. People said I was crazy for throwing my education away, but I couldn't bear to stay.'

'Where did you say you went to university? Durham?'

'Fell in love with the place when I went for an open day and knew I didn't want to go anywhere else, and Michelle felt the same. She adored the architecture. When you've grown up in a city as great as Manchester, you realise most cities are all the same. They might have their own quirks, but the high streets are full of the same shops, same restaurants and chain pubs. We didn't want that, and that's what was great about Durham. We applied to all the small-town universities, even looked at Lampeter and Aberystwyth, and they're practically at the end of the world.'

Clara laughed. 'I went on a school camp in Aberystwyth once. It did feel like the end of the world. It took forever to get there and the girl I was sat next to threw up her bag of Wotsits. Put me off them for life. I've never seen vomit that colour before or since.'

'Urgh. I don't think I'll ever eat a Wotsit again.'

'Good. Because I couldn't socialise with anyone who ate them,' Clara said with a teasing twinkle in her eye.

'Anyway,' he said, vomit another subject he was keen to avoid. 'Tell me some more about you. Besides your teenage delinquency, which your current profession suggests you've grown out of, I don't know very much about you at all.'

'There's not much to tell.'

'There must be something. Tell me about your family. Any siblings?'

'No,' she said, her face hardening. 'Only child. My parents separated when I was ten, and me and mum moved to live with my grandparents. When I was twelve we moved to Wythenshawe. I did alright at school, other than having a reputation for being a bit lippy, and even then knew I didn't ever want to live anywhere other than Manchester. It's like you said, it's got personality. It's got grit. Plus my friends are here. I didn't see any reason to go anywhere else.'

'Not even to escape the rain?'

Clara smiled. 'I even like that. When I first started working at the youth club I decided I was going to treat my mum to a holiday somewhere warm – take her away for some winter sun. We'd not been abroad since ... well, since before Dad left. We'd barely even left Lancashire, thinking about it. So I booked us this last-minute package deal to the Algarve. Nothing fancy, but it was all-inclusive. When we got there we hated it. November is *meant* to be drizzly and cold. It didn't feel right walking around in short-sleeved clothes.'

'You're close to your mum, then?'

'She's my best friend. Sounds cheesy, but it's true. I've moved back in with her since splitting up with Dean. I'm lucky, because she's always supported me without being pushy. She worked every hour she could to make sure I didn't go without, and I'll always be grateful to her for that. She's the best role model a girl could ask for.'

'Sounds like it.'

Clara eyed up the last mince pie, lonely in the centre of the plate. 'Do you want that?'

Joe shook his head. Talking about Michelle had caused his hunger to ebb away. That and the calories he'd already consumed lying heavy in the pit of his stomach. 'You have it.'

Clara unfolded an unused napkin that had been on the table as they'd been talking, and carefully wrapped the mince pie in it before placing the parcel in her handbag.

'Saving it for later?' he asked.

'Taking it for Mum,' she replied with a shy smile. 'If that's okay?'

'More than okay,' he said. 'From what you've said, it sounds like she's earned it.'

Clara

Wednesday, December 6th 2017

After she'd finished carefully wrapping the almost-square box in metallic gold paper, Clara had decided she might as well go the whole hog. In a bid to make it look like something from one of the posh shops' window displays, she'd tied a thick red ribbon around it. The fancy trimming had immediately made the present look more appealing – she only hoped Joe wouldn't be too disappointed when the gift inside failed to match up to its lavish wrapping.

Clara waited by the main door, fiddling around with the adverts and posters pinned on the notice board. She had a terrible habit of rearranging the boards, even when everything was up to date and relevant, but even though she didn't want to admit it to herself, she knew exactly why she was lingering in the hallway. She wanted to hand Joe the gift as soon as he walked through that door. Partly because she wanted to make up for the failed attempts so far, and partly because after he'd been so honest about his grief she felt more than ever that she wanted to bring positivity into his life. Nothing was going to go wrong this time. It wasn't edible, there were no stalls for it to be sold on – this gem of a gift was getting placed straight into his hands.

She looked at her watch for the umpteenth time. Half-past five. He should be here by now.

'What're you doing sneaking about?' Deirdre asked. For someone who relied on a walking stick she moved surprisingly stealthily, and Clara jumped at being caught out.

'Nothing. Just checking the notice boards are up to date,' she replied, full of innocence. 'I wanted to make sure the Christmas events were clearly advertised.'

'Have you put the poster up about the disco? I confirmed the DJ this morning. We need to make sure everyone knows about it. Hopefully they'll bring plenty of extra money to spend on refreshments,' Deirdre added, holding tightly crossed fingers aloft.

The mark-up in the fizzy drinks and crisps and sweets was where they made their money, and money was what they needed. That or more kind-hearted souls like Joe to donate their time.

'It's been up there for weeks. Shannon and the gang have spent hours trying to decide what to wear for it. They were on about getting a bus out to the Trafford Centre to splurge on new outfits. I could've sworn I heard Phoebe mentioned a sequin boob tube.'

Deirdre pulled a face. 'She's been watching too much *Strictly*.'

'Ah, give over. They're teenagers and it's their big night out. Of course they're going to want to look their best.'

'Have you thought about what you're going to wear? Because if everyone's dressing up in their glad rags you don't want to be rolling up in your jeans and hoodie.'

Clara assessed her everyday work clothes. The jeans were fine – a bit on the faded side, but they fit her well, and although the denim was thinning around the knees, soft and pliable, they hadn't yet split to reveal a flash of kneecap. The hoodie ... well, perhaps Deirdre had a point with that. It had a hole near the cuff and the print on the front had worn away from one too many cycles in the washing machine. But it was so comfortable, almost a second skin, and Clara couldn't bring herself to add it to the bag of material bound for scrap recycling. It was perfectly alright for knocking about at the club. Plus, she'd been glad of it when she'd been walking to work, doing her best to avoid the painful pelting of hailstones that had bounced around her feet.

'I won't be wearing a ball gown, let's put it that way. I'll be working. There's no point putting on my best clothes. I spent most of the last disco on my hands and knees, disinfecting the floor where Ted had thrown up.'

Deirdre wrinkled her nose. 'I'd forgotten about that. Don't let him buy any fizzy cola bottles this time.'

'I'll get the mop and rubber gloves handy instead. He spent a fortune at the tuck shop last time. We can't afford to turn him away on the off-chance he'll throw up again.'

'Some people can't handle their Haribo,' Deirdre said seriously, at the same moment as the door swung open.

Deirdre and Clara gawped at Joe's bedraggled appearance. The poor guy was soaked through.

'Hello,' he said, gingerly peeling off a soggy beanie hat. Fat droplets of water fell from it as he did so, creating a puddle on the hallway floor. Clara noticed Deirdre twitching. Health and safety...

'I'll fetch you a towel.'

As Deirdre headed to the store cupboards to see what she could find for Joe to dry himself with, Joe unzipped his coat and hung it on the coat rack. It was drenched, and Clara knew Deirdre would be in a tailspin over it dripping onto the floor. She made a mental note to get the mop and the hazard sign out of the cupboard before the kids started arriving.

'It's wild out there. Makes even this place feel tropical.'

Clara laughed. 'Don't go overboard. It's freezing in here. As always.'

The Club on the Corner was an old building with a heating system that could, at best, be described as temperamental. Stand too close to the radiators and you'd end up burned, but because of the generously sized rooms, especially the hall, it had a tendency to get draughty no matter how high the heat was turned up. Clara had got used to it over the years, but it was still a running joke that it would be a good place for wannabe explorers to come as preparation for a trip to the Arctic.

'Your jumper's soaked,' Clara observed. 'You can't wear that, you'll make yourself ill.'

'I've not got a choice.' Joe shivered, his shoulders wobbling like a set jelly. 'I've not got anything else.'

Clara shook her head firmly. 'No way. You can't sit in wet clothes all night, that's ridiculous. I'll see if there's anything in the lost property box that might fit. You never know, there might be something suitable.' She didn't add that she thought it unlikely. Joe was exceptionally tall – she'd guess well over six foot – and even the oldest boys at the youth club were far shorter than him.

Joe held up his hand, stopping her in her tracks. 'It's

alright. Simone passes my flat on the way here and she's got a key. I'll get her to pick me something up on the way. And I'll be better once I've got myself towelled down.'

Clara was annoyed that her stomach twitched at the thought. Joe was a volunteer, not one of the bloody Dream Boys. Although with his tall, broad body and attractive dark colouring, he could probably give the erotic 'dancers' a run for their money.

Clara was relieved when Deirdre appeared with a brightly coloured beach towel and threw it at Joe. He caught it expertly in one hand.

'Cheers, Deirdre,' he said, rubbing the towel over the bare skin of his shaven head. 'At least I've not got any hair to dry,' he joked.

Clara watched on as he moved the towel over his face, patting the fabric against his cheeks. But she wasn't prepared for him peeling off his jumper to reveal the damp, bare skin of his chest. She found herself catching her breath at the sight, and immediately chided herself for letting her imagination run away with her.

Clara turned her attention back to the notice board, hoping that by feigning disinterest Deirdre wouldn't pass comment.

Every part of her was itching to turn around, though. Knowing Joe was dragging that towel over his body just a few feet away was causing her heart to race. Clara could only blame her lack of bedroom action of late. It had been almost six months now since her engagement had come to an abrupt end, and there had been no one since. She was obviously turning into a sex-starved pervert.

'You put those abs away right now, young man!' Deirdre said with a chortle. 'What do you think you're playing at, flashing your body around like that? You could give me a heart attack.'

Clara was tempted to add that her own heart was beating rather fast, but thought better of it. By keeping her eyes firmly fixed on the pin board she could surely keep her mouth zipped too, even if it did take a monumental effort.

'Sorry,' Joe replied, with a teasing voice that sounded anything but. 'Simone will be here any minute and I'll cover up as soon as she brings me a dry jumper. I wouldn't want to inflict my love handles on anyone.'

'Give over,' Deirdre replied with a cluck of her tongue. 'You must spend half your life at the gym. Muscles like those don't appear out of nowhere.'

'Honestly, I don't work out. Cutting back on the drink has made a difference, though.'

'You wouldn't catch me giving up my alcohol,' Clara chimed in. She was already thinking it was well into the Baileys season and she'd not yet had her first of the year. She'd have to rectify that. Maybe she'd pop by the supermarket on the way home and pick up a bottle to enjoy over ice later. She couldn't get enough of the stuff; it was like melted ice cream in a glass. Mmmm. 'You might find yourself needing a few more drinks when you've been here a bit longer. It does tend to have that effect on people, doesn't it, Deirdre?'

Deirdre was partial to a vodka and ginger, or a gin and tonic, or a brandy and Babycham in fact, Deirdre wasn't too fussy when it came to her tipple of choice. She just liked a drink and to let her hair down.

'You make out I'm reliant on it,' Deirdre replied. 'It's a good job Joe knows me or you'd have him believe I'm drinking morning, noon and night. I only have the odd glass when it's a celebration.'

The long, loud rap on the door, followed by Simone shouting to be let in, was the only thing to halt Clara's laughter.

'There's water everywhere,' the girl said, shaking the rain out of her hair. 'I think the drains on Dirkstock Road are blocked too. The whole place is flooded. It's ridiculous.'

'Didn't you bring an umbrella?' Deirdre asked incredulously. 'Your hair's all over the shop. You look like a poodle.'

Clara smiled and turned to face Simone. She knew she shouldn't have favourites, but if she did, Simone was one of them. Slim and toned, much like Joe, her hair was usually a bouncy mass of tightly coiled curls slicked with argan oil to keep them moist. Right now they had lost their shape and their vitality, hanging like springs that had been pulled out of shape.

But it was Joe, or more specifically, his chest, who really caught her attention. He wasn't as ripped as Deirdre had made him out to be, but his pecs were defined. There was a dark scar too, sitting just above the waistband of his jeans. It was only because of the location of it, the line perfectly parallel to his belt, that Clara noticed. She opened her mouth to ask about it before reluctantly pulling her eyes away and biting her tongue. It wasn't her business, and if Joe wanted to talk about it, he surely would in his own good time. After all, he'd opened up to her about Michelle. He must trust her a little bit to willingly share something so personal.

'Want the towel?' Joe asked, offering his little sister the sodden sheet of fabric.

'It's not much good now, is it? It's soggy! Anyway, I brought you the jumper you wanted,' she said, handing the navy knitwear to her brother. 'Didn't look like it had been ironed, though,' she added with a look of disdain. Simone was at the age where she wanted everything just so. That whole group of girls were – they loved fashion and make-up and the best hair products on the market would be their *Mastermind* specialist subject. Being seen in crumpled clothing would be a fate worse than death.

'Thanks, sis,' Joe said, gratefully.

He pulled the jumper over his head, hiding the abs and the mysterious yet tantalising scar from view. Clara wondered if she'd ever ask him about it, although that would mean admitting she'd been looking in the first place. She had to admit she was curious.

'You're a star,' he said, ruffling Simone's hair in a way that only a devoted big brother could get away with.

Simone dipped away.

'Gerrof,' she growled affectionately. 'I've got five minutes to get this looking less disastrous before everyone else gets here.'

'They'll all be soaked through,' Clara reminded her. 'It wouldn't surprise me if some people don't bother coming out on a night like this.'

When the weather was extreme – either snowy, or torrential rain, or glorious sun – the number of children passing through the doors was fewer. When it snowed they were pelting each other with snowballs, and when it was sunny they hung out at the park, where they could swear to their hearts' content without Clara and

Deirdre telling them to mind their language. And when it was wet like this, they couldn't be bothered, unless their parents drove them to the door.

'Come on, time to get busy.' Deirdre headed to the main hall, where Clara had already set out a selection of board games. The kids were surprisingly into Scrabble at the moment. It made a change from their last obsession with the card game Bullshit. That phase hadn't lasted long, to be fair. As soon as Deirdre made them shorten the victory call to plain old 'bull' the cards were relegated to their usual spot at the back of the store cupboard. 'Simone, you can help me set up the table tennis.'

Simone dutifully followed, leaving Clara and Joe standing in the hallway.

'You made quite the entrance,' Clara quipped. 'Bursting in and then taking half your clothes off ... it was like the finale to *The Full Monty*.'

'Not quite,' Joe smiled. 'And I'm sorry. I wouldn't normally inflict my body on a poor unsuspecting soul. No one deserves that.'

Whether he was looking for reassurance or not, Clara wasn't sure. Joe must be aware he'd avoided being hit with the ugly stick, and even if he didn't work out, Deirdre was right – he wouldn't have a body like he did if he didn't make some sort of effort to keep in shape. Maybe it was a healthy diet and limited alcohol. Even if that was the case, it wasn't enough to deter Clara from the creamy temptation of her Baileys. She'd rather have a few curves and enjoy her treats.

'Stop doing yourself down. You're not that bad.'

'Thanks. I'll take that as a compliment, shall I?'

'It *was* a compliment.'

They stood awkwardly for a moment until Joe broke the silence. 'I'd better give Deirdre a hand. Not much use as a volunteer if I'm not actually doing anything.'

As he headed for the hall Clara remembered the gift she'd been so desperate to give him before she'd been otherwise distracted.

'Joe!'

He turned, and she held up the present, the light from the exposed bulb dangling from the light fitting reflecting in the shiny wrapping paper.

'You remembered,' he beamed.

'As if I'd forget,' she said, handing it over.

He pulled at the end of the ribbon, unravelling the bow she'd so painstakingly tied.

'It's not just for you,' she said as he peeled back the paper. 'I mean, it's yours to take home with you, if you want to. But I thought it would be good to keep here.'

Joe looked at the CD in his hand, a two-disc compilation of Christmas songs. 'I can't remember the last time I listened to a CD,' he said, beating the case against the heel of his hand. 'I download everything to iTunes these days.'

'Don't we all,' she replied. 'But there's something special about having a Christmas CD, and we've still got a hi-fi here. I think it's Deirdre's. It looks like something that came out of the ark, but it does the job.'

'Things were made to last in the olden days.'

'Don't let Deirdre hear you say that. She'd be most insulted if you insinuated she was old.'

'Ah, Deirdre will last forever, like that CD player. She's strong as an ox.' He tapped the CD case against his hand again, scanning the list of tracks. 'Thanks for this.'

'We'll put it on once everyone's arrived. Help get us in the festive mood.'

'Yeah, it's not like these songs have been on the adverts since October or anything.' Joe's voice was sarcastic, but not malicious. 'And playing in the shops. Paul McCartney was having a wonderful Christmastime in mid-November. At least, he was in Sainsbury's. These Christmas songs, I swear they're taking over the world.'

'Bah humbug.' Clara poked her tongue out. 'You can't not love these songs. Even Scrooge would find himself swaying along to "Last Christmas", so if you say you don't like them you're lying.'

'A few of them are alright, I suppose. 'Fairytale of

New York', and that Mel and Kim one ...'

'I knew it. I'll expect you to start the singing of those later, then.'

'We'll see,' he said, making his way through the door. But not before winking at Clara.

* * *

'That's not a word!'

'It is,' Cally replied indignantly. She wrinkled her nose at the suggestion she might be wrong. 'Clara,' she called, "Spleen' is a word, isn't it?'

'It is,' Clara confirmed with a nod, as she swiftly hit a backhanded shot across the table- tennis table. She'd become surprisingly adept at the sport over the years. Not professional standard, but she could hold her own against Manchester's young millennials. 'It's an internal organ. I've not got a clue what it does, though.'

The small white ball bounced off the end of the table and over the pock-skinned bat of the pock-skinned boy who had challenged Clara to a match, before hopping across the hall floor.

'Ball!' Clara called, hoping one of the kids would get to it before it rolled under the stack of chairs in the corner of the room. That corner was filthy, hiding cobwebs and crisp crumbs and who knew what else.

Clara didn't fancy putting her hand down there to retrieve a blooming ping-pong ball, thank you very much.

Joe stuck out a leg in the nick of time, the ball connecting with his still-saturated trainers and rolling back towards the centre of the room.

Clara let out a sigh of relief. 'My hero,' she joked, mocking a swoon worthy of a protagonist in a Jane Austen novel. 'You saved me from the spider's lair.'

Joe tilted his head and small crinkles appeared at the corners of his eyes as he smiled. 'Does that mean I don't have to put the CD on?'

'Don't think you're getting out of it that easily,' Clara warned. 'I've been looking forward to those songs all day.'

Joe pushed himself up off his chair, his game of Cluedo resolved (Professor Plum, in the study, with the lead piping). 'Well, if you've been looking forward to it all day, who am I to spoil your fun?'

He picked up the disc and placed it in the ancient CD player.

'Here goes nothing,' he said, pressing the play button. The opening bars of 'Fairytale of New York' started chiming out.

'It's one of your favourites,' Clara said triumphantly, bouncing the ping-pong ball once before serving it over the net. 'So you can stop moaning and start enjoying.'

She noticed a half-smile playing out on Joe's lips, and as the excited kids started singing along it broke out into a full beam of a grin. Tariq was slurring in his best Shane MacGowan impression and Clara laughed at how the usually cold hall suddenly seemed so much warmer. The tree, the music, the atmosphere ... it was what Christmas should be about. And as the Irish jig kicked in and Kirsty MacColl's inimitable voice rang out across the room, Clara couldn't think of anywhere she would rather be.

'Scumbag!'

'Maggot!'

'Cheap lousy faggot!'

The kids revelled in legitimately shouting insults at the top of their lungs (even Deirdre couldn't complain about them joining in with a classic festive hit) whilst Clara fretted in case any of the parents found out and complained about the non-PC lyrics. She hoped that by the time the adolescents got to the more innocent Christmas tunes like 'Little Drummer Boy' they'd be too busy a-rum-pa-pa-pumming to remember the start of the evening.

'You hadn't thought this through, had you?' said a teasing voice in Clara's ear. Joe's breath tickled her skin. 'They're basically hurling abuse at a hundred decibels.'

'The next song's more sedate,' she promised, although the truth was she couldn't remember which track was coming up after Queen Kirsty and The Pogues.

The ball skimmed her cheek as Tariq shouted 'Get in!' at the top of his lungs.

'Watch it,' Joe warned the boy with a point of his index finger. 'You could have had Clara's eye out.'

Tariq looked sheepish, knowing he'd taken advantage of Clara's distraction.

'Sorry,' he muttered, placing the dimpled bat down on the table before sloping off in the direction of the tuck shop.

Clara set her bat down too and turned to face Joe as the opening chords of 'Stay Another Day' started playing. She giggled, remembering Joe's comment about Dean's coat looking like something East 17 would wear. Once the giggles took hold, she couldn't stop, her whole body shaking as Brian Harvey's wide boy London accent crooned away. Soon Joe was laughing too, bent double in a fit of giggles as Clara clung to his shoulder to stop from falling to the floor in uncontrollable hysterics.

The Christmas bells were tinkling out from the stereo as Deirdre rolled her eyes to the heavens.

'You two are worse than the kids!' she declared, before turning on her heels and heading back to the calm of the office.

That only made Joe and Clara laugh all the more, until they gave in and sank to the floor, unable to remain upright for a moment longer.

Joe

Thursday, December 7th 2017

'I can't believe you've brought me somewhere this swanky when I'm dressed like this!' Clara's voice squeaked with disbelief as she drank in the fancy chandeliers, the hipster barmen complete with waistcoats and neatly trimmed beards, and the extortionate prices of the cocktails on the gold-embossed menu. This was the newest of the cocktail bars springing up in Manchester city centre, each trying to outdo the other with upmarket fixtures and fittings to match their diverse drinks menus.

'You look great,' Joe reassured her. Her flared black dress was understated and lacked the ostentatiousness of the surroundings, the white Peter Pan collar adding a girlish innocence, which contrasted starkly with her punky lace-up biker boots. 'I love your style.'

'Thanks.'

She flushed slightly at the compliment, which along with the dress and her petite stature made her look cuter still in his eyes. She could front a punk band, Joe thought, with her super-cool hair, her nose stud (and the trail of piercings that followed the outer curve of her right ear) and her clompy no-nonsense boots. Not to mention the sass. That was something she had in abundance.

Thinking about Clara's attitude reminded Joe of the conversation they'd had in the previous bar. She'd been part way through regaling him with a shocking tale, which had made him see her in a whole new light, when they'd been politely interrupted by a waitress keen to get them to order more drinks. Naturally they'd been swayed, especially Clara, who'd loved the festive drinks menu (selecting an Ice Blast – a concoction of vodka, schnapps and cranberry over crushed ice, although she'd hummed and hawed about whether to plump for a Chilly Nipple instead, purely because of the comedy name), and Joe had, in his mildly inebriated state, forgotten the conversation until now. Between the two of them the original purpose of the night, planning their presentation for the church committee, hadn't taken too long. They'd still need to get together to finalise the power-point presentation and add in the numbers Clara hadn't been able to recall from memory, but the night had descended into pleasure rather than business sooner than expected.

'You never finished telling me about Dean and the car.'

Clara twitched. 'I probably shouldn't say anything. If he wanted to, he could go to the police over it.'

'Criminal Clara strikes again,' Joe joked, taking a sip of his drink. It was pretty potent, his throat burning as the fiery mixture hit, before a warm and wonderful numbness took hold. 'So come on, spill the beans.'

She giggled as she took a large glug of her own cocktail, leaning forward with a naughty gleam in her eye. 'I keyed it. I keyed his precious convertible.'

Joe was shocked at the revelation, but it manifested itself as a nervous laugh.

'You're having me on,' he said eventually. His mouth was dry, so he turned back to his drink, hoping it'd offer him more insight. If not, at least it would act as a distraction, and as long as the slender black straw was in his mouth he didn't need to worry about floundering for words.

She shook her head, her choppy bob swinging from side to side. 'I swear, I did it. Cross my heart and hope to die.' Clara raised her index finger above her left breast and traced a large and wobbly cross. 'I didn't *plan* to.

I'm not that callous. But when I saw his car in the supermarket car park ... I don't know what came over me. I was like a woman possessed.'

'I'm lost for words.'

'What can I say? One minute I'm sweetness and light, the next my wild and untamed streak is unleashed.' Clara raised her hands in front of her face in a claw-like fashion and let out a roar before chuckling once more. 'You don't need to look so disapproving, it's not like I go around doing that to random vehicles just for the hell of it. It was one impulsive moment.'

'How much damage did you do?'

Clara's attention shifted to her drink and Joe wondered if a smidgen of shame was catching up with her. Then she smirked, a devilish twinkle in her eye. 'Enough. I ran the key all the way along one side. The paintwork was wrecked.'

'You are so naughty. I think I've got the measure of you, then you go and drop a bombshell like this and I feel I've got a lot still to learn about you.' Joe clucked his tongue, but he couldn't hide his amusement. 'Do you think he knew it was you who did it?'

'Nah, probably thinks it was a kid messing about.'

Clara sucked the remnants of her cocktail up through her straw, the noisy slurping causing Joe to raise an eyebrow.

She scooped the squidgy fruit by dragging the end of her straw along the inside of the glass, popping a raspberry into her mouth.

'I'm a good girl at heart. I don't make a habit of scratching cars.'

'That's what's so funny, you're totally dedicated to the club and you're such a great role model for the kids, and then I find out stuff like this.'

'You know what they say? It's the quiet ones you've got to watch. I think you've got to be a bit anarchic to work with teenagers. Or a lunatic.'

'I'll tell Deirdre you called her a lunatic.'

'Don't you dare!' Clara squealed. 'Even though she totally is.'

'Me and Billy used to think she was so old and boring, because she was always nagging us about something. It's only as I've got older myself I realise how cool she actually is.'

'She's incredible,' Clara agreed. 'I sometimes wish me and her were the same age. I bet she was a right hoot on a night out.'

'Her tales are hilarious,' Joe agreed. 'Did she ever tell you about the time she climbed the fence to get into Glastonbury?'

'When she was caked in mud and tried to get on the stage with Van Morrison to do backing vocals?' Clara threw back her head in hysterics. 'Yes, once or twice.'

'I'm never sure which of her stories actually happened and which are wild fantasies. Either way, she definitely believes she's experienced this stuff.'

'Exactly. Lunatic.' Clara winked.

'We all need a bit of crazy in our lives now and again,' Joe said, whilst recognising he was one of the least crazy people he knew.

Joe Smith. Even his name was nondescript.

He took the straw out of his glass and knocked back what was left of his drink, blinking as he feared he might choke on the half-melted ice cube, which lodged in his throat. He spluttered in panic at the prospect. So much for living la vida loca, he couldn't even down a drink these days without causing a scene.

'We do. But you keep on being yourself. You've got me. I can be crazy enough for the both of us.'

Keep on being yourself.

You've got me.

The words stirred something within him, and Joe began to wonder if maybe he was a bit crazy after all. Because despite all the scandalous revelations, the quirks and the flaws, he couldn't deny he was finding himself drawn to Clara.

* * *

'I might be a bit drunk,' Clara slurred, at the same moment as her ankle slipped off the edge of the kerb. She fell with a bump, landing in a pretzel knot of a heap and laughed as though it was the funniest thing in the world.

'It's Christmas. Well, near enough. You can get away with it,' Joe said, offering his hand to pull her back onto her feet.

Clara wasn't the only reveller looking the worse for wear. As they made their way down Oldham Street, past the party people spilling out of Dry Bar and Night and Day, the two stumbled together.

'Look!' Clara pointed towards the window of a record shop. Album covers were pressed against the glass, and Joe wondered what had caught her eye. There was no Avril Lavigne, as far as he could see, and the bands that made up the display were predominantly obscure indie artists favoured by Radio 6. He couldn't imagine any of them would appeal to Clara, who despite her edgy appearance seemed to favour the cheesiest music around.

'What?'

'Look at that record player! It's so cute!'

The turquoise box was propped open, looking like a toy suitcase but for the turntable and arm, and seemed cheap alongside the professional decks.

At one time Joe had considered buying a record player – swayed by an article he'd read in a music mag about vinyl's big comeback – but he couldn't get past the inconvenience of the format; not only the ability of records to get scratched and damaged, but also the faff of turning the record over halfway through. Music was so easy to access these days. All he had to do was either dock his iPod or click on one of his Spotify playlists and he'd have music sorted for the night.

'You don't strike me as a hipster. And you're not old enough to remember records being in fashion the first time around.'

'Yeah, but my gran was forever listening to records when we lived there. Never anything I liked – all really old Rat Pack stuff – but even though I'd rather have listened to chart music, the crackles and the static used to send shivers up my spine.'

'Static does that,' Joe replied, deadpan.

'You're not funny.'

'I'm hilarious,' Joe laughed. He felt lightheaded, and although he was aware that the cold air slapping his cheeks should be sobering him up, it seemed instead to be helping the alcohol in his bloodstream take hold.

'You're really not. Anyway, before you *rudely* inter-rupted, I was trying to tell you a story.' She planted her hands on her hips and jutted out her chin. 'I asked for a record player for Christmas once, way before they were back in fashion. I don't think any of the singers I liked were even bringing out their music on vinyl, but I still wanted one. I liked the way the needle moved along the grooves of my gran's records, I found it relaxing. Never got one, though,' she added sadly, reaching out to place her hand against the record player, the grimy glass the only thing between her and the object of her desires.

'Sounds like me and the limited edition Game Boy I wanted. It was ice blue and clear so you could see all the electronics inside. My mum was dead set against games consoles, though. She thought they'd rot my brain and distract me from my studies, so I was never allowed one. That Christmas morning I cried, and I never cry. That's how devastated I was. I didn't get a console until I earned enough money to buy a Wii when I was an adult.'

'I don't remember crying about the record player. I got given a doll whose hair grew when you twisted her arm, which was a pretty cool alternative. I'd forgotten about the record player by the time we sat down to eat Christmas dinner.'

'Maybe I wanted the Game Boy more than you wanted the record player, because I never forgot.'

Joe spotted a taxi with its light on passing along the

street and seized the opportunity to flag it down before anyone else snapped it up. He didn't fancy getting the last bus home with all the drunks, even though over the course of the night he'd probably matched them drink for drink.

'Clara!' he called, opening the door to the black cab and sprawling onto the pleather seat. 'Come on!'

'I did want that record player,' she said, clambering into the taxi in an ungainly motion, her eyes still fixed on the little record player.

'It's never too late. You could ask Santa for one again this year?'

Clara smiled. 'Maybe. You'll have to take me to see the big man so I can ask him.'

'And you'll have to start upping your game. Santa doesn't bring presents to people who misbehave.' Joe waggled his finger in warning. 'Belt up,' he added, as the taxi pulled away.

'I always behave,' Clara slurred as the taxi took a sharp bend. She slid along the slippery seat covering, her fastened seatbelt failing to stop her sliding into Joe with a crash.

Joe closed his eyes to block out the blur of the passing streetlights. Partly to stop the dizziness he was experiencing, but partly so he could pretend he was on a high-speed spinning waltzer; rather than being mildly turned on as a drunken Clara crushed him on the back seat of a black cab heading home via Mancunian Way.

Clara

Friday, December 8th 2017

Surprisingly, Clara had woken up feeling fresh. She knew she barely deserved it after the five strong cocktails she'd sunk the previous night. Despite her small stature she prided herself on being able to handle her drink, but the super-strength concoctions had got her rapidly drunk and left her with a throbbing head.

The sweet aftertaste of peach schnapps still lingered in the furthest crevices of her mouth and Clara was convinced her teeth were eroding even more with each passing second.

She was thankful she'd had a peaceful afternoon adding ideas she and Joe had brainstormed to the presentation and unpacking the novelty tat they were going to use for the Christmas cracker craft session at the club that night. Cutting small slips of coloured paper ready for jokes to be written on had been therapeutic (she'd have to check that none were too rude – the finished crackers were being donated to a local old folks' home. She wouldn't want the kids' risqué jokes pushing the geriatrics over the edge), and boxes of chocolates that she'd removed all the hard-centred ones from, for fear of dentures cracking. The last thing The Club on the Corner needed was a hefty dentistry bill landing on their doormat. Who knew there was so much to consider when making a few crackers out of the goodness of your heart?

Her eyes rested on the pristine white envelope propped against the mug she used to keep her pens, pencils and highlighters tidy. She'd written the letter on her lunch break, but now it was ready to be posted – right down to the Christmas stamp placed firmly in the upper right- hand corner – she was having second thoughts. She must have been drunk to have considered writing it in the first place. Or perhaps she was just desperate. Yes, that was it. She was desperate.

'Hiya.' Joe breezed in as fresh as the proverbial daisy, and Clara unthinkingly turned the envelope around so he wouldn't spot the address. His eyes narrowed. 'Been writing that letter to Santa? You'll be on the naughty list if he was watching last night. That taxi driver wasn't impressed at having to pull over so you could throw up.'

Clara buried her face in her hands, humiliated beyond belief. 'I don't want to talk about it. Oh, the shame!'

'At least you managed to get out of the cab before spilling your guts. How's your head?'

'It's been better,' Clara admitted, 'but being sick helped. I'm tired, more than anything. Deirdre reckons I'm coming down with a bug because I look so pale, and I didn't correct her. She doesn't need to know we were playing at being dirty stop-outs.'

'It was a good night. Feeling confident we can get the presentation up to scratch by Monday?'

Clara nodded. 'It'll be Sunday night before I can put the finishing touches to the slides, but yeah. I feel better now I know what needs to be done.'

'I'm happy to help you with it. It'll be a quicker job if we do it together. Two heads are better than one and all that.'

'Thanks,' Clara smiled.

Joe clocked the resources for the evening's session, piled high on the desk. 'Need a hand with anything for tonight?'

'There's not much more to do, I don't think. Once we move this lot into the hall we'll be ready to go.'

Joe scooped up a wicker basket full of novelties and plopped two half-empty tubs of chocolates, much like the one Clara had given him, on top.

'I'm looking forward to tonight,' he said, as they teetered down the staircase, arms laden. 'Simone is too, she was talking about it when I spoke to her earlier.'

'She's really arty, isn't she? Dance, singing, crafts ...'

'It's her passion. She's one of those irritating people who's good at everything, and she's always been great at sports as well as being naturally bookish, but being creative is what sparks her the most. You should see what she can do with a sewing machine. She's started making bags and selling them on Etsy, and they're brilliant. Better quality than you'd see on the high street,' he added, with evident pride.

'It doesn't surprise me. She's a talented young lady.' Clara pushed the door open with her backside before gladly setting down the items she'd been carrying on the table. 'She'll go a long way, that sister of yours.'

'She will,' Joe smiled. 'When she was four she told me she wanted to make the world a happier place. What kind of four-year-old says stuff like that? Anyway, she does make it a better place, just by being herself. My world, anyway.'

'You two have such a great relationship.'

Joe looked quietly pleased, but carried on spreading out the felt-tipped pens and glue sticks across the table tops. 'I guess. She's my sister, and I'm probably biased, but I think she's pretty incredible. I just hope Simone sees me as more than just an embarrassing older brother.'

'She doesn't think that at all,' Clara assured him. 'It's obvious how much admiration she's got for you.'

'You think so?' His eyes were alight at the suggestion.

'I don't just think so,' Clara smiled. 'I know so.'

*　*　*

'Look at all the glitter on the floor,' Deirdre grumbled, as she shuffled into the hall. 'I hope the Hoover doesn't give up the ghost again. I don't fancy sweeping this lot up with the long-arm brush,' she added, scanning her eyes across the now-sparkly surface.

The room resembled Santa's workshop, with offcuts of patterned wrapping paper strewn all around as the cracker-making factory was in full swing. The young people were enjoying the opportunity to put their creativity to the test, minus a few of the older lads, who deemed it uncool, and Tiffany, who didn't want to do anything that might mess up her newly applied nail extensions. Clara had to admit they looked pretty badass – blood red like a cartoon villainess except for the ring fingers, which were silver and glittery – and for a fleeting moment she wished she was the type of woman who had the energy (and the finances) to prioritise manicures. She'd only had two in her life: once when she was a bridesmaid for her cousin and they had a pamper party as part of the hen do, and once when she'd decided to go all out for her birthday celebrations. New hairdo, spray tan, false nails and every available surface waxed until it was as smooth as a baby's bottom. Dean had barely noticed her efforts. Even when prompted he'd only offered 'you look good', rather than the 'stunning' or 'beautiful' she'd hoped for, and it had made her doubt it was all worth it. Whilst she still swore by her regular cut and blow-dries at her favourite salon, she wasn't falling into the trap of paying a small fortune to a beautician if it made little to no difference to her overall appearance. None of it had felt like her style, anyway. It had all been a front, a mask, and an expensive and elaborate one at that.

'If it's not, we'll get this lot picking up every last speck of glitter,' promised Joe. He had a mischievous glint in his dark eyes as he added, 'Can't see you helping out with that, though, Deirdre. Not with your old knees.'

'Less of the old,' warned Deirdre, pursing her lips tightly together. 'I'll have you know these knees aren't complaining because of their age. If anything, they're worn out from overuse!'

'How do you overuse your knees?' asked Simone. 'All

the gymnastics you were telling us you used to do?'

'The gymnastics played its part, but it was the all-night raving at the Hacienda that did the lasting damage,' she said, mournfully. 'I was always the first on that dance floor and last off it,' she said with a faraway look on her face. 'Those were good days.'

'I don't think anyone needs to know about your nights out on the town,' Clara interjected with a pointed look. She'd heard stories of party-girl Deirdre before, and they weren't suitable for easily influenced teenage ears. 'Look at how well we're doing with the cracker- making.' She gestured towards the plastic crate overflowing with finished handmade crackers. 'Joe's checked every single joke to make sure they're alright.'

He looked up, worried. 'I don't think they'll be rivalling the Morecambe and Wise Christmas Special any time soon, but there's nothing rude. This is as bad as it gets,' he said, passing Clara a slip of card with a cheeky joke written on it. The writing was barely legible.

'That's not rude, that's just rubbish,' said Clara, laughing despite herself before handing the joke to Deirdre.

'Tariq thought it was hilarious,' Joe countered.

'I should have known it would be one of his,' Deirdre said with a fond smile. 'Bless him, he's not got a future as a stand-up comic.'

'We're running out of stuff to put in these crackers,' Clara remarked, noting how the tacky gifts and chocolates were now looking decidedly sparse. She suspected the kids had made a dent in the chocolates, especially given the tell-tale chocolatey residue in the corner of Brianna's lip creases, but she didn't feel she could judge them for nibbling, not when she'd munched her way through a good percentage of the toffees earlier in the day as she worked on the presentation. She'd been glad of the sugar kick. 'Do you think we'll have enough to take with us when we go?'

'Oh, that looks like plenty,' Deirdre said. 'But why don't we make up more to distribute to other groups in the area too. I bet the food bank would be glad of them.'

'That's a great idea,' Joe enthused. 'Some of those families won't be getting presents this year, so a seasonal touch will make all the difference.'

'Then it's decided,' Deirdre replied, her accompanying nod laden with finality. 'We've got the carol singing at the old folks' home tomorrow night, and any crackers left over can be taken to the food bank with the other donations. We're going to make up food parcels there next week,' she reminded Clara. 'Quite a few of this lot have volunteered to help out already, including Tariq and his terrible sense of humour.'

'I'd not forgotten, I've started stockpiling hot-chocolate sachets and mini marshmallows to donate. It doesn't seem much, but it screams Christmas to me. It's not fair that the people who rely on the food bank miss out on treats at this time of year, so I wanted to donate more than dried pasta and tins of baked beans.'

She thought back to the hot chocolate she'd had with Joe, the memory of the rich flavour flooding her mouth. It had been Christmas in a cup, and although what she could offer these families wouldn't compare to the out-and-out luxury of that drink, it felt nice to know that her little gesture might make someone's Christmas that bit more memorable.

Joe sidled up to Clara, before leaning down so his mouth was close to her ear.

'Simone's been busy making gifts to donate too,' he revealed, his voice low and deep. 'She wanted to give something special too.'

'That's so sweet.' Clara's heart swelled at the thought of Simone going the extra mile to help the families who were in need. What a lovely family the Smiths were. 'What's she been making?'

'She's crocheted flower brooches and sewn some patchwork cushions too. And she's going to make some dolls' clothes on her machine with fabric that was donated to the church. It's good quality, but too small to make anything bigger with. One of the parishioners works at a factory so she rescues any offcuts that she thinks might be useful.'

'Are you coming to the food bank with us?' She mentioned the date and Joe checked the calendar on his phone. 'We'd be grateful for an extra pair of hands. It can be a bit like organised chaos when this lot try to "help", she said, raising her fingers into quotation marks.

'It's an odd-numbered day, so I should be taking you somewhere Christmassy.'

'I'll probably be too tired after,' Clara said, with a pout of sadness. 'It's physically demanding lifting those boxes of tinned foods, and mentally exhausting keeping this lot in check.'

'Looks like I'll have to come along then, and we'll add that to our list of Christmas experiences,' Joe said.

'Great.' Clara smiled in return, a warm fuzzy feeling filling her chest. She was enjoying the time she was sharing with Joe. 'We're doing a good job of keeping the countdown going.'

'We are,' Joe agreed, 'although I've not had a present yet today.'

'If that's a hint, it's not very subtle.'

'I wasn't going for subtle, I was going for sledgehammer,'

he grinned. 'I could get used to having a present to open every other day.'

'They're not much to get excited over,' Clara said apologetically, 'especially today's.' She picked up a home-made cracker from the top of the filing cabinet and handed it to Joe. 'I made you a cracker.'

Joe laughed as he accepted it, rattling the cylindrical core to try and guess the contents.

'I made sure to put one of the highest quality gifts inside.'

'Hmm,' he said, bringing the tip of his index finger to the corner of his mouth. 'Could it be a fake tattoo or one of the joke spiders?' he teased. 'I could have great fun with my mum with one of those. She hates creepy-crawlies, especially spiders. That one scene in *Home Alone* had her screaming in terror.'

'I can confirm there are no mini arachnids. It's much better than that.'

'Can I open it now?'

He fingered the wisps of red floristry ribbon that kept the cracker tied. Clara had used a scissor's blade to curl it into tight ringlets, which added a professional flourish. It had a more finished look than the ones the children had made, except for Simone's, which were reminiscent of something you might find in a gift boutique. She'd added tiny bells she'd brought from her own craft box, along with shiny silk ribbon that she'd tied into perfect symmetrical bows.

Clara shook her head adamantly. 'Not until we've got this lot packed away. I think we're about done, though, so you won't have to wait too long.'

Joe groaned. 'I don't want to wait at all.'

'The sooner you get cracking with the Hoover, the sooner you'll be able to open it.'

'Never have I been more desperate to tidy up,' he said, with an exaggerated sigh, placing the cracker back on top of the cabinet.

'It'll be worth it,' Clara replied, before adding, 'even if you are *destined* to have to wait a little while longer.'

She laughed at her own joke, knowing the contents of the cracker. She was still laughing as Joe lugged the heavy upright Hoover out of the cupboard.

* * *

It was very nearly ten o'clock by the time the hall was in a decent state, and Clara was struggling to stifle a yawn as she stacked the plastic chairs away. Whether it was the previous night's antics catching up with her, or simply the result of a long day trying to control a group of over-excited teens and pre-teens she wasn't sure, but either way she couldn't wait to get home, pull on her favourite brushed-cotton pyjamas and fall into bed.

'This'll do,' Joe said, propping the mop he'd been using to scrub the most persistent sticky marks off the floor against the wall. 'It's not perfect, but it's been given a good once-over. Do you think it'll get the Deirdre seal of approval?'

As though on cue, Deirdre entered the room, smothered by her patterned rain mac. The leopard print wouldn't have looked out of place on Scary Spice back in her heyday, but Deirdre looked worn out, and Clara could tell the walking stick she was increasingly relying on was bearing more weight than usual.

'Looks clean enough to me. Let's get off home. It's been a long day.'

Clara caught sight of the cracker, still on top of the cabinet where Joe had left it before catching his eye. They couldn't leave until he'd seen what was inside.

'I'll lock up.' Clara reached down to check her keys were attached to the belt loop of her jeans with a climbing hook, the way they always were, and felt a rush of relief when her hand connected with the coolness of the metal. 'We're almost finished here, so you go. You look done in.'

'I feel it,' Deirdre pushed her glasses back up onto the bridge of her nose with a laboured sigh. 'I wouldn't last an all-nighter at the Hacienda these days.'

'You wouldn't be able to. It's all apartments these days,' Joe pointed out. The conversion had been a major news story, with some music fans up in arms that such a significant city landmark could be repurposed for housing, whilst other dedicated musos (and ageing nostalgics looking to recapture their hedonistic youth) clamoured at the opportunity to claim a piece of Manchester's musical heritage.

'Alright, clever clogs, stop being pedantic. I meant my dancing days are long gone. A mug of Ovaltine and *Coronation Street* on catch-up and I'll be ready for bed, and I won't take much rocking.'

'Sleep well,' Clara called, as Deirdre waved and headed into the corridor. 'See you tomorrow!'

The banging of the heavy front door echoed through the old building. Clara shuddered. She'd been here alone many times before, and despite the vast spaces and creaky floorboards (not to mention the unfounded rumours that the place was haunted) she'd never felt anxious. Not that she felt anxious now, but there was something about being here, in an otherwise empty building, with Joe, that was different to being with him in a pub, or a coffee shop, or a crowded Christmas market. It was more intimate here, somehow.

She giggled nervously as she reached for the cracker. 'It's time for you to find out what I put in here. I thought long and hard about it, so you'd better appreciate the effort.'

'Want to pull it?' he asked, gripping one ruffled end and pointing the other in Clara's direction. The cheap wrapping paper crackled in his fist. 'You never know, you might get lucky and win the goodies yourself.'

'Surely that'd defeat the object. It's a gift. I made it for you.'

'In that case, I'll rip it,' he replied with a grin, pulling at the paper until it unfurled. The contents of the cracker spilled out onto the floor below. 'Wow,' he said, taking in the amount of goodies that had been released. 'You certainly packed it full.'

There were the chocolates, a varied selection to make up for the box she'd given containing only toffees. A stick-on moustache, because they'd been joking about how Tom Selleck was the only man able to sport a caterpillar on his upper lip and still look sexy. Her favourite joke, written in her neatest writing on a slip of lilac paper. He groaned as he read it aloud.

' "What kind of bees make milk? Boo-bees." That's terrible, Clara. Worse than the ones Tariq was churning out at a rate of knots.'

'I'll have you know that was my favourite joke as an eight-year-old.'

'And still your favourite twenty years on?' he said, a twinkle in his eye.

'Nineteen, actually. But yes, it's a classic joke that stands the test of time and appeals to all audiences. I can't bear pretentious quips that try too hard to be clever. I prefer to keep it simple.'

'What's this?' he asked, bending down to retrieve a small plastic packet from the floor. 'I didn't see these on the tables earlier.'

'That's because I bought it especially for you,' she said. 'Haven't you seen a fortune-telling fish before? Every year I used to get one in my Christmas stocking. Taking turns for the fish to tell us our emotions was one of the best bits of the day.'

Joe shook his head. 'I haven't got a clue what you're on about.'

'Hold out your hand,' Clara instructed. He did as he was told as she took the flimsy red cellophane fish out of the packet and placed it in the palm of his hand. It curled immediately, the head and tail meeting to form a circle. 'That means you're passionate,' Clara said with a confident laugh.

'That proves it's not the most reliable form of fortune-telling. I've been single for years. There's something fishy about this fish,' he punned. 'Come on, let's see what it says about you.'

Clara obediently held out her hand and Joe carefully placed the fish in the curve of her palm. She felt a rush of warmth dash up her arm at the contact, but the fish didn't move, not even a flicker.

'Uh oh. That doesn't look good,' Joe said with a grimace.

He studied the piece of paper to read what the lack of movement predicted for Clara's future.

'You don't have to tell me what it means,' Clara replied sadly. This had this happened to her before. Only once – the Christmas after her dad had left. 'Dead fish. I'm destined for a lonely existence with nothing but a house full of stray cats to keep me company. I should have known. There's you with a future chock-a-block with passion and I'll be alone with no one to love or love me,' she said melodramatically.

'It's a piece of cellophane,' Joe reminded her sensibly, removing the motionless fish. Even as he picked it up between his thumb and forefinger it curled. 'It has no bearing whatsoever over your future.'

'But what if it does? What if I *am* destined to be alone? I might never find another person who'll love me.'

'Not possible.'

'It might be, if I don't learn to trust again.'

'Anything that knocks us takes time to recover from.

It's part of the process. You trust me, don't you?'

Clara's heart pounded as their eyes connected. She could have sworn he was looking right into her soul.

She did trust Joe. It was her own judgement she doubted. She'd fallen foul of giving her trust to those who hadn't earned it before.

'I don't want to be bitter forever.'

'You won't be,' he assured her. 'The right person will come along and everything with Dean will become a distant memory.'

'But what do I do in the meantime?'

'You eat chocolate and lots of it.'

'Now you're talking my language,' she replied, forcing a smile. The dead fish had thrown her more than she wanted to admit. 'Chocolate might be the answer.'

He handed Clara a caramel keg. She gladly accepted.

'There's no might about it,' Joe said emphatically. 'What you need is chocolate and friendship, and I'm here to offer both, if you'll accept.'

Clara's chest constricted at his kind words, and for a moment she thought she might start to cry. The emptiness of the club, the fortune-telling fish, the overwhelming exhaustion – it was all a bit much. And that was without attempting to decipher what that spark of energy between her and Joe might be trying to tell her.

Instead she took a deep breath, oxygen rushing to

her brain as she inhaled, and that, combined with the chocolate and the promise of Joe's friendship, was enough to make everything bearable.

'Thank you,' she said finally, breaking the silence. 'I do.'

Joe

Saturday, December 9th 2017

There was a distinct smell to the place; a lingering whiff of bleach that clung to the air, mingled with the stench of boiled cabbage and old age. It was reminiscent of hospitals, actually, and made Joe's head spin.

The residential home itself was inoffensive – the old, stone-fronted house had its own private grounds, and although the interior décor wasn't to Joe's taste (dark regency shades and hard settees that didn't look at all comfortable) it was clean and warm and had a nice overall feel.

'Come in, come in,' said the cheery care assistant, guiding the young people into the community room. It was a large space with a polished floor, warranting a more ostentatious presentation than the few paltry carols they'd been practising at The Club on the Corner.

'We've been looking forward to this. It's all Joanie's been talking about, having you lot come.'

'You hear that?' Deirdre said, ushering the last reluctant stragglers in through the door. Shannon had her coat pulled up at the front so it covered her nose, and Joe knew she'd clocked the unusual aroma of the Autumn Days Rest House. It was hard to miss, to be honest. 'You might not think you're doing much by turning up here and singing a few Christmas tunes, but for some of these folk it's the highlight of their day. Hard to believe, I know,' she added with a chuckle.

'We'll be coming to see you in here soon, Deirdre,' Tariq joked, his thick Manchester accent laced with laughter. His laughter didn't last long. The look she gave him was enough to curdle milk and Tariq acted suitably admonished as he mumbled his apology.

'I can't imagine Deirdre in a rest home,' Joe said tactfully, even though he was amused by Deirdre's insistence that she was in her prime. 'She's too stubborn, for one thing, and too independent, for another. Anyway, she's far too young.'

Deirdre nodded her approval, 'Exactly. I'm a spring chicken. My autumn days are a long way off, thank you very much.'

Joe didn't point out that however much she said she was coping, the discomfort of each step was showing on her face. Then there were the wrinkles around her eyes, the grooves far more pronounced now than they'd been when Joe himself had been a member at the club. Deirdre wasn't that old in the great scheme of things – probably only ten years older than his mum – but she wasn't young either. The finish line of retirement was within her sights, not that she'd be likely to give up The Club on the Corner any time soon. It meant too much to her.

'They are,' he said kindly, holding the door to the community room open for her. 'You're going to outlive the lot of us.'

'Probably,' she replied amiably. 'I put it down to having a nightcap. I swear a little snifter knocks me out and ensures I get a decent night's sleep. Then I'm raring to go the next day, not sat on my arse like this lot, staring at a TV screen.'

'You watch all the soaps religiously,' Clara laughed. 'If you miss even one episode you get antsy and restless.' She turned to Joe, who was telling Tiffany to remove her gum before the performance started. 'Just be glad you weren't volunteering earlier this year. There was a funeral on Corrie and she forgot to tape it. You'd have thought she was missing out on paying her respects to one of her oldest friends, the way she went on about it.'

'She was one of my favourite characters,' Deirdre sniffed. 'And she'd been in it so long, it felt a bit like losing a friend. You can make fun all you like, but I don't have a family of my own, not even nieces or nephews. Other than the kids that come through the club, they're the closest thing I've got to someone to worry about. I know people think I'm foolish investing my time in fictional characters, but I couldn't give a monkey's. Those programmes make me happy.'

'And that's what matters,' Joe replied, directing a look of warning at Clara. There was a sharpness to Deirdre's tone, which probably signified nothing more than the hectic schedule in the run-up to Christmas combined with the stress of running the club on a shoestring. Nevertheless, it made Joe uncomfortable. Deirdre looked worn out of late. 'You work hard, so deserve to relax when you get home. How you choose to do that is up to you.'

'I was only joking,' Clara said, part apology and part on the defensive. She'd lengthened her small frame by a good two inches, her back straighter, as though she was a puppet being pulled taut.

'I know, love. I know.' Deirdre sank into the chair provided by a matronly member of staff at the care home, the relief at taking the weight off her legs apparent from the happy sigh that escaped her lips.

'Come on, then, which of you two is taking charge and getting the carols started? And make sure the kids are smiling. These oldies look bloody miserable,' Deirdre boomed. 'They could do with cheering up.'

'They're not the most enthusiastic audience,' Joe agreed, but his voice was more subdued. 'Although, how anyone can fail to be entertained by this lot is beyond me. I'm sure Ted will have them in the palm of his hand when he starts his acoustic rendition of "Silent Night".'

The residents were slumped in their chairs, crocheted blankets tucked tightly around their knees, their lips puckered inwardly.

'And if not, there are always Tariq's jokes to fall back on,' Clara suggested, referring to the plan for each young person to give a resident one of the carefully crafted crackers at the end of the evening.

'We'll have to make sure we get out quick, before they read them,' Joe said.

'Although this lot probably wouldn't be able to read a thing anyway,' Deirdre interjected, her tone pithy. 'Not without their reading glasses.'

Joe didn't mention the wire-rimmed glasses slipping once again down the sharp slope of Deirdre's nose. Instead, he strode into the space that had been sectioned off for the performance, introduced the club, and counted in the first carol, 'Once in Royal David's City'.

*   *   *

All was going well. The renditions of the first three songs on their 'set list' had caused a stir – at least as much of a stir as the Autumn Days crowd could muster – with one game lady, who Joe presumed was the afore-mentioned Joanie, swaying with arms aloft as she sang along.

'Joe.'

The hissing of his name was almost drowned out by the choir of the youth club members, who were practically shouting out the chorus of 'O Come All Ye Faithful', but then he heard it again, probably not loud enough for anyone else to pick up on, but noticeable to him.

A panic-stricken Phoebe was gesturing to him from within the huddle of youths. It was as Joe made his way into the centre of the group that he noticed the blood streaming from his sister's nose. Digging into his pocket for a tissue he hoped was clean, he passed it along the line and the blood seeped into the tissue as Simone pinched the bridge of her nose.

She'd not had a nosebleed for years, although she'd suffered badly with them when she was small. Joe had become adept at dealing with them when Simone was a toddler, teaching her how to lean forward and breathe through her mouth whilst clamping her thumb and forefinger around her nose to stem the flow. He'd not liked blood even then, but he'd loved his little sister so much that he'd been able to push his unease to one side. Since the car crash it had become a genuine cause of anxiety.

Joe gulped the air as a lightheadedness took over. He hated the disorientated feeling, as though his own blood was draining from his head and pooling in his feet, fixing him helplessly to the spot.

The singing carried on around him, although it sounded further away to Joe's ears, and he wondered if he was actually swaying or if the giddy sensation was tied in to his fear. His vision blurred and it was only when a warm hand gripped his wrist that he realised how untethered he felt.

Clara – soft-focus, head tilted in concern – steadied him; her muffled voice asking if he was okay.

Joe tried to nod, although wasn't sure he succeeded. He wasn't sure of much. His body had forgotten how to stand. He was leaden yet weightless, floating yet rooted.

'It's Simone,' he mumbled, his voice lost to the airless room. 'Nosebleed.'

'It's stopped. It wasn't a big one, and she's fine. Look.'

Clara gently spun Joe to face his sister again, and as Simone came into his eye line Joe could see Simone was singing along with her friends, every ounce of her creative body loving the moment.

His head defuzzed, everything clearer with the knowledge that things were back to normal. Simone was fine, he was fine, everything was fine. Clara's hand on his arm suddenly felt unnecessary and unnatural.

'Oh,' he said, overcome with embarrassment. 'Yeah. Of course she is.'

'And you're sure you're alright?' Clara probed. 'You looked on the verge of passing out. You frightened me.'

Joe looked at her more closely. Two vertical lines creased between her eyebrows. Questioning. Wondering.

'I'm not good with blood.'

'That's nothing to be ashamed of,' Clara replied, massaging her hand against his arm. The wool of his jumper spread the motion until he was aware of the life pulsing through his veins.

'I'm not ashamed. I've nothing to hide,' he said, but it wasn't how he felt. He felt helpless and he wished he could run, away from the cheery singing, the weird-smelling building, Clara.

He might be saying he had nothing to hide, but that wasn't the truth. There were parts of him he was keeping buried, words he wanted to say but couldn't formulate. Moments from his history that weren't easy to relive – the ones he replayed to himself in the desperate early hours as he lay awake tossing and turning, praying for peace.

'I was trying to be nice,' Clara said, retracting her hand as though she'd been burned. Perhaps his voice had been a touch snippier than he'd intended.

The singing continued around them, as Joe turned on his heels. He noticed Deirdre watching, but that didn't stop him heading for the sanctuary of the hallway.

The dizziness returned, the piercing lights burning his eyes and his brain, so he fumbled for the light switch, plunging the hallway into darkness as he sank onto the bottom step of the stairs.

For a moment he was sure he could feel Michelle there with him. Her long, flyaway hair tickling his cheeks, a hint of her laughter wrapping him in an embrace ... But it was impossible. She was gone, dead long ago, and he was very much alive. The guilt consumed him whole, as it so often did. Why had he survived when she hadn't? There was no rhyme, no reason.

'Rejoice, Rejoice, Emmanuel ...' The voices of the young people were louder now, and a glow of light seeped into the hallway from the gap between the door-frame and the door. The uplifting melody brought him back to the present, along with the sight of Clara, who had flicked on the light.

Joe blinked as his eyes adjusted.

'You didn't have to follow me,' he said.

'I needed to make sure you were okay.'

'I was thinking, that's all.'

'Anything you want to talk about?'

'Do you ever feel as though the past is holding you back? Stopping you from making the most of the present?'

'Everyone feels like that at one point or other in their lives. It's human nature.'

Joe's eyes met Clara's, and the tears brimming over her lower lids told him she knew exactly what he meant.

'It's this time of year ... it's so difficult. It doesn't feel right to celebrate.'

'Because of Michelle?' Clara's voice was soft.

He nodded. 'That's a big part of it.'

'She loved you, Joe. Michelle loved you. Whatever you think or feel, she wouldn't want you to be miserable, especially after all this time.'

The words were simple and rational. He could live in the past, determined to allow every joyous element of Christmas to be blighted or he could choose to be free from the painful memories of Decembers past.

Did he really want to carry the weight, the pain, with him for the rest of his life? Joe knew the answer. He didn't.

'You're right.'

'I know I am. I'm always right.'

He smiled at her sass. 'And you're cocky. I'd love to be as gutsy as you.'

'I'm not gutsy. Not all the time, anyway.'

Her smile was flimsy.

He raised his eyebrows in a question, wondering if her comment related to her earlier tears. Maybe she was missing Dean. He might be an arse in a crap coat who'd cheated on her, but he was also her ex-fiancé. They'd had a future together all mapped out. Their situations weren't that different at the core.

'I'll tell you about it one day,' she promised. 'But for now we'd better get back to the kids. They'll be giving those crackers out to the residents.'

'We'll need to prepare for a quick escape before they get to Tariq's jokes.'

'Not sure Deirdre's got much of a rush in her today. We'll have to hope they save them for Christmas Day instead,' she smiled.

Clara disappeared into the function room and Joe was alone once more. He took a deep breath, smiled and allowed himself to believe that moving forward was not just a possibility, it was a reality. *His* reality.

As he followed Clara's footsteps, Joe thought that maybe – just maybe – the future could be bright after all.

Clara

Sunday, December 10th 2017

'What a day.'

'Oh, it's not been so bad,' Clara said cheerfully. She'd enjoyed the evening session at the club, especially as miserable weather had meant it was quieter than normal for a weekend. It had given her and Joe a chance to talk about what they needed to finalise for the presentation, although the serious conversation they'd shared in the hallway at the residential home had been left firmly in the past.

Deirdre did look tired, though. The drooping bags that sagged under her eyes were dark, and Clara noticed she was hunched over her stick.

'I swear my back's splitting in two.' Deirdre pushed her shoulders back and stomach forward in a stretch. 'I don't think I'm going to hang about tonight. A couple of Paracetamol and a medicinal brandy will work wonders, I'm sure.'

'You do too much,' Joe said, eyebrows raised into judgemental arches. 'There's no shame in knowing when to slow down.'

'Agreed. Go home and put your feet up or you'll be no good to anyone tomorrow.' Clara was all but shooing Deirdre out of the door, and for once it wasn't taking much persuading to get Deirdre off the premises.

'Make sure you set the alarm before locking up,' Deirdre reminded. Clara had never forgotten to in all the years she'd worked at The Club on the Corner and she'd done her fair share of being last out of the door, but Deirdre was especially cautious following an attempted break-in back in the summer. Clara had tried to make light of it at the time – after all, any burglars would be sorely disappointed by the lack of cash, gadgets or other items of value on the premises. Unless they were on the lookout for well-used sports equipment or board games with half the pieces missing, they'd be leaving empty-handed. Deirdre had found it harder to laugh it off.

'I will,' Clara promised. 'Double-locked, as usual. Fort Knox has nothing on this place.'

'Stop fretting,' Joe called, as Deirdre collected her coat from the hallway, 'this place will be secure. Promise. It'll be as safe as if it had overnight security guards on the premises.'

'And mop that patch near the stage where Ted spilt that can of Sprite. He did say he'd cleaned it up, but I bet he's not done a thorough job. Teenage boys ...'

'Yes!' Clara exclaimed with frustration. 'We're on it, or rather we would be if we weren't having this conversation with you,' she added, the sarcasm laid on thick.

'Alright, alright, keep your hair on. I'm gone. Hope you get everything done that you need to ready for the presentation. See you tomorrow, Clara. See you tomorrow, Joe.'

The two let out sighs of relief as the door slammed shut behind Deirdre.

'I thought she'd never leave.'

Clara bent down, dustpan in one hand, brush in the other, and swept up a pile of crisp crumbs. You'd think it had been feeding time at the zoo.

'She doesn't know how to rest, that's the problem. Her mind's hyperactive, but her body's ageing.'

Joe rubbed the table top, his hand moving the blue and white cloth in a circular motion across the surface. He increased his force to try to budge the stubborn streak of silver nail varnish that glittered against the dull brown surface.

Shannon had brought her supplies and set up a salon

to rival Manchester's top nail bars. It was a surprise the kids weren't high as kites from the fumes, although going on the silliness – which Deirdre had passed off as festive high spirits – Clara was convinced they were giddier than usual. Shannon had even given Ted a layer of polish – a very neutral shade of taupe that was hardly noticeable – insisting all the top male musicians were androgynous, and that Ted's middle-of-the-road haircut and lack of guy-liner was going to hold him back in his quest for international stardom. She'd wanted to get her hands on Joe's nails too, but he'd been adamant – not to be mistaken with Adam Ant, Joe's style was decidedly more mainstream than the eighties icon – Shannon's nail varnish was going nowhere near his fingernails.

'I'll tackle that patch Deirdre was on about. She'll go bananas if there's even a hint of stickiness on that floor when she comes in tomorrow.'

'Sticky patches. The bane of lives the world over,' Joe said with a cheeky laugh.

'Joe Smith!' Clara retorted, eyes wide and mouth open as she pretended to be flabbergasted, although the more time they spent together, the more she appreciated he had a wicked sense of humour. 'You dirty bugger!'

'I didn't mean it like that,' he replied, although the

naughtiness was evident in his eyes. He might be the son of a vicar, but he still had plenty of innuendo in his locker.

'Liar. You definitely did.'

'Okay,' he admitted. 'I did. I wanted to see if you'd be shocked.'

'I'm not shocked. More surprised.'

She reached for the slate-grey mop and the matching bucket filled with diluted bleach, squeezing the excess fluid from the twisted fronds of the mop-head before thoroughly scrubbing the floor. Deirdre had been right – Ted hadn't done the best job of cleaning. The resistance of the mop against the tackiness of the liquid-cum-solid residue of the sugary substance gave Clara added purpose, and a sense of satisfaction as the mop moved more smoothly over the floor. When she was happy the job was complete she carried the bucket to the toilets, emptying the dirty solution down the sink before flushing it through with tap water.

Joe had folded the tables away by the time she re-entered the hall. As usual the space looked much bigger now it was clear. The Christmas tree still looked as beautiful, though, standing splendid and majestic, as though it were watching over proceedings.

'Just the tree lights to switch off and then we can make a start on that work for the presentation, if you're sure you don't mind helping?'

'No problem at all. I did promise.'

'If you switch the lights off, I'll lock the cupboards,' Clara said, reaching for her belt loop to retrieve her keys. The only thing she could feel was the rough denim of her jeans, so she patted again but still met the same result. When she looked down she discovered what she already feared. The keys weren't there. 'Shit.'

Joe looked up. 'What's the matter?'

'I can't find my keys. Did you notice them when you were cleaning the kitchen?' Her aversion to washing mugs meant she'd allocated that job to Joe. 'I might have taken them off when I unlocked the cleaning cupboard.' It was a long shot, but a possibility. Clara was always extra careful to ensure she'd locked the chemicals away.

'Nope. The sides were clear and the cupboards locked.'

Clara's eyes scanned the room. The keys weren't on any of the window ledges, or on the stage.

'I don't know where else they'd be,' she said, a bubble of panic starting to swell in her chest. 'Deirdre's gonna go ballistic if I've lost them.'

'They can't be far away,' Joe answered calmly. 'Retrace your steps. Where did you have them last?'

Clara thought about it. It must have been in the

kitchen, when she was mixing up the bleach. She could clearly recall that she'd filled the mop bucket, put the bottle of bleach back in the cupboard and locked it straight away. Then she remembered being called into the hallway by Simone and Cally, the last two kids to leave that night, as they were getting a lift. She'd put the keys on the work surface near the microwave as she'd said goodbye to the girls. Then she'd come back into the hall and swept up, before going back into the kitchen for the mop, dustpan and brush. The keys had definitely been on the side then, immediately before Deirdre had left. Maybe they'd fallen on the floor.

'They were in the kitchen, I'm certain. Near the microwave.'

The pair made their way to the kitchen, switching the light back on. No keys on the work surface. No keys on the floor. Clara even checked in the sink, just in case, but no. They weren't there either.

'They're not here.' Joe's comment was so unhelpful, so blatantly obvious, that Clara snapped.

'No shit, Sherlock! I can see they're not here! But this is where I left them, so where the hell have they gone?'

Joe shrugged, timid and mouse-like.

'I'm going to have to phone Deirdre and ask her to come back. She shouldn't be far away, and if she lets me borrow her keys we'll still be able to get the presentation done,' Clara said. She reached into her handbag for her mobile, scrolling through her contact list for the number. When she found the entry she was looking for, she pressed the 'call' button and put the phone to her ear. She held her breath as she waited for her boss to answer, and when the phone clicked she started speaking at pace, before realising it wasn't Deirdre at all.

'It's gone to answer phone,' she told him dejectedly.

'If worst comes to the worst, we could always set the alarm and drop the Yale lock?' Joe suggested.

Clara shook her head. 'No way. Deirdre would flip if she turned up in the morning and I hadn't double-locked the door. In her eyes, that's a sackable offence.'

She dialled Deirdre's number again, punching the 'end call' button in annoyance when it once more went through to the machine.

'Why don't we get cracking with that presentation? We can keep trying to get hold of Deirdre as we work.'

Clara sighed. 'Okay. I've saved what I've been working on to the laptop. Why don't we go up to the office and see what's left to do?'

An hour later, when the final slide of the presentation was complete, they still hadn't been able to get hold of Deirdre and Clara was insistent that she couldn't leave the premises without double-locking the door.

'Look, you should go,' Clara said. 'You've been here long enough as it is.'

'You've been here longer,' Joe rightly pointed out.

'Still, I get paid for being here. You're here out of the goodness of your heart. You don't have to stay any longer than you need to.'

'I'm not leaving you here alone,' he said. 'Give it another five minutes. She's probably on the phone.'

'Who to?' Clara asked. 'It's only me she ever phones, other than her sister. But she wouldn't be ringing her at this time of night.'

'Maybe her battery's dead, then.'

Clara frowned. 'I've got a bad feeling about this.'

'We could go and wait out the front? It can't be any colder out there than is it in here,' he suggested.

Joe rubbed his hands together, blowing on them. Now Clara thought about it, her own digits were feeling the nip. That was the trouble with the club, as soon as the heating clicked off. It was as though it had never been on in the first place.

'We could get some chocolate from the newsagents while we waited,' Clara thought out loud. 'So long as one of us is on the steps waiting for Deirdre.'

'Sounds like a plan.'

Joe made his way down the stairs and into the hall, lifting his coat from the hook before wriggling into it.

Then he handed Clara her jacket, which was tiny in comparison.

'Cheers,' Clara replied, grabbing her stuff. As well as her handbag, there was a plastic bag containing Joe's countdown gift. She was particularly happy with this one, even though it was a bit of a cheat as she didn't want him to open it until Christmas Eve. She'd spent her morning searching the high street shops for a comedy onesie (she'd opted for one of the Teenage Mutant Ninja Turtles – maybe Donatello? Was he the purple one?), because no matter how little money they'd had, Clara's mum had always made sure she had new pyjamas on Christmas Eve. It had added to the magic. She could recall the soft flannel against her skin as her mum tucked her up, warning her to fall straight to sleep or Santa might not come, and the anticipation as she closed her eyes whilst her mum read her *The Night Before Christmas*. Clara had bought a copy of the Clement Clarke Moore book to go with the onesie, and she'd written a note explaining the significance of the gift on a card she'd thought Joe would like.

Joe reached for the handle, cocking his wrist ninety degrees as he attempted to open the door. It didn't budge.

'You've not taken the latch off.' Clara shook her head in despair.

'I have.'

Joe pointed to the rugby-ball-shaped brass knob on the Yale lock. He was right. It was definitely not dropped.

'Then, why's it not opening?'

Joe examined the thin crack between the doorframe and the door. 'It's been locked using the key, so that Yale lock won't make any difference. Until we get hold of Deirdre, we're going nowhere.'

Clara groaned. Since she'd got the idea of chocolate in her head she'd almost been able to taste it.

'I'll try ringing again.' Joe pulled his phone from his pocket and made the call.

Clara watched on hopefully, but could feel the sag in her shoulders as Joe shook his head.

'Nope. Still going through to answerphone,' he said.

'Try her home number?' Clara suggested.

Joe did, but it rang out. Either Deirdre wasn't home yet or she was already upstairs, with no intent of answering her landline.

'It's no use standing around. We could be here a while.'

'We could be here all night,' Clara pointed out. 'Let's go back upstairs. It's not as draughty up there.'

The pair made their way to the office, their footsteps reverberating around the otherwise-empty building. It made Clara shudder, the echo creeping her out.

'We'll be alright up here,' Joe said cheerily, his eyes resting on a box of Ferrero Rocher on the bookcase. 'Look, there's even chocolate. We didn't need the news-agents after all. Isn't there a blow-heater too? We can plug that in.'

'If we're here all night I'm putting the heating on. I'll pay the bill out of my own pocket,' she shivered. 'I don't understand what happened to my keys, though. I could have sworn they were in the kitchen. Now it looks like we're here for the long haul.'

'You make it sound like it's a fate worse than death, being here with me,' Joe joked, sinking into the hard-backed desk chair.

'Oh, stop fishing for compliments.'

'I wasn't! But with all your grumbling you're doing a great job of giving me an inferiority complex.'

'My fiancé cheated on me. I think I'm entitled to a bit of a wallow once in a while.'

'You can't have the monopoly on misery. Morrissey claimed it already.'

Clara smiled the most fake smile she could muster, and Joe laughed.

'Heaven knows I'm miserable now,' she deadpanned.

'Well, let's see if I can cheer you up,' he said, turning on the small portable radio perched on the windowsill.

The melancholy melody of the theme tune from *The Snowman* was playing, and Joe joined in, swaying from side to side, eyes closed as he over-enunciated the words like a young Aled Jones.

'Are you part of the choir at church?' Clara enquired. 'No.'

'Good job,' she said cheekily. 'You're flat.'

Joe leant over and swatted her arm and Clara pretended to be put out, although the banter was exactly what she needed. That and some additional warmth. She turned the switch on the blow heater, the fan inside whirring to life as the heat blew out into the room (along with an unpleasant smell not dissimilar to singed hair).

'At least it made you crack a smile.'

'Surprised it didn't crack the windows too.'

'You're vicious.' Joe clutched his hand over his heart. 'I'm hurt.'

'Diddums,' Clara laughed, pressing the redial button on her iPhone.

'I should probably be grateful you're not keying my car,' Joe muttered, the flicker of a smile creeping at the corner of his lips.

If it had been anyone else, Clara would have given them the middle finger, but it was Joe – sweet, sweet Joe – so instead she poked her tongue out.

The automated voice started talking immediately, and Clara hung up. No point listening to that when she wasn't going to leave a message. Deirdre had obviously turned her phone off for the night.

'Still nothing,' she said. 'I'll give the landline one more try.'

When that too turned out to be futile, they admitted defeat.

'We could ask someone else to go round to hers to collect the keys?' Joe suggested.

'At ten at night?'

'Hmm, yeah. I forgot it was that late.'

'Deirdre sleeps like a log anyway. Once she's asleep there's no waking her. We went on a residential with the kids a few years back and I had to share a room with her. I've never heard anyone snore so loud in all my life. I swear a pneumatic drill would have been quieter.'

'The only other option is to set up camp for the night,' Joe shrugged. 'Not sure it'll be very comfortable, though.'

'I fell asleep in my friend's front garden once.'

'Camping?'

Clara shook her head. 'Nah. After a particularly heavy night out I decided I couldn't manage the last ten steps to make it into her house, so laid down on the lawn.

Next thing I knew I was dreaming that I was swimming in the ship canal.' She grinned. 'I was using a giant doughnut as a rubber ring. That was a great dream.'

'You must have been hammered.'

'Totally blotto. That was the wake-up call. Not knowing where I was or how I got there made me realise how fucked up I was. Work all day, drink all night and repeat it all again the next day, it wasn't sustainable, any of it. I was out of control.' She remembered that feeling, of everything spiralling until she couldn't focus; not only because of the drink, but because of the hurt and the heartache. 'Things had to change. I made a decision that morning, lying on the dew-covered grass. I wasn't going to let Dean and his cheating ruin my life. I picked myself up, brushed myself down and moved on. Literally.'

'I know I've said it before, but he didn't deserve you.'

Clara felt the blood rush to her cheeks, and she hoped they hadn't gone scarlet with embarrassment. She didn't take compliments well, and Joe was generous with words of kindness. If he picked up on it, she'd have to say it was her body reacting to the change in temperature. The blow heater was doing a good job, even if it was stinking the place out.

'Thanks.'

'Are there any blankets?'

Clara thought for a minute before remembering a stash of fleecy blankets that they'd used as rugs at the family picnic back in the summer. They'd been shoved in a cupboard since July, so Clara expected them to smell musty, but when she retrieved them they were in a plastic container, lid clamped shut. Although not line-fresh, they didn't smell bad.

'We'll probably need a couple of these each to stay snug,' she said, throwing Joe two. 'Although this reminds me – I've got today's present for you too. I was going to tell you to keep it under the tree until Christmas Eve, but these are extenuating circumstances, and it might make tonight more comfortable for you.'

She took the sizeable package out of the bag, dumping it unceremoniously on Joe's lap.

'That's a big one.'

'Back on the innuendo again, are we?'

Joe snorted. 'I meant the present. It's only you and your filthy mind hearing anything other than that.'

He peeled carefully at the end of the Sellotape, as though trying to save the paper. Clara's mum used to do that so she could reuse it another time; when money was tight savings had to be made where they could. It seemed to take an age for Joe to reveal the fleecy green onesie, and as he unfurled the material he burst out laughing.

'This is incredible,' he said, looking genuinely thrilled. 'Where on earth did you find an adult-sized turtle onesie?'

Clara tapped the side of her nose. 'Not telling. But I hope it'll fit you. It might be adult sized, but you're taller than average.'

'Turn around,' he instructed, in a voice that was as bossy as Joe ever got. 'I'll try it on.'

He was already out of his coat and halfway through peeling his jumper over his head, giving Clara another flash of that mysterious stomach scar, but when his fingers reached for the buckle of his belt, she spun quickly to face the wall.

Clara could hear the clunk of the metal and the heaviness of his jeans dropping to the floor, and she gulped. It had been a while since she'd been in such close proximity to an almost-naked man. A handsome almost-naked man too, even if it was just Joe.

Clara shifted her weight between her feet.

'You can look now,' Joe said, after what seemed like an age.

Clara turned around and burst out laughing at the image before her. To give him his dues, Joe hadn't done this by halves, his face shrouded by the oversized hood, its purple mask covering his eyes. The onesie fitted him in the body – probably because he was slender – but both the sleeves and legs were half-mast on his gangly limbs.

'It's not that funny!'

'It is,' Clara said, clutching her side. There was the first biting niggle of a stitch coming, a result of laughing so much, and it was funny to think that just moments before she'd been feeling something akin to attraction. Joe looked hilarious. 'Sometimes I forget what a giant you are.'

'I'm not a giant, you're just tiny.'

'I'm short, but you're still giant.'

'Mutant. Like the turtles.'

'Did you see the book?' Clara asked, noticing the hardback had slipped down the side of the chair.

Joe twisted to follow Clara's gaze.

He picked up the book, running his hand against the smooth dust jacket.

'I love this,' he said eventually. 'My mum would always read it to me on Christmas Eve, even though I'd be half asleep by the time we got back from midnight mass. I think they took me along in the hope it'd give them longer in bed on Christmas morning.'

'Did it work?' Clara asked.

'Did it heck! I was up at five o'clock, begging to open my presents. Dad had to be up to lead the Christmas Day service anyway. By the time I was a teenager and would happily have lazed in bed until dinner time, Simone had come along and taken over the "Wake up, it's Christmas" baton.' He smiled. 'I didn't mind, though, because seeing her face as she opened the presents was worth being dragged out of bed for.'

He sat at one end of the settee, pulling a cushion up behind him before wrapping first his coat and then the two blankets over his knees. Clara sank down into the other end, where the cushion was saggy with Deirdre's indent, and tucked her feet under her body.

'Give it here.' Clara held out her hand in demand.

Joe did as he was told and handed the book over, before burying his hands under the cover and allowing his head to flop back against the settee. His mouth dropped open into a yawn.

'Tired?'

'Shattered,' he admitted, yawning once more.

'Let me read to you,' Clara said, opening the book. She loved the imagery of the famous poem, the rhythm of it, and soon she was lost within the winter fairytale, not stopping for breath until she reached the final line.

She snapped the book shut and looked up to find Joe's eyes closed and mouth open, the steady rise and fall of the blankets echoing his peaceful sleep-filled breathing pattern. He looked younger now he was asleep, smaller. Child-like, although that might have been because the hood of his onesie was askew. He looked half sleepy human, half cock-eyed turtle.

'Goodnight,' she repeated in a whisper, as she stretched her arm out to flick the light switch to the off position. 'Sleep tight.'

The room went black, the only light the silvery flash of crescent moon peeping in at the window.

Clara didn't fall sleep straight away. Instead, she listened to the pattern of Joe's ragged, barely-there breathing as she shivered in the darkness; whilst resisting the inexplicable urge to snuggle with him on the half of the settee he had claimed.

Joe

Joe yawned.

He'd not slept well last night, and woken up stiff and sleepy, momentarily confused about where he was. Then he'd seen Clara, peacefully sleeping underneath her blankets, and remembered the previous night's unexpected lock-in. He'd called Deirdre straight away and was relieved when she answered on the second ring. She'd not sounded surprised to hear from him, even at that early hour, and when Joe had explained the predicament Deirdre had searched her handbag and found that she'd somehow managed to take both sets of keys. She'd arrived soon after to let them out, and Joe had had time to get home and shower (and, most importantly, brush his teeth – he hated the slimy feeling of unbrushed teeth) before heading for his shift at the hardware shop. He'd left an emotional Clara berating Deirdre. She was still emotional nine hours later.

'I'm getting nervous.'

Joe could tell. Clara had been jiggling in her seat for the past fifteen minutes – twisting her rings distractedly round and round her fingers, tapping her feet against the tiled floor of the corridor, leaning first forwards and then backwards in her seat, as though fighting to get comfortable.

'You've nothing to be nervous about,' he replied softly. 'The presentation is great – it's got all the facts and figures and enough emotion to tug on the heartstrings of the committee too. They'd have to be soulless crea-tures not to take pity on the club.'

'It's more that I'm nervous about getting up there and talking in front of them all. What if I get flustered and end up missing out key points?' Clara wrung her hands together, before wincing and adding, 'My palms are sweaty. I thought that was just a saying. I didn't think it actually happened in real life.'

'You're not going to miss out anything, and even if you did it's there on the slides for them to read for themselves. Honestly, the run-through you did earlier was brilliant. I was on the verge of tears myself, and I helped you put the whole thing together.'

Clara smiled at that, which gave Joe a warm feeling

in his core. It felt good to be able to put her at ease.

'I knew they were tears I saw building in your eyes!' she said with glee, before her smile faded and she added, 'I'm not confident about speaking in public, and this feels more important than any of the times I've had to stand on stage in the youth club and ask families to give generously.' She fidgeted again. 'I'm genuinely not sure if I can do this.'

Joe smiled kindly and reached out to place his hand on hers. Clara's constant twitching was making him feel restless too, so smothering her delicate hand with his meant neither of them were able to squirm.

'You can do it. I know you can. And I'll be right there next to you. If it does get to be too much then give me the nod and I'll take over.'

Clara sighed a sigh that Joe thought was most likely of relief. 'It's reassuring to know I'm not going into this alone. I don't want to let Deirdre down by letting my nerves get the better of me, that's all.'

'Sshhh,' Joe said, with a stern look. 'You wouldn't be letting anyone down. The Club on the Corner is in your heart – in your bones, even. No one would ever question how much it means to you.'

'That's not enough, though. Love alone won't keep the place going. We desperately need to find money from somewhere if we can open our doors to everyone on that waiting list. And if we had money to give the place a facelift too ... there's so much potential to make it amazing.'

'It's amazing already,' Joe corrected. 'True, it would benefit from some work, but I'm confident we'll get funding from somewhere to spruce it up. I tell you what, if we don't get lucky with this, I'll write to one of those TV shows that turn up and blitz the place in a day.'

Clara giggled. 'It'd take a lot of MDF to fix everything that needs fixing at the club.'

Joe laughed along with her, until the door to the church hall opened and his dad invited them in.

The committee were at the far end of the hall, sitting behind a long row of tables that made Joe feel as though they were auditioning for *X Factor*. Reverend Smith was in the seat at the end of the row, less judgemental than Simon Cowell, but equally as expectant. Joe and Clara's presentation was the fifth and final one of the day and Joe hoped the committee weren't flagging. A plate at the centre of the table was piled high with custard-cream biscuits and Joe willed them to pick up one of the little rectangles and get a sugar-hit so they'd be able to take in the information Clara was about to present.

'Whenever you're ready, Clara,' Reverend Smith said.

Clara looked at Joe, the fear evident in her eyes. Then,

with a smile, she walked towards the long table and handed a copy of the presentation to each of the committee, before starting her spiel.

'I'm Clara O' Connell,' she began, 'and I'm the deputy manager at The Club on the Corner. The youth club has been using the building since the 1980s, providing a safe place for young people within our community to socialise with each other. The building was originally multi-purpose, but we are now the only users.' Clara took a breath, Joe nodding his encouragement. She continued with confidence, sharing the club's current plight and the ambitious renovation plans and the ideal staffing structure, not once faltering over the numbers she'd been so afraid would trip her up. When she finished talking through the final slide, Joe wanted to whoop with pride and delight, and he gave a thumbs-up as he took to the floor to invite any questions.

Five minutes later they were out, Clara placing the flat of her palm against her chest.

'My heart's still pounding!' she exclaimed, as they walked down the winding pathway through the church grounds. It was not long after four o'clock, but due to the season it was already pitch black but for the luminous white glow of the ankle-high lamps that marked out the walkway.

'You were brilliant. So cool and calm. I'd never have

guessed you were as nervous as you were.'

'I'm good at hiding my feelings.' Clara shrugged as Joe looked curiously on. 'When my dad left I pretended I wasn't hurting. Didn't want to upset Mum any more than she already was, because I could hear her crying at night as I lay awake in bed. I had to be strong for her, so I put on a brave face and a smile and hoped she wouldn't notice my heart was breaking as much as hers was.'

'Oh, Clara.'

'I was the same with Dean. I knew things weren't right but I hid behind a mask, clinging grimly on to the future I'd thought we'd have. I've become quite adept at making out things are fine when inside I'm crumbling.'

'That's so sad.' Joe fought the urge to reach out and hug her, instead saying, 'Don't ever feel you have no one to talk to. I'm always here with a shoulder to cry on. Two actually,' he said with a smile, trying to lighten the mood.

'Thanks,' she said, folding her arms in front of her chest. A body-language expert would probably have said this was Clara closing herself off again, but Joe knew it was nothing more than her way of wrapping herself up against the grim weather of the evening. 'And the same goes for you. You can always tell me anything that's bothering you. Nothing's too small or too silly.'

Joe's heart plummeted until he could have sworn it was in his gut, every throb uncomfortable and unpleasant. He wished he could tell Clara what was bothering him, what had been continually bothering him for the last eight years. But sharing would mean facing up to old demons, and so, instead, Joe clenched his lips shut, keeping both his guilt and his grief bottled up, the way he always had.

Clara

Tuesday, December 12th 2017

'Cally! Get down from there this instant!'
Deirdre's panic was evident as the chair Cally precariously balanced on teetered, quivering like a wobbly bottom lip of a toddler caught doing something it shouldn't, before tipping backwards.

Cally landed on the floor with a dull thwack, which reverberated around the room.

'What did I tell you?' Deirdre chastised, fisted hands pressed into the folds of her ample waist. 'I knew that was going to happen. I could see it coming a mile off.'

Clara, who was closer to the incident, hurried to the scene, the usual hubbub of the club hushed into an ear-piercing silence.

'Deirdre –'

'You're not an infant, Cally, and you've been coming

here long enough to know I won't stand for you acting like one. This is no time to act like a jackass!'

'Deirdre.' Clara adopted a no-nonsense tone. This wasn't the time to be criticising. It looked as if Cally could have done serious damage. 'I think we're going to have to get her to A&E. I've got Mum's car with me today as she's not working, so I'll drive if you ring her parents and tell them what's happened. They can meet us at the hospital.'

Cally's arm was bent at a right angle, but not at her elbow. Clara's stomach churned at the sight, salty bile rising in her throat. She wasn't the squeamish sort, but Cally's arm was in such an unnatural position that she could hardly bring herself to look.

Poor Deirdre's face fell, her jowls dropping a good inch and a half as the severity of the situation hit home.

'I'm so sorry, Cally. I shouldn't have ranted and raved without making sure you were alright. Does anywhere else hurt?'

'Just my arm,' Cally replied, through tightly gritted teeth. Her right hand was tentatively protecting the left arm, despite the damage already having been done.

Clara gently offered her support as the teens watched, both horrified and enthralled. It was like a car crash, but on a smaller scale. Chair crash.

'What can I do?' Joe asked.

His stance suggested discomfort and Clara was aware of the shakiness of his body, but the determination in his face was stronger. However, after their conversations about Michelle, Clara was wary of taking him to the hospital. Cally's situation wasn't life or death, but he'd still have to face up to ambulance sirens and overworked doctors. It might bring back bad memories.

'You stay here and help Deirdre and Lynsey tidy up. It's nearly time for this lot to be heading home anyway.' The clock on the wall indicated it was closing in on nine.

'Are you sure you'll be alright on your own?'

Clara nodded. 'Cally's family will probably get there just as quickly as we will, but I don't want to risk it. She'll need a cast to reset this arm.' She had to concentrate really hard not to gag at the thought. 'Come on,' she said, holding the door open for a whimpering Cally, 'Let's get going.'

As she allowed the door to shut behind her, Clara could have sworn she heard Joe say something, but it was indecipherable and she didn't have time to turn back. Cally's arm was far more pressing.

*   *   *

By the time Clara was leaving the A&E department her

head was splitting in two. The stark strip lighting had made her head hurt and the *noise* – it wasn't as though she was used to silence, she worked with young people, after all – but what with the high-pitched wails of babies with red faces and high temperatures, and the babbling chatter of anxious parents, she'd been relieved when Cally's parents appeared through the revolving doors.

Wrapping her coat across her body to protect herself against the cold, Clara made her way towards the over-flow car park, her eyes firmly fixed on the glistening pavement ahead. The streetlights bounced off the frosty ground, making the usually dull-grey tarmac look as though it had been covered with a dusting of glitter, and she sensibly shortened her stride in response. She didn't want to fall head over heels. One broken bone was enough for one night.

'Hey.'

Clara jumped back with a start.

'Joe! Hey.'

'I wanted to check Cally's parents had arrived. Has she been seen yet?'

'A triage nurse saw her pretty much straight away. She's ninety-nine per cent certain it's a break but they're waiting for an x-ray to confirm it. Thank God for the NHS. What they do is bloody amazing.'

'We're so lucky,' Joe agreed. 'It's a national treasure.'

'Cally's parents weren't impressed that she'll likely need a cast,' Clara said with a wry smile. 'She's already broken her wrist, two fingers and her ankle. Sounds as though she's a bit of a calamity.'

'At least they won't blame the club for not looking after her properly. We've avoided the lawsuits yet again, hopefully.'

'I don't think they're the 'where there's blame, there's a claim' type.'

'You're right. Her mum goes to church and she's the gentlest woman I've ever met. So softly spoken and wouldn't say boo to a goose. Definitely not the type to drag us through the courts.'

The two of them started walking, Clara matching his long stride despite her fears. At least if she did fall, now Joe was here she'd have someone to get her medical attention.

'Where are you parked?' he asked.

'The car park on Upper Brook Street. You?'

'I'm on the road. Couldn't find a space and took a chance,' he said, before wryly adding, 'I think your rebellious streak must be rubbing off on me.'

Clara cocked an eyebrow.

'What?' he said with mock innocence.

'You make out I'm wild, when in reality I can't wait to get home and have a long soak in the bath, if my mum's not used all the hot water already.'

'It's been an eventful day. Wanting to relax doesn't make you any less wild. I bet even Russell Brand baths, now and again.'

'I'm not sure,' Clara replied, scrunching her lips until her nose wrinkled. 'He always looks a bit ... crusty.'

Joe threw back his head in a laugh, his breath visibly billowing as he exhaled. 'I bet you wouldn't say that to his face.'

'I doubt he'd care. He's too busy being outrageous.'

'So were you that night we went to town. Don't you remember that bar where you got up and started dancing?'

'What are you on about?'

'That last bar, the one with all the wood and the posh lights? You were throwing all kinds of shapes.'

Clara raised her hand to her mouth as vague recollections of shouting about her ability to do the Macarena wormed their way to the forefront of her mind. The Macarena hadn't even been playing. There had been a pianist ... Oh dear.

'Let's not talk about that,' she said hastily, 'and you don't have to cross the car park if you're not parked up here. I can already see Mum's car.'

As though to prove her point she pulled her keys from her pocket and pressed the unlock button, her headlights flashing in response.

'I don't mind.'

A comfortable silence enveloped her as Clara reached for the handle on the driver's side. As she lifted the lever upwards she gasped. 'I nearly forgot to give you your presents. It's a good job they're in the car. Why don't you get in and I'll drive to where you're parked. It's too cold to walk when you don't need to.'

'If you're sure,' Joe said, gratefully climbing into the passenger side.

Clara was briefly ashamed of the sweet wrappers that had amassed in the foot well. There was quite the collection, enough that Joe's shoes crunched as he pushed the seat back to accommodate his long legs. He was much taller than Clara, who usually occupied the seat.

'Your presents are on the back seat,' she said, pushing her keys into the ignition and checking her mirrors as Joe purposefully clicked his seatbelt. She noticed him pull on it to check it was secure, but didn't pass comment. 'Help yourself.'

Joe reached over as she reversed out.

'Are both of these for me?'

'Yep.'

'I'm touched, but you didn't have to. This is only meant to be a bit of fun, not making more work for you when you're already rushed off your feet.'

'It *is* fun,' she insisted, her eyes remaining fixed on the road, even though she wanted to see his reaction to the gifts. 'Anyway, you're making as much of an effort as I am.'

'It's my pleasure. I'm enjoying our time together.'

She could see his fingers pulling open the paper bag out of the corner of her eye.

'It's not much,' she said quickly.

'It's fantastic,' he replied.

Clara glanced over as she paused at the T-junction, pleased to see Joe examining the craftsmanship of the wooden nativity scene as closely as he could in the dimly lit car.

'I saw you admiring it at the markets,' she admitted.

'You noticed.' He smiled as he ran his hand over the wood.

'I notice lots of things.' Clara pushed firmly forward on the gearstick as she pulled out onto the main road. 'Eagle-eyed Clara, that's me.'

'I love it,' he said, carefully returning it to the bag and folding a purposeful crease in the top. 'I'll put it out every Christmas and think of you and that night at the market.'

'And nutjob Miranda,' Clara chuckled.

'I'd tried to forget her,' he said, joining her in the laughter.

'The other present's more generic,' she apologised, 'and impossible to disguise so I didn't bother wrapping it.'

Joe held up the red-and-white-striped candy cane, an emerald-green ribbon tied beneath its hook.

'And it's edible,' he said, immediately peeling back the plastic shrink-wrap that covered it. 'Which is perfect because I'm starving.'

The pepperminty scent filled the car, fresh and invigorating and totally encompassing Christmas.

'Phew. I was worried you'd think that was a cop-out.' As Clara rounded the corner and saw Joe's little red Ka parked, wheels mounting the kerb, she felt a pang of sadness that he was going. He was so easy to be around. 'Here we are,' she said as she pulled in.

'Here we are,' he echoed. He opened the door and a blast of freezing-cold air filled the car, diluting the essence of mint. 'Cheers for the lift, and for the presents.'

He held up his bag and what was left of the candy cane. The hook was already gone and it now resembled a skinny sick of rock.

'You're welcome.'

The door slammed shut and Clara inhaled sharply as Joe turned to wave.

The car suddenly felt hollow, empty. *She* felt hollow and empty. And as she flicked on her indicator and pulled out onto the street, she was already wondering where the Christmas Countdown would take her and Joe next. She could hardly wait. She missed him already.

Joe

Wednesday, December 13th 2017

It was a nippy night, and after standing in the cold for fifteen minutes waiting for Clara to arrive, Joe was beginning to have doubts about everything. His coat, which was way too thin for the current temperature. The pasta he'd eaten before he came out, because the sauce had been garlic-heavy and he didn't want his breath to smell. The pasta was weighing on his stomach too, which was churning with nerves.

Most of all he was wondering whether bringing Clara here was a bad idea. He'd not been to this theatre in years, the last time being when he and Michelle had watched a pantomime. Was it disloyal to her memory to bring another girl here? Joe wasn't sure, but he felt guilty even so.

Oxford Street was bustling, as usual, and as he stood

outside The Palace Theatre Joe was very aware of looking like a man who'd been stood up. He couldn't help glancing at his watch for the umpteenth time. They'd arranged to meet at seven, but it was already gone ten-past, and although the performance wasn't due to start for another twenty minutes, Joe had expected Clara to have arrived. People were streaming in through the ordinary brown doors, dull in both colour and style, which disguised the opulent plush red velvet seats and ornately gilded décor of the theatre within.

Joe loved watching the people arriving – the suited men and smartly dressed women, and the little girls in their frilly princess dresses. A night at the theatre encouraged people to make an effort with their appearance, and Joe had tried to scrub up too. He'd pulled out a slate-grey woollen blazer that he'd bought on a whim the previous winter and teamed it with stiff black trousers and a powder-blue shirt. He'd toyed with the idea of a tie, before deciding that was too formal, instead unbuttoning his top button in a semi-casual style. Joe hoped he looked smart and that Clara would appreciate seeing him in something other than his usual sportswear or polo shirt and jeans combo, but with every second that passed he was convincing himself Clara wasn't going to turn up at all.

He sighed as he looked at his watch again, then out to the passersby. Students mainly, what with the campuses for both Manchester University and Manchester Metropolitan being in such close proximity. Then there were the commuters hurrying towards nearby Oxford Road station to get their trains back to Warrington or Widnes or Stockport, or one of the other outlying towns that people travelled into the city from. But although there were plenty of people, weaving in and out of each other in a dance all of their own, there was no Clara.

A stocky gentleman wielding a briefcase shoulder-barged past him. Rain was falling – he could see it in the beams of the streetlights and as the passing cars sprayed puddles over unsuspecting bystanders – but even the miserable weather wasn't as gloomy as the thought of Clara standing him up was making him.

He stared out blankly into the December rain, trying to decide what to do. Would it look desperate and needy to phone her? She wasn't all that late, not really, but it was so cold and damp that his feet felt like ice blocks.

He was reluctant for his hands to leave the warm confines of his pockets, but was ready to pull out his phone to see if she'd sent a message, when he felt the tap on his shoulder. Joe was relieved to find himself greeted by a somewhat bedraggled Clara. Her hair was sticking out at jaunty angles under the navy beanie hat she was wearing, beads of sweat building on her exposed forehead.

'I'm sorry,' she panted. 'The bloody bus didn't turn up and so I had to walk from the club, and it's further than you think and it's raining again ...' She paused for a moment to catch her breath. 'I'm so annoyed with myself because I'm never late, but I was trying to finish off this application form at the club and when I looked at the clock it was already almost six and I thought I'd have to get the bus. Then when it didn't come ...'

'Ssshhh. It's fine. You're here now and it's still early. Come on, let's get inside and dry off.'

He held the door open and Clara stepped into the foyer, still chattering on about how bad she felt for keeping him waiting.

'Clara, don't beat yourself up about it. We're here and we've still got time to buy an overpriced bag of jelly babies, so there's nothing to apologise for.'

'And a programme,' Clara added, pulling off her hat and shaking out her hair. The way it stood on end made it look as though she'd just rolled out of bed, and that thought made Joe's stomach muscles clench. 'I don't know anything about *The Nutcracker* except what you told me, so I'll need all the help I can get to follow the story.'

'You won't, I promise. Even if you don't know the story you can enjoy it as a real spectacle. I guarantee you'll know more of the music than you think, too. But if you want a programme, I'll buy you one.'

Clara shook her head vehemently. 'I'll buy one myself. I wasn't expecting you to get me one.'

'I know you weren't,' Joe replied, 'but I want to. It'll give you a chance to find out more about your name-sake. That was another reason I wanted to bring you here, because the girl in *The Nutcracker* is called Clara too.'

'I'm so underdressed,' Clara moaned, pulling at the hem of her burgundy jumper dress as she cast her eyes over the well-dressed theatre-goers. 'Everyone else looks like they're going to a wedding.'

'You look great,' Joe assured her, thinking that she really, really did. Whilst other women were wearing strings of pearls or had their hair coiffeured into well-sprayed up-do's, Clara's look was understated and effortlessly cool. Her ruffled hair (the result of the weather and the hat) along with her heavily lined eyes gave her a rock-chick edge, but she carried herself with class. Other people – lesser people – might not be able to pull it off without looking scruffy, but Clara fitted in, despite her outfit being more casual than those being worn by the rest of the crowd.

'I planned to go home and get changed before I set off, but with the paperwork and waiting for Lynsey to arrive ... time slid away from me.'

'More bids for funding?'

'Yeah, I'm feeling quietly hopeful about this one. It's specifically for youth groups in the North West, so we've got a decent chance. The form went on forever, though.'

They shuffled forwards in the queue for the confectionery kiosk, and Joe was glad they'd not decided to join the clamouring crowds waiting at the bar. There was a lone harried-looking lad serving, slick, long hair the colour of spun gold tucked behind his pixie ears as he desperately tried to meet the needs of the punters impatient for their large red wines and gin and tonics. Poor guy. Joe would have put money on him counting down the minutes until the bell rang and everyone filed into the theatre, leaving him in peace until the fifteen-minute interval, which was probably even more hectic for him.

The young girl in the kiosk had it easy, in comparison, and the smile she gave Joe as he placed his order suggested she was happy in her work. She handed over a sunshine-yellow bag filled with gelatinous coloured men, and Joe and Clara made their way up the staircase to the circle. The doors were open, closely guarded by ushers wearing starched white shirts and carrying armfuls of programmes. Joe took one from the ruddy-faced lady, who ripped their tickets.

'For you,' he said, trying to hand the programme to Clara as they entered the theatre, but she wasn't listening. She was too busy taking in the beauty surrounding them, the swirling carving that edged the boxes and the proscenium arch frame, the shimmering gold against the deep red of the seats and the bunched curtains at the edge of the stage.

Joe smiled at her reaction. He'd felt the same way himself the first time he'd first come here. It was a magical place – a beautiful place – and Joe found it charming that Clara too was falling under its spell.

'It's quite something, isn't it?'

'It's ... wow. I must have walked past this building hundreds of times, but I never knew it was decked out like this inside.' She looked up to the ceiling, taking in every detail of the intricately patterned coving. 'Thank you, Joe. Thank you for bringing me here and showing me a part of my own city that I never knew existed.'

Her reaction was enough to assure Joe that bringing Clara here was the right thing to do. A warm rush pulsed through him, and although he knew he was probably being ridiculous, he took it as a sign from Michelle. It was as though she was giving her approval, letting him know it was fine.

'You're welcome,' he said, tentatively placing his hand on the small of her back to encourage her to move along. There was a backlog of people trying to enter the auditorium now, with showtime nudging ever closer. 'We'd better move. People are wanting to sit down.'

'Yes. Right. Of course.'

She moved, somewhat reluctantly, Joe thought, along the row to their seats, which were positioned slap bang in the centre of the circle. When they'd removed their coats and settled in the flip seats, he was finally able to hand over the programme he'd bought her.

'You won't really need it to follow the story, but it can be a souvenir. A way to remember the night.'

Clara reached out to squeeze his hand as the lights dimmed.

'How could I ever forget this?'

Joe couldn't explain away the sadness he felt when she retracted her hand from his, so instead, as the opening bars of Tchaikovsky's famous score played, he pulled open the bag of jelly babies, selected one and promptly bit its head off.

*   *   *

Joe was distracted. Although he was enjoying the ballet, every so often he'd steal a glance at Clara, trying to gauge her reaction to what was playing out before her. Although there had been one moment where she'd full-on beamed, it was hard to decipher her thoughts through the semi-darkness. It had been a relief when the houselights had come up for the interval and Clara full-on enthused about the costumes, the staging and the rather prominent bulge in the dancer who was playing Cavalier's tights.

'This is supposed to be a night of culture,' he said with mock horror. 'I didn't pay good money for tickets for you to eye up some well-hung dancer.'

An elderly lady with a felt hat propped on top of her tightly permed steel-grey hair turned and glared and the pair of them giggled at her obvious disapproval.

'Stop making out I'm a pervert,' Clara said with a laugh, playfully swatting his arm. 'Even you noticed. Anyone would have, it was just ... *there*.'

'I was admiring the beautiful *port de bras*, actually.'

'Bra?' Clara looked puzzled.

'The positions of the arms,' Joe explained, showing a perfectly rounded third position. 'It's French.'

'Oh.' She laughed again, and it sounded like a song. 'So nothing to do with underwear.'

'Not all of us have a mind as mucky as yours,' he answered.

'It's brilliant. I wasn't sure I was going to like ballet,

but this is amazing. And it's so Christmassy!'

'I hoped you'd like it. Simone's a big fan of *The Nutcracker*, and she was gutted when I told her we were coming tonight.'

'You should have brought her along. I wouldn't have minded, she's a great kid.'

'She's involved with a concert at school. Mum and Dad have gone to watch.'

Clara's face fell. 'Are you supposed to be there too?'

'She didn't ask me until this morning, so I'd already bought the tickets for this. She was fine about it, though. She's part of the choir, so it isn't like she has a solo this time.'

'But she'd still have wanted you there,' Clara replied. She suddenly looked very sombre and serious. 'I know how close you two are.'

'Simone's old enough to know that I don't have to be physically with her to be rooting for her. And I'm sure she'll tell me about it tomorrow, or maybe even tonight. She's obsessed with WhatsApp. And I'll tell her all the details about this.'

A mischievous glint appeared in Clara's eyes. 'Even about the well-hung dancer?'

Joe rolled his eyes. 'No,' he replied drolly. 'He's all yours.'

'Good,' Clara smiled, wrapping her arms tightly

around her chest. 'Because I do like a man who knows how to move.'

Joe thought of his shoulder, still bruised from his recent foray back into the world of breakdancing. He knew how to move, sort of. It was just his body was out of practice.

'Fancy an ice cream?' he asked, nodding towards the lady selling tubs from a tray around her neck. It looked uncomfortable, he thought, weighing her down, and he wondered what the person who came up with the idea of wearing a food stall had been thinking. It looked borderline torturous.

She nodded. 'Do you think they'll have strawberry?'

'I'll see what I can do.'

He sheepishly stood up, hyper-aware of the annoyance of the row who were having to stand up to make way for him to squeeze past, and smiled at how glad he was to be here with Clara.

As he paid for two tubs of ice cream, he signalled a thumbs-up in her direction to show her that her luck was in – he'd managed to bag the last pot of Strawberry Delight ice cream – and felt a familiar yet long-forgotten flip in his stomach as she smiled back a lop-sided gratitude.

Oh dear, he thought. This has the potential to become messy. Awkward and messy.

* * *

By the time they were gathering up their belongings, the auditorium was half empty. People were keen to get away, either to carry on their night with a late dinner or a nightcap, or to get home to the comfort of their beds.

'I'm fascinated by how quickly everyone leaves,' Joe observed. 'Five minutes ago there wasn't an empty seat, and now look. There's only us.'

'It's a bit creepy,' Clara added. 'All this space ... It's so beautiful, but I wouldn't want to be here at night. It'd be even scarier than being in the club.'

'Then we'd better get moving. They'll be locking up soon.'

The staff were cleaning around them, obviously wanting everyone out as quickly as possible, but that didn't stop Clara whipping out her phone and taking a selfie of her and Joe with the empty stage as a backdrop. Joe saw his smile on the screen, too wide and too toothy, but he couldn't rein it in as Clara pressed on the screen to snap the photo. He'd had a fantastic night.

'That's a keeper,' she said. 'I'll send it you later.'

'Thanks.'

The prospect of having a photo of the two of them together on his phone sent a ripple of delight through him, which in turn set off a flicker of panic about what the recent stirrings in him meant. Could he really be falling for Clara? And did she see him as anything more than a friend in need?

He didn't know. But as they descended the stairwell back towards the street, the echoes of their footsteps satisfyingly hollow, what he did know was that something had changed in him tonight. Something inexplicable and exciting and super-charged, and that frightened him in the best possible way.

Clara

Thursday, December 14th 2017

Clara had been humming 'The Dance of the Sugarplum Fairy' all day long. Talk about an earworm. It had kept her company on the bus, on the walk to the club, when she'd been to the bakery to buy a vanilla slice...

Clara stopped short as she entered the office. It looked different.

'Deirdre? Have you been tidying my desk again?'

Clara wasn't sure why she was even bothering to ask. It was obvious her boss had been on one of her tidying sprees. They were few and far between, but once Deirdre got a bee in her bonnet, she'd not stop until she'd blitzed the club from top to bottom.

This was one of those days. The usual piles of paper were missing, for one thing, the empty mugs waiting to be washed no longer sat on the windowsill for another. But most importantly, Clara noticed the stack of envelopes was no longer piled up ready to be taken to the post box at the end of the road. Her heart sank.

'I couldn't stand the sight of that paperwork building up for a minute longer,' Deirdre called from the store-room across the landing. 'I moved it into your drawer.'

Clara released a sigh of relief as she reached for the small brass handle and pulled open the drawer, imme-diately spying a stack of half-finished forms for additional funding and a leaflet advertising training courses that sounded useful but were way outside the non-existent training budget the club currently had. She pulled the wedge of paper out, placing it in the centre of her desk, knowing that if it stayed hidden she'd keep procrastinating. That wasn't an option. The club needed money, and it needed money fast.

'I took those letters down to the post box on my break too,' Deirdre said proudly, brandishing a fluores-cent-pink feather duster like a weapon as she entered the room.

Clara took a deep breath in at the comment. 'Which letters?'

'The ones that have been sat on your desk for ages! You do realise it's Christmas? If you don't get these things posted they'll never arrive on time.'

'All of them?'

Clara's mouth felt dry. She tried to recall what time the postie collected from the vibrant red box down the road. Was it four o'clock? Or five? Clara wasn't sure, but it didn't really matter – the clock on the wall was already showing twenty to six.

'Thought it'd save you a job.' Deirdre spun her duster like a magic wand, a fine layer of dust particles filling the air and causing Clara to splutter. 'Plus I'm trying to be more active. The doctor says if I don't keep moving with my knee I'm going to be referred for physio. The last thing I want is Bella or one of her sort fiddling about with my joints.'

'Can we not talk about her?' The thought of the letter winging its way across Manchester at this very moment was already making Clara feel nauseous. Add Bella to the mix and she might vomit for real. 'And I don't want to talk about Dean either.'

She couldn't begin to predict how he'd react when the letter arrived, whether it'd even reach him. She'd deliberately addressed it to the football club rather than to his home, even though she could have easily sent it to him there. After all, she knew the address off by heart. She'd lived there herself for the best part of two years. The city-centre apartment had been a far cry from what she'd been used to, shiny and new and immaculately presented. She'd loved living in the heart of Manchester with the pulse of people around her, vibrant and vital. But she'd still missed the familiarity of her own home, her own community. There wasn't that sense of looking out for each other – she hadn't even known the names of her neighbours until one day when she'd taken a parcel in for them.

'I'm sorry, love. I didn't mean to stir up bad memories.'

'You didn't.' Clara's voice was clipped and she knew it.

'I've said it before, and I'll say it again. He's scum, and you'll find someone worthy of your love one of these days. There must be plenty of men out there looking for someone like you.'

'Someone like me?' Clara laughed at the absurdity. She was barely staying afloat. The club, her personal life, not to mention the current political climate, which was enough to make anyone feel bereft. If it wasn't for the escapism of Joe and the countdown, she'd probably have resorted to alcohol again to numb the pain.

'Don't do yourself down, Clara. You're ballsy. Any man worth his salt will find that sexy as hell, and those who don't aren't worth your time. You're full of Northern grit, but not hard-nosed. That's important too. Strong women are punchy without being bitchy.'

'That's something I learned from you. And from

Mum. Everything the pair of you do you do with love, but you won't stand for being played for a fool either. Nothing ever scares you. You're good role models to have.'

Clara blinked away the tears that were prickling at her eyes, making a conscious effort to take on some of the bravery of the women who inspired her.

'We all have fears, Clara. Sometimes the best thing to do is face them head-on.'

Clara digested Deirdre's words.

So what if Dean did get the letter? Nothing that terrible would happen. At best he'd respond positively, and at worst he'd ignore it. Unless he thought the whole thing was laughable and turned up on her doorstep to rip it up in front of her very eyes...

But she couldn't worry about what might be. There was no point. Anyway, history didn't repeat itself that often, did it?

* * *

'What do you think of my lashes, Joe? Nice, huh?'

False eyelashes were the latest fad with the girls at the club, the thicker and longer the better, in their eyes (or at least, around their eyes), and Tiffany fluttered hers purposefully in Joe's direction.

'Erm ... yeah. Great.'

Tiffany beamed in delight at the half-hearted vote of confidence, before returning to her girl gang, singing the praises of the lip gloss she'd found at the market for a fraction of the price it was on the high street.

Joe mouthed 'help me' in Clara's direction as soon as the girl's back was turned.

Clara could hear the group talking in hushed tones, punctuated by coy giggles and sideways glances in Joe's direction. Aha, she thought. Tiffany's got a crush.

'She terrifies me.' Joe said.

'Oh, I love Tiff. She's a real character.'

Clara looked over at the girls, who were now pouting wildly. She supposed they were trying to look sexy, aiming to perfect their duckfaces for the numerous selfies they'd undoubtedly be uploading to Instagram later that night.

'She's certainly that.'

'She reminds me a lot of myself at her age. I thought I was the bee's bloody knees back then.' Clara shook her head at the memory, and at how far off the mark she'd been. What she'd give to have even a fraction of the confidence she'd had back then, now. 'And I loved my make-up, and was just like her, always seeking out the best bargains because we didn't have money to fritter away on anything that wasn't essential.'

'You found a way to get what you wanted, though,' Joe said knowingly.

Clara's face formed a puzzled frown.

'Taking the lipstick from the magazine cover?' Joe reminded her.

'Sssh! Don't go mentioning that! Anyone could hear.' She looked over her shoulder cautiously.

'No one's listening,' Joe confirmed. 'Your secret's safe with me.'

'Can you keep another secret?'

Clara locked eyes with Joe, hoping she could trust him not to laugh or judge. She needed to talk to someone about the letter. Deirdre couldn't have noticed it amongst the stack of Christmas cards and applications for funding, because if she had Clara wouldn't have heard the last of it. Deirdre would have wanted every detail about what the letter contained.

Joe lowered himself so he was sat on the edge of the stage, his long legs dangling down. Clara mimicked his movements, although her legs were far farther from reaching the floor of the hall.

'Tell me anything. I promise it'll go no further. I'm all ears.'

Clara giggled, although she couldn't explain why she found it so funny. Maybe because, if she was being really harsh, Joe's ears were on the large side. Not quite on a par with Gary Lineker, but they were noticeable. Sticky-outy, but not in a bad way. In fact, they were kind of cute.

'What?' He frowned.

'Nothing,' Clara said firmly, trying to calm herself from the inside.

'What's this secret you've got to share, then? More acts of crime? Should I get Greater Manchester Police on speed dial?'

Clara swatted him as he grinned at his own joke.

'No. I'm worried I've made a fool of myself, though.' Her heart was racing. 'I hadn't even decided if I was going to send the letter in the first place, but now it's out there and all I can do is wait and see what happens.'

'You've lost me. Start at the beginning.'

Clara wove her hands together, tapping her fingertips against the knuckles of the opposite hand.

'I'd been filling in all those forms about funding. There were so many of them asking the same questions and wanting to know the club's incomings and outgoings, how many kids we get on an average night, boring stuff that they use to make a decision, when the truth of the matter is they don't have a clue about how we work and what everyone here needs. It just seemed so pointless.' She remembered how defeated she'd felt as she fought against the endless reams of paper. 'I thought about what would make a difference to these kids, what we could do if we had more money. Most of the kids here won't get a Christmas like the ones they show on the telly. They won't be having turkey with all the trimmings, presents piled high under a tree that skims the ceiling in their living room. You know yourself, most of the families don't have surplus money to throw around. And I was thinking about Jordan, whose Christmas Day will be the same as any other, caring for his mum. He's fourteen! He shouldn't have that responsibility.'

She paused, and Joe waited patiently for her to continue. Clara was thankful that he wasn't putting pressure on her to talk.

'So I thought about what would make his Christmas memorable, something that he'd really love. If anyone deserves a treat, it's him.'

'Tickets to a United match, surely. Football's his passion.'

'Exactly.' Clara flinched, embarrassed. 'And I thought of a way we might be able to make it happen, not just for Jordan, but for the rest of the kids too. I'm such a fool.'

'Some of those funding places let you spend the money on anything so long as you can prove it's beneficial. You can make an argument that these children would learn from the experience of going to a match. I don't think anyone would think that was foolish.'

'You don't understand.' She examined her fingernails, bitten down way too low. It was a bad habit, but one she couldn't stop. 'I wrote to Dean. I thought he might be able to use his connections to pull some strings. He was in the youth team at Man U for a while,' she explained. 'He's still in touch with some people that work there.'

'So that's what you're worrying about.' Joe bit down on his lip. 'I can see why, but I don't think you need to. He might be an idiot for playing around when he had you, but there must have been something good about him. You wouldn't have been with him in the first place if he was a completely callous human being.'

'What if he knows it was me who scratched his car? It's beyond cheeky to ask for anything from him when I've behaved like I have.'

'He behaved far worse,' Joe reminded her. '*Far* worse. Maybe he'll surprise you.'

'I hadn't even decided if I was going to post it. I'd left it on my desk to mull it over, but Deirdre had one of her cleaning frenzies and thought she was doing me a favour by posting it.'

'That desk was getting out of control –' Joe began.

'It's organised chaos,' Clara interrupted. It might not

look like much of a system to anyone else, but it worked for her. 'I can put my hands on anything you ask me to in seconds.'

'Whatever you say. I believe you.'

'It's true.'

'It's a disaster area. But you keep on fooling yourself,' Joe said, but not unkindly. 'Anyway, for what it's worth, I don't think you need to get het up about it. And if he comes up with the goods it'll be well worth it. Jordan would be over the moon.'

'Can you imagine?' Clara replied, smiling at the thought. 'He'd be so impressed.'

'Fingers crossed.' Joe held out his crossed digits in front of him.

'Fingers crossed,' Clara repeated emphatically, surprised by how much better she felt for offloading. Joe was a good listener – there was no judgement with him, just kind words and a reassuring smile. Most importantly, she trusted that her secret would go no further.

'We'd better get back to work.' Joe slid from where he'd been perched on the edge of the stage. 'And I'm looking forward to seeing what treat you have in store for me tonight too.'

Clara brought her hands to her mouth in horror. With everything else that had been happening, she'd forgotten her plans to head to the supermarket to get Joe a present.

'I'm so sorry. What with all the paperwork and how busy I've been, I totally forgot.'

'Oh.' Joe smiled, but Clara wasn't sure it reached his eyes. What was that look? Disappointment? 'Don't worry about it. You're still free tomorrow night, though? Meet me in town after work? I'll message you with the details in the morning.'

'Sure,' Clara replied, still annoyed at herself for breaking her part of the Christmas Countdown deal, especially after such a fabulous evening at the theatre the night before. She'd been looking at the photo of the two of them together, their faces luminous and radiant, and it made her chest hurt. They were so different in many ways, but she was beginning to realise they were very alike in all the ones that mattered. 'I'll look forward to it.'

But she wasn't sure if he heard her, because he was already heading towards Jordan and Tariq, who were glued to their phones at the far corner of the hall, and she feared her words had been swallowed up, drowned out by the noise.

Joe

Friday, December 15th 2017

'I don't think I've ever felt as cultured in my life as I have this past week,' Clara laughed as they headed towards the imposing cathedral. It was another landmark Manchester building she'd told Joe she'd not set foot inside before. 'First the theatre, now this.'

'Don't say I never take you anywhere.'

'You take me everywhere! I don't think I'd leave the house except to go to the club without you to encourage me.'

'Pppfff. You would,' Joe assured her, 'and probably somewhere more raucous than Handel's *Messiah*.'

'I'm looking forward to it, actually. I've never been to anything like this before.'

'It's something new for me, too.'

Clara looked surprised. 'Really? I thought you'd have

seen it every year, what with your dad being a vicar and all.'

Joe shook his head. 'This is my first time. Dad recommended it, but it's a busy time of year for him. He likes to really focus on outreach work during Advent, so he never gets the chance. I think he was a bit envious of us for coming. He took Mum to see *Messiah* on their first date, thirty-two years ago.'

'Thirty-two years and they're still going strong.'

'I know. It's quite something. They've taught me what a marriage should be. And it all started with a night out like any other. Dad jokingly said it's the perfect way to woo a girl.'

He inwardly cringed at his words. It sounded like a cheesy chat-up line.

'You've been telling quite a few people about where we've been going, having you?' Clara said, eyes narrowing. 'First Simone with *The Nutcracker*, and now your Dad about this.'

'They don't know about the Christmas countdown, just that we're spending time together.'

He swallowed nervously. Was she ashamed to be seen with him? Is that why she seemed so reluctant to tell anyone about the countdown?

'It's fine,' she assured him, nuzzling her nose down into the folds of her scarf. 'But you know what they're like. It's the whole *When Harry Met Sally* thing, where no one believes men and women can be friends. Deirdre's already got plans to marry us off.'

She rolled her eyes, as though it was the most ludicrous thought ever, and the crushing sensation of rejection contracted in Joe's chest.

He let out an uneasy laugh, relieved when someone he vaguely knew interrupted to say hello. By the time they'd found a space on a pew near the back, Clara was talking about the kids at the club, which Joe found a much more comfortable topic of conversation.

'And then he asked me if I'd seen Take That first time around! Do I really look old enough for that? I know I've got a few wrinkles around my eyes, but I didn't think I looked that ancient.'

'I can't believe you've been to see Take That at all,' he joked, shaking his head. 'That's not something to be proud of.'

'Until you see them live you can't judge,' Clara insisted. 'They're Manchester's finest. Next tour you can come along with me, as long as you're prepared to queue to get near the front. Thatters are hardcore. If you want the best spot you have to put the hours in.'

'I wouldn't have thought you'd be into Gary Barlow. I thought you had better taste.'

'I'm a Howard girl,' Clara confessed with a wink. 'It's

that thing about being attracted to good dancers again. Plus his abs are a work of art.'

'He must be old enough to be your dad!'

'Age ain't nothing but a number, Joe,' she said seriously. 'And if you come with me to a show next time you'll end up harbouring a man crush on at least one of them. Probably all of them, actually.'

'Hmmm,' he replied noncommittally. 'Perhaps.'

He preferred his music louder – still favouring Foo Fighters and Blink 182 – and Billy would never let it rest if he found out he was going to a Take That concert. Although if he mentioned he was doing it for Clara he was sure his friend would forgive him. Billy was keen for Joe to join the 'settled down and shacked up' club as quickly as possible. His interest came from a good place, Joe knew, but Billy's perfect little family was a reminder of what he was missing out on.

The choir filed into the pews ready to begin the performance, and a hush of anticipation silenced the audience.

As the recital began, Joe allowed the music to sweep over him and around him and through him, stirring his emotions, and he was reminded of the power of music. Of how not only one genre can bring you pleasure; sometimes something completely different to what you think you like reminds you how wonderful it is to be alive. And as he stole one last look at Clara he thought that perhaps going to see Take That with her might not be so terrible after all.

* * *

'So, what did you make of it?' Joe asked as they made their way back along the aisle towards the exit of the Cathedral. He was curious to know what Clara had thought of the performance. Much of it had been passive listening, until the 'Hallelujah Chorus', where the audience were invited to get on their feet and belt out the rousing chant.

'I don't know if I'd want to see it again,' Clara answered diplomatically, 'but I'm glad you invited me. And the Cathedral looked beautiful all decorated for Christmas. I was mesmerised by the candles. That, along with the haunting melody moved me more than I expected.'

'It was kind of hypnotic, wasn't it? I feel like I've been under a spell.'

They each took a mince pie that was being offered by a portly gentleman on the door who wished them a Merry Christmas and a safe journey home, and as the succulent mincemeat flooded into Joe's mouth, a boozy aftertaste assaulting his taste buds, the realisation hit that they were already more than halfway through Advent.

Joe wasn't ready for their time together to be over, and the Christmas Countdown was the perfect excuse to spend time with Clara away from the club. He'd taken to going home from The Club on the Corner and looking fondly at the gifts she had given him. Everything from the cheesy CD to the fortune-telling fish, which had caused so much upset revived flashbacks that caused him to smile to himself, knowing no one would understand the significance of these items except himself and Clara. It felt special.

Clara was special too. She had character, and was funnier than he'd given her credit for. More sensitive too. She was kind-hearted and willing to try new things, and so committed to keeping the youth club running. He couldn't help but be attracted to that wholehearted enthusiasm. But he was taken aback by how the more he liked her, the more physically attracted to her he became. She was striking, with her angular haircut and sharp jawline, almost elfin in appearance; and so far from the type of girl Joe usually went for that it had caught him by surprise how she suddenly seemed beautiful to him. But she *was* beautiful, so totally, utterly beautiful in his eyes, and it was hard to believe he could ever have thought otherwise.

The twinkling city spread out before them as they headed towards the tram stop, and as the headlights of the yellow-fronted vehicle came almost immediately into view, Joe could barely hide his disappointment. The night was coming to an end all too quickly for his liking.

'Thank you for taking me,' Clara said, as the tram drew to a halt besides the otherwise empty platform. 'I'd never have gone to something like that without you inviting me. You're broadening my mind.'

'It was my pleasure.' Joe pressed the button to open the sliding doors and a beeping sounded out in the darkness. 'I had a great night.'

'Me too.'

And before he could process it properly, she'd risen onto the tips of her toes and stretched up to planted a kiss on the underside of his jaw, before boarding the tram and leaving him, bewildered, on the platform.

As the tram pulled away Joe touched the spot where her lips had been with his fingertips. If he didn't know better, he'd have sworn his skin was aflame.

Clara

'I can't believe it.' Joe's face was alight with joy. Clara highly doubted there were many people, least of all men of Joe's age, who'd be as thrilled to receive a Game Boy this Christmastime. 'Where on earth did you get it from? It's not like you can walk into John Lewis and pluck one of these babies from the shelf.'

'Tell me about it,' Clara replied with a laugh. The hours she'd spent scouring the internet for the exact model Joe had lusted after were worth it, though. He was beaming with out and out delight.

'So where *did* you buy it?' Joe persisted. 'EBay?'

Clara nodded. 'I got involved in a bidding war for this. It was almost as bad as the time I set my heart on replacing the Wedgwood vase of my gran's that I broke.'

'Oh dear. How did you break it?'

'Playing with one of those little bouncy balls. I insisted I'd be able to catch it and kept throwing it against the lounge wall, even though she told me not to. She'd warned me I'd end up breaking something and, of course, she was proven right in the end when her favourite vase was smashed to smithereens on the hearth. She didn't shout at me, but the disappointment on her face was enough to make me cry my eyes out. I felt so guilty.'

'When was this?'

'Ooh, I must have been ten. I'd got the ball out of a party bag from Millie Ferdinand's birthday trip to McDonald's and it was all I'd played with for a week, until that day. After that I threw in it the bin in a rage.'

Clara felt a pang of mournful longing for the cheap toy. She'd barely thought about it for years, other than when her regret had caught up with her and she'd put her heart and soul into replacing the much-loved vase. Her mum had never been keen on balls in the house, mainly because her gran was a big fan of porcelain. Figurines of smartly dressed women in flowing ball gowns, mugs commemorating royal weddings (the mugs had lasted longer than the marriages in most cases, Clara realised), and the favoured vase which Clara had never seen filled with flowers of any kind. 'It's far too precious for that,' her gran had exclaimed, aghast at the suggestion.

'And you replaced the vase?'

'Years later. I found an identical one on eBay and thought it might ease my conscience, but I didn't know it was worth as much as it was. Maybe it wasn't, I could have been totally swindled out of my money.'

'I hope you didn't pay over the odds for this,' Joe said, holding the bright-blue Game Boy aloft. 'Although whatever you paid, it was worth it. You've made eight-year-old Joe Smith very happy indeed. And twenty-eight-year-old Joe Smith too.' He looked in the bag to where a collection of small game cartridges were sealed in individual air-tight ziplock pockets. 'There are all the classics in here.' He pulled one out at random, marvelling at it and Clara couldn't hold back her laugh. He might just as well have been eight years old again, because his excitement really was that of a kid at Christmas.

'Don't worry, I didn't rob a bank to fund it.'

'I wouldn't put it past you.' Joe grinned.

'Ha-ha,' Clara replied. 'As if.'

'It's perfect,' Joe said, wrapping his arms around her. Clara was so taken aback by the unexpected contact that she almost lost her balance. The height difference between them put her at a distinct disadvantage when it came to staying upright, and Clara automatically wrapped her arms around Joe's waist to stop herself from falling. She found her cheek pressed hard into his chest, so hard that she feared the pattern of his knitted jumper might leave an imprint on her skin. 'Best present ever.'

'Better than a Teenage Mutant Ninja Turtle onesie?' she asked, eyebrow cocked.

'Yep. That was a great gift too, but I've wanted one of these for twenty years.' He looked down at the gadget in his hand, his face lighting up as though love-struck. 'Imagine how you'd feel if you finally got the present you always wanted as a kid.'

When he pulled back, the gulf between them seemed enormous to Clara. With yesterday's kiss and then the hug, their relationship had taken a turn to becoming more physical.

'The little record player,' Clara said with a mournful pout. 'If only. I doubt my mum even remembers I wanted one in the first place.'

'That's what Christmas lists are for,' Joe prompted. 'You should write one to give to Santa. If you're good between now and then he might pop down your chimney to deliver you one on Christmas night.'

'We haven't even got a chimney.'

'Then how does he bring you your presents?' Joe asked.

'He's got a magic key, obviously,' Clara said, her tone light. 'It lets him in to all the houses and flats that don't have a chimney to come down. That's what my mum always used to say.'

'And that's supposed to be reassuring? I'm not sure the idea of a strange man with a key that can open any door would help me get to sleep on Christmas Eve.'

'Even if he was bringing presents?'

'I can't be bought,' he said, piously.

Clara spluttered. 'Coming from the man who's rubbing his hands together with glee every time he gets a countdown gift?'

'That's different,' he said, carefully putting the handheld console back in the bag with the cartridges.

'How so?'

Joe looked up, and Clara sensed a strange tension. She understood now what people meant when they said the air could be cut by a knife, because that's how she felt, as though she was suspended or frozen. The world seemed to be in slow motion, then Joe turned away and the spell was broken.

'Forget it,' he said finally, before smiling and holding the bag of goodies aloft. 'You're probably right.'

There was an uncomfortable pause. Usually their silences were peaceful rather than empty. Something had shifted, but Clara couldn't put her finger on what.

'I'd better go and find Deirdre,' she said finally. 'She wanted me to help her with something.' She didn't elaborate. She *couldn't* elaborate, because it was an out and out lie.

'Thanks again,' he called, as Clara left the hall and made her way up the staircase.

She ran her hand along the banister, reassured by the solidity of it against the palm of her hand, and she suddenly wondered why she was running away. They were friends, that was all. Nothing to be scared of, nothing to flee from.

Clara inhaled, dust and Pledge filling her nostrils. Then she turned around, skipped down the stairs and, head held high, walked back into the hall, where she found herself face to face with Joe.

'If I start my letter with an apology, do you think Santa will forgive me for all the bad things I've done this year?' she asked with a grin.

Joe grinned back, all awkwardness alleviated. 'It's worth a shot,' he said.

'Then I'd better get writing.' Clara reached for a pen and piece of paper from the cupboard and took both items to the table, before starting to furiously scribble words on the page. She glanced at her watch. 'Ten minutes until we open the doors and mayhem ensues. Do you reckon I can get it done before then?'

'With all the sins you've got to own up to, I doubt it,' he ribbed.

'Oh, go and polish your halo somewhere else,' Clara said jokily. 'Some of us have grovelling to do.'

But Joe didn't go. Instead he pulled up a chair next to her, switched on his Game Boy and lost himself in his game, the high-pitched bleeping background noise as Clara scrawled her wish list on the page.

Joe

Sunday, December 17th 2017

'Joe? Can you help me please?'

Tiffany was struggling, a fully stuffed bag for life in each perfectly manicured hand. Shannon's handiwork had lasted.

'Coming!'

The food bank was loud – or rather the kids were – and their enthusiasm for the task at hand was almost tangible as they sorted through the packets of pasta and porridge. Some of these kids didn't have much themselves, but behind their bravado and attitude they loved helping others. The carol performance at Autumn Days had shown it, and this only proved the point further.

He relieved Tiff of the weighty bags and heaved them onto the long table that ran along the back wall of the room.

'Here you go, Jordan. A few more bags for you to sort through.'

'It's never-ending.' Jordan's tone wasn't accusatory. It was matter of fact. The people of Manchester had given generously to the appeal, either buying extra to leave in the donation bins at the local supermarket or bringing it directly to the food bank. But Joe knew that although it might look like a lot, what the charity had to give barely scratched the surface. Demand was at an all-time high.

'I'll give you a hand,' Joe replied, pulling a family-sized box of Cornflakes from one of the bags and adding it to the crate marked 'cereals'. 'Clara's got some of the others unloading a delivery of donations from the back of a van. It's come from one of the local pre-schools. I guess everyone wants to help out someone in need this Christmastime.'

'It's good that people want to help at Christmas, but how does the food bank survive the rest of the year? There must be families who rely on places like this to eat all year round, not just in December.'

Joe nodded, impressed by the youngster's thought process. Then again, Jordan was mature. He'd had to grow up fast, what with the responsibilities of looking after his mum.

'They're always appealing for donations. The church

has a basket where people can donate, and I know some of the local supermarkets do too. But you're right, I think Christmas makes people more aware, both of how much they're spending and of how lucky they are.'

'I know I complain sometimes, but at least I never go to bed hungry.' Jordan added a pot noodle and two packets of Cup-a-soup to a box marked 'just add water'. 'The lady who showed us the system for sorting donations told us some people that come here don't have any way of cooking food, not even a microwave. That's why there's a box for hot food that just needs hot water. Makes me feel grateful.'

'You're right, we've got lots to be thankful for. But that doesn't mean you have to be strong all the time, or that you can't have a moan now and then. Sometimes it's good to let it out and clear the air.'

Joe bit his tongue as he realised his words were nothing more than lip service. He'd still not told Clara the whole truth about Michelle. He was frightened that to say the words out loud would ruin everything, just as he was starting to live again.

'No one likes a whinger.'

'You're far from a whinger,' Joe said. 'I know your mum's grateful for all you do.'

The more he'd heard about Jordan's situation, the

more admiration he had for the lad. Not only did he care for his mum, he also looked after his younger brother. The Club on the Corner was his respite, a break from supermarket trips and hurried school runs, the Hoovering and pegging out the washing.

'Anyone would do the same.'

The boy's body language signified that the conversation was closed, although Joe silently thought there were many Jordan's age who wouldn't do the same. Jordan never made a fuss, he accepted his role and went about it methodically. Joe could see why Clara had a soft spot for him – he was a good lad.

'Incoming!' Clara's voice boomed out around the room, and as she entered, followed by an entourage of kids armed with further supplies of dried and tinned foods. 'This should keep you lot busy for a while.'

Rather than the groan Joe would have expected, the teens set straight back to sorting the food and toiletries. They saw it as a challenge, one they were totally up for.

'They're doing us proud, aren't they?' beamed Deirdre. 'Miranda can't sing their praises highly enough.'

'They have good auras, these young people. Every one of them has a pink glow. That's indicative of a positive, caring energy,' explained the woman. Joe recognised her immediately. She might not be wafting her homemade candles about and wittering on about

Clara's exceptional sense of smell, but her wiry auburn hair was impossible to mistake.

'Hi, Miranda,' he smiled feebly, hoping she wouldn't remember him.

'I've seen you before,' she said, thoughtfully bringing her finger to the corner of her lip. 'Miranda never forgets a face, I pride myself on it.' She scrunched her eyes into slits as she mused, her lips pursing as she took in every pore of Joe's face. 'Don't tell me, it'll come.'

Her intense studying of his features left Joe unnerved, and in the end he couldn't take it any more.

'Were you at the Christmas market?' he asked, knowing full well that was the only place the two had ever crossed paths. If he'd seen her elsewhere he would have remembered – and probably crossed the road to avoid her.

'That's it!' she exclaimed, clasping her hands together. 'Now I remember. You were with that pretty little thing who had an incredible nose.'

'Clara's not a thing,' Joe mumbled under his breath, but Miranda's eyes widened and he knew she'd heard. Either that or she'd read his mind; he'd not put it past her.

'Yes,' Miranda continued, brushing her cloud of hair over her shoulder, 'Your girlfriend has quite the gift. There aren't many people who can distinguish between my unique blends as well as she can.'

Joe coughed, which extended into a splutter. 'She's not my girlfriend' he stuttered when he finally managed to control himself. 'We work together.'

'Oh, is she here?'

Miranda's face lit up like a Belisha beacon at the news. Between that and her flame-like hair she was practically florescent. Joe had no experience of auras, positive, negative or otherwise, but if Miranda had one, he'd have bet on it being luminous orange.

She pushed up onto the balls of her feet, creasing the leather of her battered cherry-red Doc Martens as she scanned the room. Her eyes flickered rapidly, skittish like butterfly wings.

'Coo-eee!' she called as Clara entered the room, barely visible behind the enormous cardboard box she was cradling.

'Hello?' Clara answered.

'It's me, Miranda. Creator of the most unique and sensual candles this side of the Pennines.' The joy at their reunion was evident in her voice, but Joe heard the despondency in the generic greeting Clara returned.

'For heaven's sake, let Clara put the donations down first. She's only small. She'll have arms like Mr Tickle if she carries that lot for much longer,' Deirdre replied bluntly.

'Here, let me.' Joe stepped forward to take the box from Clara. His arms ran parallel to hers as they cradled the corrugated cardboard, and the hairs on his arms prickled to attention as their eyes connected.

'Thanks,' she said. 'It's more big than it is heavy. I'd have managed.'

'I know you would.' His eyes sparked. 'But this way you get more time to talk to our old friend Miranda.'

The profanity Clara muttered made Joe chuckle. 'What's she doing here?'

'She's one of the coordinators of the food bank, apparently, so perhaps we shouldn't be too hard on her. She's obviously a good person to freely give her support.'

'As long as she doesn't mention my aptitude for aromas,' Clara replied drolly. 'I don't think I can handle being made out to be the next Jo Malone.'

'Sssh, she'll hear.'

'Good! Maybe then she'll keep a wide berth.'

'Not much chance of that,' Joe said, spying Miranda working her way towards them. 'She's coming over.'

Clara was still groaning as Miranda wrapped her in an embrace, a knockout waft of patchouli accompanying the flamboyant flinging of the arms.

'Sorry to separate you two lovebirds,' Miranda cooed as she finally disentangled herself from an unimpressed Clara. 'The bond between you two is electric. I could feel the charge from across the room. It was the same at the Christmas market, that's why I remembered you,' she said, placing a hand on Joe's arm. He pulled back as abruptly as he could without appearing rude.

'Sorry, but there's no electric bond here. Friends and colleagues,' Clara replied.

The denial stung Joe's soul. He liked Clara a lot, and if it wasn't for the burden of guilt he was carrying, he may even have made an attempt to tell her just how much she meant to him.

'You can't fight what's written in the stars,' Miranda said, with a mystical swish of her hand.

'I don't believe in the stars.' Clara smiled a blank smile, which Joe could tell threw Miranda off her stride, even if only momentarily.

'Oh, but they believe in you, Clara. They believe in you. You'll see.'

And with that, Miranda turned on her rubber soles and was lost, disappearing amongst the teenagers stock-piling tins for the people of Manchester who needed a helping hand this Christmas.

* * *

'Attention, everyone,' Deirdre called, her hand cupped into a fleshy megaphone her already amplified voice didn't need. 'It's almost nine, so I'm afraid it's time to call it a night. If you're midway through preparing a food parcel, finish it off, but otherwise it's time to down tools.'

The youngsters' enthusiasm hadn't waned as the evening had progressed, but their energy levels had, and Joe suspected they'd secretly be glad to get home. His own limbs were aching, the bending and stretching, lifting and carrying taking its toll.

'Are you as exhausted as me?' Clara asked, blinking. 'I can barely keep my eyes open.'

'Pretty shattered,' Joe admitted. 'If Miranda could see me now all my aura would be telling her is that I'm ready for bed. I seriously underestimated how physically demanding this was going to be.'

'Muscles I didn't even know I had are screaming at me.'

'Same. I've not been sleeping well lately.'

'Something bothering you?'

This was his chance. But he was too exhausted to even know where to begin, so instead he shook his head.

'We've made a dent sorting through the donations,' Clara observed, taking in the bags and boxes that had been made up. 'I wish I could be here to see them being collected.'

Joe noticed a flicker of sadness in the twitch of her smile. He put it down to exhaustion, until she said, in barely more than a whisper, 'We relied on food banks for a while.'

'Lots of people do,' Joe replied, trying not to pry, even though he desperately wanted to know the circumstances. This was unchartered territory, part of Clara's life he didn't know about.

'My mum wanted to move out of my grandparents' as quickly as she could. She's a proud, independent woman. But when we got rehoused it turned out the money she made cleaning didn't stretch very far.' She shrugged. 'She's stubborn and refused to tell my gran and grandpa how tight things were. Donations like these stopped us going hungry. I'll forever be grateful to the people who helped us.'

'I never realised.'

'I never told you. I'm not ashamed. There was never reason to say before.'

Joe was filled with a warmth that Clara had felt able to open up to him. Normally she was a powerhouse – a small but fierce dynamo – but right then she looked breakable, and Joe wanted to wrap her up in a protective hug, to be her bubble wrap. If it hadn't been for all the people around them, he might have, too.

'I'm glad you felt able to tell me. It means a lot.'

'You're really easy to talk to, you know that?'

'Thanks. You're easy to talk to, too.'

He swallowed down the lump in his throat, ignoring the voice telling him to share his own secrets.

'That must be the bond between us that cuckoo Miranda was insistent about,' she grinned. 'Although I do sometimes wonder what I did without you.'

Joe wondered what he'd done before he knew Clara too. His life was different now.

He felt different too, he realised.

Happy, that's how he felt. He felt happy.

Clara

Monday, December 18th 2017

As she dodged her way through the relentless Manchester rain, the plastic bag containing her latest gift for Joe swung gleefully at Clara's side. She smiled, pleased that this gift was not only full-on festive but also entirely practical.

She'd visibly reeled when Joe had mentioned what he was planning on wearing to the disco. Admittedly, there wasn't as much emphasis on what the staff wore as there was on the kids. Phoebe and Tiff would make sure they were dressed head to toe in the most desirable garments, and there'd be a fair few 'designer' outfits that had fallen off the back of a lorry.

Clara skipped through the door, dripping onto the tiled hallway floor. Relieved to be in the dry, she pulled back her hood and unzipped her coat, giggling at the

Christmas jumper beneath. That was exactly why she'd chosen it. It was her new favourite. Others might have cheeky slogans or over-the-top designs, but this was outstanding. She'd even relegated her classy Scandinavian design for this newest recruit to her festive knitwear collection. Gaudy red, the same colour as traditional phone booths and letterboxes nationwide, with a large, spiky splash of emerald green slap bang in the centre. There was a shiny gold star atop the knitted tree, which gleamed as it caught the light. But the best bit, the *piece de resistance*, were the flashing fairy lights. This jumper perfectly embodied all the tacky joys of Christmas.

'Look at you!' Deirdre shook her head. 'You're like the Blackpool Illuminations.'

'That's me,' Clara grinned, twirling to show off her latest purchase. 'Bold and brassy.'

'Whereas I'm beginning to feel that what Blackpool and I have in common is that we're tired and dated,' Deirdre sighed. 'I've been feeling my age these past few weeks.'

'It's the stress of worrying about this place.'

'True. It's non-stop at the moment. But mustn't grumble, tonight's party night and we need to get the place fit for a disco. I want tonight to go off with a bang.' The smile faded from her face. 'I have a feeling this might be the last Christmas disco The Club on the Corner plays host to.'

Clara patted her boss's arm, hoping to offer comfort. 'Don't say that. The church committee are making a decision this week. Maybe we'll be lucky. And if not, we'll find a way to keep this place going, we always do.'

Clara's eyes fixed on a large cardboard box in the corner. 'What's that over there?'

'Just a few bits and pieces,' Deirdre mumbled defensively. 'To make it a bit more exciting for the kids.'

Clara pulled back the flaps of the lid, taking in a mish-mash of accessories, predominantly from the decade taste forgot. There were day-glo headbands, *Fame*-inspired legwarmers, enormous tortoiseshell glasses that the NHS would have struggled to give away if it wasn't for Morrissey making them fashionable in a geek-chic kind of way...

'What is this stuff?' Clara asked, recoiling as her fingers met with the coarse curls of a cheap-looking blonde wig.

'I thought we could make one of those photo booths with the props. This stuff's been stored in my garage, but with one of us armed with a camera we could get some shots of the kids laughing at my former fashion disasters.'

Clara picked up a black-and-white-striped fur hat and balanced it on top of her head, ignoring the fine layer of dust that floated in front of her eye line. 'Look at this! It's hideous!'

'Oi,' Deirdre replied, retrieving it from Clara's head and pulling it protectively close to her bosom. 'I'll have you know, that was a favourite of mine. I wore it to a Duran Duran gig in the eighties, and I'm convinced Simon le Bon was eyeing me up.'

Clara swallowed down a laugh. Deirdre was the polar opposite of the singer's model wife Yasmin. If Simon *had* been looking at her, it was probably because he was wondering why one of his fans had a raccoon on her head.

'Well, it's certainly eye-catching.'

Deirdre lovingly placed the hat on top of the jumble of eighties paraphernalia.

'We could set it up on the stage if we pull back the curtain. It would work as a booth and the backdrop would look professional.'

Clara scooped up the box, the raccoon hat tickling against her nose until she feared she might sneeze.

'Leave it to me,' she said. 'You just make sure the tuck shop is set up. You know how they love those sweets.'

As Deirdre unlocked the store cupboard, which held the sweets and crisps, Clara set up the makeshift photo booth. Deirdre was right, the lustrous velvet curtain would be a perfect background; and if she repositioned the tree, she could block off the corner so the posers could vogue to their hearts' content without being watched. Clara sorted the accessories into the buckets usually used to store footballs and tennis balls. She wasn't foolish enough to believe the hats and props would stay as organised, but at least this way she'd know she'd tried.

'Hello? Anyone around?'

She scrambled to her feet at the sound of Joe's voice.

'Over here,' she called, peeking out from behind the curtain. 'Deirdre had an idea about setting up a photo booth, so I'm trying to get it ready.'

'Oh, I love those,' Joe replied, bounding over like an enthusiastic Labrador. 'They had one at Billy and Emma's wedding and the photos were hilarious. It's fair to say I didn't really pull off the blue wig. And it itched like mad.' He scratched his head.

Clara laughed. It was hard enough to imagine Joe with hair, let alone *blue* hair. 'Now that I'd have liked to see.'

'I'll bring in the photos some time,' he smiled. 'I was quite conservative with my choices compared to some, though. Billy put on everything he could get his hands on, all at once. He looked like Elton John in his *Rocketman* phase.'

'He's been your best friend for a long time, hasn't he?'

'Elton? Nah, I don't know the guy,' Joe joked, before adding, 'Yeah. From the first time we met, we just clicked. He bought the last packet of Beef Monster Munch from the tuck shop and we almost came to blows, because no one wants to be stuck with the pickled onion ones. They burn your mouth. Anyway, he offered to swap them for Hula Hoops. We ended up sharing, and that was that. We've been best friends ever since. He's more like family, really.'

'That's lovely.'

Clara had always felt on the periphery, never having one best friend. She got on with most people, except those who couldn't handle her sometimes cutting remarks, but there had never been one particular friend who she could turn to in a crisis. Although, when she thought about it, recently she'd been opening up to Joe more than she'd opened up to anyone before, even her mum or Deirdre.

'I'm lucky to have him. He's seen me at my worst and always been there to pick me up.'

'Do you get on with his wife? No jealousy that she swooped in and took your best friend away from you?'

'Emma's cool. She's not the kind of woman to take any nonsense, and that's exactly what Billy needed. Give him an inch and he'll take a mile, but she made it clear from the off that she wouldn't stand for any nonsense.'

'Oh?'

'He went through a wild stage,' Joe explained. 'When I was away at uni he got involved with a gang. They could tell Billy was daft. He's the kind of person who'll do anything for a laugh. They thought they could get him to take the wrap for all the chaos they were causing.'

'What kind of chaos? Graffiti? Stealing hubcaps?'

'It started off with small stuff, but that was basically an initiation to see if Billy was up to the task.' He sighed, dejection oozing out of him. 'They all carried blades. In the end Billy did too.'

Clara's eyes widened. 'Knife crime? Shit.'

'It wasn't for long, thankfully. The police started patrolling the neighbourhood when reports of muggings and threatening behaviour went up, and when the ringleader got arrested the whole thing fizzled out. But it felt like I'd lost him for a while; it was like going through a break-up. I'd think of something I'd want to tell him and then suddenly remember that he wouldn't be interested, because the only thing he cared about was pleasing the gang.'

'That sounds awful,' Clara replied, with a sympathetic smile.

'It was, but as soon as he met Emma he settled down. He's four years older, but even as a sixteen-year-old she was ballsy as anything. She told him in no uncertain terms that if he wanted to be with her, he had to give up that life. He was so smitten he turned his back on it all. Thankfully the scrote that got him into it went to prison, which made it easier. When I came back after Michelle died he was so loved up, really soppy. He'd changed for the better.'

'It's frightening how people can get swept up so easily by gangs. That's why I fear for some of these kids.'

'That's why places like this are so important. Helps give them focus, encourages them to take ownership of the community. That can make all the difference.'

'I hope you're right. And I hope we can find a way to open our doors to more of the young people who need us. There was another "sorry, but we can't offer assistance on this occasion" letter arrive today,' Clara replied.

'I'm sure things will get easier soon,' Joe said optimistically. 'I've got a good feeling about it.'

Clara hoped Joe was right. She couldn't bear it if this was the last Christmas disco The Club on the Corner would ever hold. Somehow, *anyhow*, she had to make sure this place kept going.

* * *

The kids thought Deirdre's accessories were hilarious.

'Did you actually used to wear this stuff?' Jordan asked bluntly. 'Like, seriously? Not for fancy dress?'

Deirdre looked most put out and Clara had to wrestle back her laughter.

'The flaming cheek! These were the height of fashion,' Deirdre replied. 'They weren't cheap either. I scrimped and saved to get enough money together for that faux-fur coat.'

Shannon was parading around in it as though she were Naomi Campbell. Her lips were jutting out so far that she was little more than a pout on her twig-like legs.

'I like it. All this vintage stuff is back in fashion. The Northern Quarter's full of it,' she said, tossing her hair like a goddess. 'I reckon I can pull it off. I wouldn't wear real fur, obv, but this is so warm and snuggly.'

'You look like a polar bear,' said Cally dismissively, but Clara was sure there was a hint of jealousy buried deep in the comment. Shannon looked good, there was no two ways about it. With her cropped blonde bob and blood-red lips she looked like a young Debbie Harry, and had more style in her manicured little finger than Clara had in her whole body. Not that Clara was bothered, her Christmas jumper was festive and practical, and although she was worried the lights were going to burn out any minute and the jumper's appeal would diminish as a result, they'd held out so far.

'I like polar bears,' Shannon fired back. She had the confidence to carry off her quirky fashionista style, knowing her own taste and trusting in it. Clara's wardrobe as a teen had been Top Shop and New Look. She'd diversified as she'd grown in both years and confidence, but never to Shannon's degree.

'Right, get into position,' said Clara, holding up the camera. She was aware of a restless queue building behind her. Shannon placed one hand on her cheek and gazed beyond the camera in a totally fey pose, whilst Simone grinned from behind a pair of mirror shades, which she'd inexplicably teamed with an Everton scarf that Clara had no idea how Deirdre was in possession of. 'Gorgeous,' she smiled, as she clicked the button and caught the Polaroid that spewed out. 'Go on then, girls. Have a dance for a bit.'

'I'm not taking this coat off,' Shannon said, pulling it tightly around her. 'Deirdre, can I buy it off you? My parents asked what I wanted for Christmas and I couldn't think of anything, so they said they'd give me money instead. I'd give you a fair price.'

'Alright,' Deirdre said. 'If it'll stop you going on at me.' Deirdre was making out she was hassled but Clara could tell she was secretly chuffed to have found someone who appreciated her past style. 'But I've no idea what a fair price is. It's been in that box for at least ten years. I'm amazed a family of mice haven't found it and used it as a nest.'

'Let me know how much you want,' Shannon called over her shoulder as she descended the stairs onto the makeshift dance floor, her strut ramped up a notch at the result of bagging her much-coveted item. 'I'll bring it tomorrow.'

'You're so soft,' Clara said. 'You'd get more money selling it on eBay.'

'Better it goes to someone who loves it, though,' Deirdre answered. 'Her face lit up when she put it on, and if that's not an indicator that it belongs with her, then I don't know what is.'

A gang of three boys were rifling through the accessories, discarding eye patches and feather boas before settling on a random selection of baseball caps (worn backwards) and posing like gangsta rappers. Clara snapped the moment for posterity, and then felt a tap on the shoulder.

'Is it our turn yet?'

The brilliant white of Joe's new jumper dazzled her. Two big black lump-of-coal eyes stared out from his pecs, and a three-d carrot poked forward from a point just above his navel.

'I like the jumper,' she said approvingly.

'Some nutter who's really into Christmas bought it for me,' he replied with a grin. 'I'd never have predicted I'd be the kind of man who'd be wearing this sort of get-up.'

'Ah, but you're a youth worker now,' Clara replied. 'Everything goes out of the window when you enter this weird and wonderful world.'

'You're right. I thought the days where a group of people would be chanting 'Go Joe, go Joe, go Joe' to try and get me breakdancing were well behind me. Turns out I was wrong.' He pulled a face. 'I did a couple of helicopter spins to keep the crowd happy and I think I've done my back in as a result.'

Clara laughed. 'Now, that I'd have loved to have seen. Perhaps you can show me later. I'll ask Disco Dan to play some Run DMC so you can show me your moves.'

'Nuh huh. I wasn't joking when I said my back was killing me. If you want to see back flips and head spins you'll have to watch some Diversity videos on the internet when you get home.'

'That's an average night for me,' she joked. 'Let's face it, Ashley Banjo is easy on the eye.'

'So they say. My mum watches that dance show he judges without fail, Simone too. What is it about that man that has females of all ages falling at his nimble feet?'

'He knows how to dance. Plus, tall dark and handsome became a thing for a reason.'

She flushed as she took in Joe. Well over six foot tall. Black skin. And undeniably gorgeous, especially in a goofy Christmas jumper that was slightly too small for him. Yep, and he had some of the Banjo charm.

'It looks like you've been busy up here. Deirdre's idea wasn't as crazy as we thought after all.'

'This lot are the selfie generation,' she said. 'Their motto is "photos or it didn't happen", so we shouldn't be surprised it's gone down a storm. They're liking the novelty of an actual printed picture too. Most of them store their pictures on their phones and don't bother getting a hard copy.'

'Sounds like me,' Joe admitted. 'I've got about 500 photos on my phone that I keep meaning to print them out, but I never get around to doing it.'

Clara wondered if he'd kept the shot of the two of them at the theatre. If he'd looked at it like she had, trying to decide if they looked good together.

'Well, let's get a photo of us now it's quietened down,' she said, pushing her thoughts aside. 'Record that Christmas jumper for the ages.'

She held out the camera, lens facing towards them, and prepared to shoot.

'Not yet!' Joe exclaimed, grabbing a fez and popping

it on her head before standing back to appraise her. 'That's better. Now you really look the part.'

'If that's the way we're playing it, you can wear these,' she laughed, handing him some large glasses with a plastic moustache dangling from them.

He gamely put them on.

'I think we're ready.'

She leaned in towards him and quickly took the shot. The flash caused her to blink, but didn't stop her carefully catching the photo between her thumb and forefinger, determined not to touch the developing print.

'I wasn't ready!' Joe protested, mock-scowling at her from behind his disguise. 'I think my eyes were closed!'

'Ah, it'll be fine,' she said with a flick of her hand, just as Disco Dan announced (in a typical party DJ manner) that Joe was needed to assist Deirdre and Lynsey with serving the hot dogs. That explained the sudden exodus of the kids from the photo booth, thought Clara. They were bottomless pits, eating anything they could lay their hands on.

'I'd better go,' he said, pulling off the glasses and tossing them back into a bucket. It wasn't the right one, but Clara didn't say anything. As predicted, everything was in a muddle anyway. 'Deirdre will be on the warpath otherwise.'

She thought there was a reluctance hidden in his

words, as though he didn't want to go.

'Okay,' she said, placing the camera down on a chair. 'See you later. And save me a hot dog!'

She watched as he made his way to the far corner of the room, the primary coloured lights of the disco reflecting off the pure white of his jumper. The kids swarmed around him, eager for food.

Clara looked at the now-developed photo, still in her hand. The image showed her gurning at the camera, clutching the lop-sided burgundy fez with one hand as she poked out her tongue. Joe's eyes weren't closed, she noticed. They were looking at her.

Clara pocketed the photo, then promptly forgot all about it as she headed towards the food stall, where a hot dog smothered in tomato ketchup was waiting for her.

Joe

Tuesday, December 19th 2017

'Nice wellies,' Joe observed, as Clara rounded the corner.

'They are, aren't they?' she replied cheerfully. 'When you said to wear something suitable for walking, I thought I'd better come prepared. You didn't say whether we were staying on the beaten track or if it'd be wet and muddy.'

'Everywhere's wet and muddy. It's Manchester in December. But we're not going into the woods or anything, you'd have been fine with trainers,' he said, balancing on one leg and waving a black Adidas samba in front of him.

'Are you going to let me in on where we're going? This is a bit of a weird meeting point.'

They'd arranged to get together outside the newsagent's. No one else was around, not even the kids who gathered there on their bikes and loitered until the newsagent sent them packing. It was cold, bitterly so, and even the teenagers would rather be inside than hanging about on street corners on a night like this.

'We're going to do the Advent window walk,' Joe explained. 'Dad's organised it through church. This is the starting point,' he said, pointing towards a home-made stained-glass window. Bright-yellow tissue paper allowed the shop's light to shine through, creating a vivid image of a star, radiant beams shooting from each of its pointed tips, as a red number one blazed in the corner.

'I'd wondered what this was about,' Clara said. 'There's another window like this in the florist on Beesham Street.'

'There's a whole trail of them. The idea is that you follow the windows through Advent and then on Christmas Eve the final window display goes up at the church hall. Some are in shops, some in houses. It's a different way of doing an Advent calendar.'

'A way without chocolate,' Clara said. 'That's tragic.'

'Not if we go and buy some supplies first. We'll need fuel to get around the whole walk, won't we?' he said, pushing open the door to the shop. A welcome surge of warmth hit him. 'Come on, I'll treat you.'

Clara grinned. 'Now this is beginning to sound like my kind of walk. But how do I choose between a Dairy Milk and a Twix?' she asked with a shrug, mitten-encased palms upright.

Joe leant in.

'You know what,' he whispered flirtatiously. 'I'm feeling wild. Have both.'

* * *

By the time they reached window nineteen, Joe and Clara had been walking for the best part of two hours. It shouldn't have been the most appealing route, the rows of terraced houses laid out in a grid-plan style little more than Lego houses, but walking along these streets – not far enough out of town to be suburbia, but not buried in the heart of the city itself either – felt right. It was neither here nor there, a hazy in-between, but to Joe this area was, and always would be, home. There was a charm in the way the front doors led straight to the pavements (although no one ever used the front doors – they were usually blocked off by a settee or a coffee table to make the most of the small living space that passed for a front room. Entry was almost always via the yard and kitchen). Joe might have grown up in the detached rectory next to the church, but all his closest friends from both school and youth club had lived in the back-to-back red-brick terraces.

'This is where Billy used to live,' Joe said, pointing to one of the houses. He didn't mention Michelle, although he thought of her as he looked at the upstairs window. It was slightly ajar. A small Christmas tree stood in the window, flashing white fairy lights chasing each other around its branches. 'His parents still lived here until a few years ago. So many happy hours spent in his room playing on the PlayStation and listening to Foo Fighters CDs on repeat.'

'It's funny how buildings hold so many memories, isn't it? Logically I know they're nothing more than bricks and mortar, but it's as though they absorb the lives of the people who spend time there. My grand-parents lived in the same house for forty years, and when me and Mum moved in with them, Mum slept in the room she'd had as a girl. It still had the same carpet down too, this flecked lavender and purple monstrosity. It was like a strange time warp where every-thing stayed the same.'

'Our house is a bit like that,' Joe admitted, before remembering he didn't live with his parents any more. 'Mum and Dad's, I mean. When we first moved in it was all done out fresh. I was only young but it's clear in my mind. Mum was very excited about choosing the wallpaper for the hallway, but I don't think she'd expected it to still be up now.'

'I can't imagine your mum ever choosing anything less than tasteful,' Clara replied. 'Every time I've seen her she's perfectly turned out, like a fifties film star.'

'I'll tell her you said that. She'll love it.'

'It's true,' Clara insisted. 'She looks amazing. No wonder Simone's so confident about her own style with her as a role model.'

'They are pretty cool women,' Joe smiled with pride as they continued to the end of the street. An imposing pub stood before them. It looked warm and inviting, and even the off-key screech of a guitar from the weekly open mic night wasn't enough to quell the temptation. 'Fancy a quick drink and a warm?'

'That sounds great,' Clara replied, 'My feet are numb. And sore.'

'Have you been here before?' Joe asked, pushing open the large wooden door. The heat hit them in a wave, the same way it does when you take your first steps on land in a foreign country.

Clara shook her head. 'Have you?'

'Hi, Joe!' called the barman with a wave. 'Not seen you in here for a while.'

'I'll take that as a yes,' Clara laughed.

'This place was a regular haunt when we were teens,'

Joe said, raising his hand in reply to the barman. 'They never bothered checking ID, so we knew we'd get served without any bother.'

'Let me guess, Billy again?' Clara grinned. 'He seems to have been the one who always led you astray, so underage drinking is par for the course.'

'Along with a few others. When we were sixteen or seventeen we'd come here on our way home from the youth club for half a pint and they always sent me to the bar. I was the tallest, see, so the staff would ask less questions. To be honest, I think they were just glad to have some customers, even though they must have known we were underage. Back then Billy was about four-foot nothing,' he laughed, 'not that he's much taller now'.

'I'd like to meet him one day. It sounds like he's played an important part in your life.'

Joe caught his breath. This was the moment. He couldn't hold back any longer.

'He has, and not only because he's my best friend.' Joe blurted the words out quickly, hoping it would make them easier to say. It didn't. 'Billy is Michelle's brother. Her twin brother.'

Clara stared, then finally, after what felt like hours, said, 'That explains why you're so close. When you've been through something like that, it's inevitable. It must have been awful for him, too.'

Joe nodded, unable to express just how awful. He'd hoped once he started talking the whole story would rush out, but he couldn't formulate the thoughts, let alone the words. His head was swimming, his stomach felt as though it was being sliced in two. The red and gold of the damask wallpaper blurred until it looked like blood. He was glad they were at the bar, so he could hold onto the wooden counter.

'It was.'

Clara must have noticed his discomfort, because instead of pressing for more information she pulled out her purse.

'I think we could both do with a drink,' she said.

They placed their order – a dry white wine for Clara and a pint of lager for Joe – before moving to a table in the snug, as far away from the current wailing wannabe as possible. The sound travelled regardless, but at least they didn't have to see him and his predictable leather jacket, ripped jeans and white t-shirt combo.

'You know I said my feet were cold?' Clara said, sinking down into a soft chair. 'They're suddenly boiling.' She looked mournfully at her wellies. 'Do you think I could take them off, or would that be weird?'

Joe was relieved that the conversation had moved on.

'In most places it'd be weird, but some of the sights I've seen in here over the years are far stranger than socked feet. I'm not sure you'd want to walk on this floor, though,' he said, pulling a face.

The wooden floor was definitely of the permanently sticky variety, years' worth of spilt drinks building up to create a viscous layer that required strong legs to prise the soles of shoes off them.

'I'd better not. People will look,' she said, scanning her eyes around the pub as though people had anything better to do than examine her feet.

Joe shuffled out of his coat and sat down on a chair on the opposite side of the low square table.

'It is warm,' he agreed, loosening his scarf. He had originally thought it was him, but when he touched the radiator, he retracted his hand on contact. 'Yep, the heating's on as well as the log fire. That'll be why it's super-toasty. The total opposite of The Club on the Corner.'

'It's alright for you,' Clara grumbled. 'Your feet aren't coated in a layer of plastic half a centimetre thick.' She looked down at the trainers, flimsy by comparison, and exhaled.

'If you're that embarrassed, I'll join you. Come on,' he said, pushing the toe of one foot against the heel of the opposite trainer in exactly the way mums always tell their children off for, saying it'll ruin the shape of the shoe.

'What are you doing?' Clara's voice was pitchy and high, laced with giggles.

'Taking my shoes off. You must be sweltering with those wellies on. No one's looking. Might as well be comfortable.'

Joe saw her throw one more fleeting look around the pub. Everyone was chatting with friends, watching the performers act as though they were playing Wembley Stadium rather than a backstreet Manchester pub, except for the lurcher laid out in front of the fire, enjoying having his belly rubbed.

'Alright,' she conceded. 'But I'm hiding them behind the chair so no one knows.'

She took off the wellies and quickly shoved her feet under the table in case anyone should decide now was the time to inspect her footwear. Her striped socks (complete with a hole in the right one where her big toe was peeping through) were a statement, but not the sort she'd ever want to publicly make.

'Surely someone can come up with a way of making plastic shoes that are comfortable. It reminds me of the jelly shoes I used to have on holiday for paddling in the sea – they used to rub like anything too.'

'Can't say I ever had any myself,' Joe said, 'although

I did own a pair of Crocs once.'

Clara's jaw dropped. 'And you're openly admitting that? And here was I complimenting your family on being bang on trend. You obviously don't take after your mum.'

'Everyone does say I'm more like my dad,' Joe smiled. 'Although I've no plans to follow him into a liturgical life. I don't think I could rock a dog collar.'

'But imagine how cool you'd look in a cassock. You could pretend to be a Jedi. Or a Disney princess.'

'I'm happy in my jeans, thanks.'

They sat in quiet companionship, a sedate acoustic artist picking out a heartfelt melody on his guitar. It wasn't a song Joe was familiar with – perhaps self-penned – but it was tuneful and melancholy and kind of beautiful.

'Thanks for keeping me company tonight,' Joe said. 'I wouldn't have wanted to be alone.'

'Oh, it's no problem,' Clara replied breezily.

'No,' he insisted. 'I wouldn't have wanted to be alone tonight.' His eyes connected with hers, as he pressed for her to understand. 'And I couldn't have coped with a night in with my family, Mum looking pitifully at me across the lounge. It's eight years since ... since Michelle died.'

'Michelle's anniversary,' Clara said, bringing her hand

up to cover her gaping mouth. 'I'm so sorry, Joe. I didn't even think. And I've been prattling on about wellies all night.'

He held up his hand to halt her flow. 'Sssh. There's no need to apologise. This ...' he swept his hand around the pub, '... It's exactly what I need. What you said before was right. Michelle wouldn't have wanted me to be miserable. She loved to laugh.'

'It's easier said than done, though, sometimes, being upbeat.'

'I don't do crying.'

'Not because you're trying to fit into some macho stereotype, I hope?'

'Do you know me at all? No, I've just never found it easy to cry. I feel it all in here ...' He patted his chest twice in quick succession, 'But for some reason the tears don't often come.'

'As long as you don't feel you can't.'

'I'm fine, Clara. Live music, a roaring fire, a beer in my hand ... it's not all bad.'

Clara smiled. 'Not to mention my scintillating company and conversation.'

'That's been the highlight,' he teased. 'How do you know I'm not actually a secret collector of wellies? I might have a whole room dedicated to them, for all you know.'

'That might be the end of our friendship. I'm calling it – wellies are officially the worst footwear in the world. Along with all other plastic shoes, of course.'

'Of course,' he said, taking a large swig of his lager. The pint glass was half empty now, or half full, depending on how you looked at it. 'But seriously, thank you. I've enjoyed tonight, and I never would have expected to find myself saying that when I left the flat. The anniversary is always difficult.'

'Thank you for showing me the Advent windows. I had a great time, although I'm sure I can feel blisters swelling up underneath these socks,' she said, peeping the colourful striped socks out from underneath the table and playfully waggling her toes.

'Sounds painful,' Joe said, with a nod that suggested mock sympathy. 'Maybe another drink is the answer? It might help numb the pain.'

'Go on, then,' she said, knocking back what was left of her wine. 'Purely for medicinal reasons.'

'Of course,' said Joe with a wink as he pushed himself out of the chair. 'These are on me,' he added, patting the bulge his wallet was making on his hipbone. 'And thanks again for being such good company.'

As Joe made his way to the bar, Clara's smile turned into a full-on laugh. Joe's besocked feet were padding mutely across the filthy floor.

When Joe reached the bar, he turned to look at Clara. He trusted her. He wanted to tell her everything.

Clara

Wednesday, December 20th 2017

'This isn't a traditional Christmas present,' she said apologetically. 'Not like the others.'

Joe feigned a look that Clara assumed was supposed to register 'aghast'.

'Surely the Christmas queen isn't running out of ideas? I thought you'd have an endless list of perfect festive gifts compiled.'

'Oh, I do,' she laughed. 'I'm like Santa himself, making a list and checking it twice, three times, four times ...'

'I hope I'm on the nice list,' Joe replied, 'after taking you to some of the best places Manchester's got to offer.'

'If Santa's been keeping an eye on you you'll have plenty of presents under your tree next week. I've loved every minute of our adventures. Although you wouldn't know it from what I'm about to give you.' She reached into her bag and pulled out a small brown paper bag that doubled as wrapping paper. 'It's really not much,' she said apologetically, 'and I'm having a bit of gift-buying regret. I was in a bit of a silly mood. I blame the wine last night. I swear I was still drunk when I woke up. You should have stopped me!'

They'd stayed at the pub much longer than they'd planned, eventually getting thrown out at closing time, with Clara grumbling about having to encase her feet in the offending wellies, especially as on inspection they had caused some rather nasty blisters on her heels. She'd lost count of how many drinks she'd had altogether, but she'd estimate five. Or maybe six. No wonder she felt as if her brain cells were imploding. The Alka Seltzer had helped but hadn't yet restored her to the best version of herself. Urgh.

'I drank as much as you, but I made sure I had two pints of water before going to bed,' he said virtuously. 'That always keeps the hangovers at bay.'

'You should have made me drink water too,' moaned Clara.

'I did. Don't you remember? When we stopped off at the chippy?'

'We had chips? I don't remember.'

'Large chips, cheese and gravy,' he corrected. 'And a bottle of water each.'

'Why don't I remember that? That's my favourite meal.'

'Erm ... because you were drunk?' Joe laughed. 'Surely you remember going to the park?'

Clara shook her head blankly.

'You were insistent that we went on the swings. And the slide. And you wanted to go on the monkey bars too, until you realised that even you were tall enough to reach them without your feet leaving the ground.'

'Oh, the shame.' Clara could feel her cheeks flushing. 'I'm a terrible drunk, always making a fool of myself. At least I wasn't sick this time.' When Joe failed to reply she panicked. 'I wasn't, was I?'

'You weren't,' he reassured her. 'It was fun, and I was as bad. I pretty much bullied you into going on the seesaw, because despite being almost thirty I love a seesaw.'

Clara giggled, a vague recollection of Joe whooping as he flew into the air coming to mind. 'It was a good night, wasn't it? And good to talk. Although it's a shame we won't get to see the rest of the Advent windows.'

'We could do the last few another time, if you want to. Maybe on Christmas Eve, before the church service.'

'Don't talk to me about that. The thought of us not being selected as the charity of the year makes me feel a bit sick. Those donations would make such a difference to a group like ours.'

'It'd make a difference to whichever charity gets chosen,' Joe corrected, and Clara immediately felt guilty. Just because The Club on the Corner meant so much to her, it didn't mean the other charities weren't also worthy recipients. She just wanted to give kids like Jordan somewhere safe and supportive to go.

'I know, and they all make this a great community to be part of. But it'd be brilliant if we could get some help. More income would mean we could let more kids through the door. We might even be able to give the place a bit of a facelift too. Look at the walls in here! It must be years since this room had a lick of paint.'

'Do you want to see something?' Joe said, beckoning her towards a corner of the room.

Clara followed, curious.

'You'll have to bend down,' he said.

Joe crouched, and Clara mirrored him, unsure what he could be showing her in the corner of the games room. They hadn't used it for anything other than storage for the past year – partly because of the shabby paintwork and partly because it was one less room to heat – and first impressions didn't suggest there was anything out of the ordinary about this particular corner.

'Look.'

Joe pointed to a gap between the skirting board and a plug socket. When Clara couldn't see what he was trying to show, she lowered herself to her knees.

There on the wall, in tiny script, she saw his name.

'When did you do this?' she asked, rubbing her finger over the writing. The blue biro was as vibrant as if it had been put there only yesterday.

'I can't remember exactly. Years ago. Forever ago.'

'This shows you can be a rebel, once in a while,' she said with a smile.

'It shows how long it is since this room's been redecorated,' he corrected. 'But maybe it'll be restored to its former glory before too long. We need to have a little faith.' He nodded at the gift she was still holding. 'Am I ever going to get today's present?' he asked with a smile.

'It's not at all Christmassy,' Clara apologised, 'but after our conversation last night I saw this and it made me think of you.'

'This is great,' he said, immediately taking the mug out of its box and smiling at the image on the front. Dave Grohl's face looked warped on the curved surface of the mug. 'I'll always love Foo Fighters and this is perfect. Thank you. I'll leave it here so I won't have to drink out of the awful mugs from the cupboard any more.'

'That's what I thought. You've lasted this long, so you earned a mug of your own.'

Most of the mugs at The Club on the Corner were functional but ugly, mainly freebies advertising local businesses. Clara, Deirdre and Lynsey had their own, brought in from home and closely guarded, and she'd noticed him looking mildly envious whenever they brewed up and he had to make do with a receptacle advertising landscape gardeners or double-glazers.

'And Foo Fighters too. Best live band on the planet, bar none.'

'You'll not be saying that after I've dragged you to see Take That,' Clara said, a naughty gleam in her eye.

'Did you watch the Foo Fighters when they headlined Glastonbury back in the summer? Hit after hit and they got better as the night went on. Overran, but no one cared because they're epic,' he enthused. 'Dave Grohl is a legend. I could listen to him play forever and my ears wouldn't tire of it.'

'They're not my cup of tea, but I'm glad you like the mug. Might encourage you to do the tea run a bit more often.'

'Thanks, Clara,' he said, pulling her in for a hug. He squeezed her close and she could smell his aftershave, a dark, mysterious aniseed aroma.

'Not just for this,' he clarified, 'For last night too, and

for being such a good friend.'

'You're welcome,' she breathed, not rushing to disentangle herself from his embrace. Because, as much as she hated to admit it to herself, being close to Joe was a pleasure and a thrill.

*   *   *

The kids had all gone, leaving the hall in disarray, and just Joe and Clara to tidy the mess. Deirdre had left early to celebrate her neighbour Enid's birthday. Enid, a spritely one hundred today, wanted to show off her birthday cards, particularly the one from the palace. She was a staunch royalist.

'I haven't got the energy tonight,' Clara said. 'Shall we just chuck all the resources into the storage crates for now and sort it out properly tomorrow?'

'Sure,' Joe replied, getting stuck into the tidying straight away. 'Then maybe I'll put the kettle on and have another cup of tea. I swear it tastes better out of my new mug.'

Clara chuckled. 'I'll join you. Let's take this stuff through to the games room first, so it's out of the way.'

Between the two of them it didn't take long to collect up the books, games and craft activities. It was as they were putting them into the storage space that Clara thought she heard Joe speak. This voice was exceptionally quiet, and it wasn't until he repeated himself more loudly that Clara heard what he was saying.

'I should have died, not Michelle.'

She turned to face him, lowering the plastic crate to the ground. His features were crumpled, his eyes brimming with tears. Seeing him in such obvious pain hurt her, and Clara instinctively placed her hand on his shoulder in an attempt to offer comfort.

'We were in the car together, on our way home from a party. It was a Christmas do someone on her course had organised. We hadn't even wanted to go.' He laughed bitterly. 'I'd been drinking, so Michelle said she'd drive. It wasn't far, five minutes at the very most, and the roads weren't busy. It was the middle of the night.'

He paused, closing his eyes. Clara waited, not wanting to push him. He would talk when he was ready.

'We got into the car and she put on her seatbelt. I didn't bother. Didn't think it was worth it for such a short drive.'

Clara thought back to the night when they'd taken Cally to the hospital and he'd taken such care to ensure his seatbelt was secure. Vaguely recalled a comment about getting strapped in when they'd shared a taxi together after their night on Oldham Street.

'We were almost home, literally at the junction at

the end of our road, when it happened. Someone pulled out at high speed.' He wiped the back of his hand under his nose and sniffed before continuing. 'They smashed into us with force. I went straight through the windscreen. My torso was cut to ribbons but by some miracle there was no internal damage. I've got the scars, though.'

That explained the marks she'd seen.

'Michelle wasn't as lucky. The other car had hit her side. The seatbelt, the air bag ... none of it was enough to protect her. None of it was enough to keep her alive.'

Clara didn't know how to respond. Words didn't seem adequate, somehow.

So instead, she put a lesson she'd learned from her mum into action and said, 'Let's finish talking about this over a cup of tea.'

Joe

Thursday, December 21ˢᵗ 2017

'Ouch!'

Joe rubbed his ribs, which had been elbowed by an overzealous woman determined to get her greedy mitts on the last copy of the latest album by the boy band of the moment.

'Are you okay?' Clara asked, with concern. 'We should have known better than to come to the Trafford Centre four days before Christmas. It was never going to be anything other than a total nightmare.'

'It's my own fault. I shouldn't have left it to the last minute. Or I could have done it all online from the comfort of my own sofa. That would have been less painful.'

'In every sense,' Clara added, with a grin that infuriated Joe. Not because he couldn't take a bit of ribbing

305

– he could hold his own when bantering with his mates – but because she looked so damn cute with that cheeky look. Like a little elf, or something, but not one of those creepy ones. More like Zooey Deschanel. Impish and mischievous and one hundred per cent adorable.

This was what he'd discovered about Clara O'Connell. She had the capacity to be a minx one minute, but a confidante the next. They'd spent the previous night talking, crying and laughing together, and he'd told her things he'd not revealed to anyone before. He'd been surprised by how much it helped, and how she'd known when to talk and when to merely listen.

Joe scanned the rows of DVDs and Blu-rays that made up the charts, desperately hoping he'd find the one Simone had her heart set on. She'd given clear instructions. It had to be the limited-edition version as it had extra features – outtakes and a director's cut and an interview with the household-name actress who played the lead.

When he recognised the shiny green box from the picture his sister had sent him on WhatsApp (she'd sent it four times, just to make absolutely sure Joe knew what he was looking for) he felt a wave of relief. What's more, there were at least ten copies of it, so he wouldn't have to fight anyone for it. Thank goodness Simone wasn't into boy bands. He wouldn't have been able to face traipsing around endless shops looking for that must-have CD, and anyway, the lead singer freaked him out. He had the most ridiculously high quiff that must require a crazy amount of gel to stay upright, especially when gyrating around on the stage. Maybe Joe was jealous because his own hair had receded early. He'd decided to shave the lot off to save the hassle.

'Very funny,' he said drily, as he took the Blu-ray off the shelf and placed it into the plastic basket alongside a Stevie Wonder CD for his mum.

'That's another tick on your list,' Clara said. 'So who else do you need to buy for?'

'My dad. Billy and Emma. Something noisy for Roman. And I probably ought to get Deirdre a present too, although I've no idea what.'

'I've already bought and wrapped all my presents.' She was borderline smug.

'Of course you have. You're the sort of person who ties them up with curling ribbon.'

Clara jutted out her chin. 'I like things to look nice.'

'I've noticed how neatly the countdown gifts you've given me are tied. There's been a perfectly symmetrical bow on almost every gift.'

Clara's cheeks went scarlet, making her look even more like one of Santa's little helpers. All she needed was a green and red hat and she'd be set, Joe thought with a smile.

'You'll have to wait and see the full force of my wrapping prowess when I give you your final present for Christmas Day.'

Joe's head cocked. He hadn't been expecting a present to go under the tree, not when Clara had already been giving him gifts for the best part of a month.

'You don't have to get me anything. Honestly, you've given me more than enough already. Save your money,' he begged.

'Too late. I told you, I bought all my gifts weeks ago.'

'You didn't have to ...' he started.

'I know I didn't. I wanted to.'

He couldn't deny the glow that built inside him at that comment, and even though he knew Clara had only bought him a present because she was a kind-hearted Christmas fanatic, who'd use any excuse to buy and wrap another gift, Joe liked that she'd thought of him.

'Santa will be transferring you to the nice list at this rate,' Joe replied. 'It was worth posting your letter after all.'

Clara had considered waited in line to meet the main man, but when it became evident they'd be waiting all night to see Santa along with every child in the shopping centre, she'd settled for leaving a letter in his special post box. Joe had loved seeing her so giddy, so childlike, as the grotto had come into view.

He was still in his dreamy bubble when a tall, burly man in a puffa jacket barged into him, bringing him right back down to earth.

'Sorry mate,' came a gruff voice.

Joe's heart sank further as Clara stood frozen, mouth agog.

Dean.

Dean with a woman in a navy-blue tunic with a fob watch pinned over her breast pocket, who Joe suspected was the woman he'd cheated on Clara with.

* * *

'I'm sorry,' Clara said, rapidly flapping her hands in front of her face. Joe knew she was fighting back angry tears. 'I shouldn't have run like that.'

'You can't help how you feel.'

Joe emptied a sachet of sugar into his coffee, although it was probably sweet enough already, what with the festive vanilla spice syrup he'd asked the barista to add. All the same, it had suddenly become a day where sugar seemed necessary.

'I don't feel anything!' Clara's voice was high and pitchy. 'I'm just angry that he's parading around with her on his arm. And when he tried to strike up a conversation ...' Clara let out a puff of frustration. 'What would I have to talk about with him? I had to get out of there, and fast.'

Clara slid the palm of her hand around the enormous cup of hot chocolate she'd ordered – the biggest they offered at the coffee shop she and Joe had stopped at – took a sip, then slammed it down on the dark wood table with force. Whipped cream drizzled down the side of the mug.

'Now look what he made me do,' she said, her face etched with frustration as a creamy pool formed against the polished surface. 'It's gone everywhere.'

Joe bit his tongue, not wanting to point out the obvious – that Dean was long gone and the loss of the swirly, chocolate-dusted cream was nothing to do with anyone but Clara herself. There are times in life where it pays to remain silent, and Joe recognised this was one of those times.

Noddy Holder was less considerate, screaming 'It's Christmas!' at the top of his lungs, as Slade's Christmas classic blared out over the speakers without a second thought for Clara's heartache.

She glared in response, Joe noting the rare moment of Christmas antipathy from Clara.

'Here,' he said, handing her a napkin. 'Use this.'

She dabbed at the spillage until the liquid seeped through the pure-white tissue.

'Thanks.' Her voice was clipped. 'And I'm sorry,' she added, with a sigh. 'I'm angry, that's all. I don't have feelings for him any more, but he still hurt me more than I can say. Seeing the two of them touched a nerve.'

'That's natural,' Joe replied gently. 'You were together for a long time.'

'Four years,' Clara whispered. 'And he threw it away like it was nothing.'

She circled her hands around the cup before bringing it to her mouth and sipping the hot chocolate. She had the merest hint of a whipped-cream moustache for a moment before her tongue licked her upper lip and it was as though it had never been there.

'I'm sorry,' she repeated. 'You don't want to listen to me going on about it.'

'If it hurts, let it out. I want to listen. You listened to me. Last night ... you were amazing, Clara. I was so scared you'd judge me, but you didn't. You ... you made it easy to talk about something so hard.'

She smiled weakly.

'There's nothing to say, really. It was a good relation-ship, until it wasn't.' She shrugged. 'At the time I thought it was for keeps, but in retrospect I wonder if I was kidding myself all along. I don't want to have to see him around, though, and I certainly don't want to speak to him.'

'Do you think you're blocking it out so you don't have to face up to it?' Joe asked. 'That's what I do. Bury my head in the sand and pretend everything's fine, even if I'm falling apart. When Michelle died, I didn't cry a single tear. I told everyone I was doing okay, even though I was a mess. But you don't have to pretend with me. You can tell me anything, any time.'

She looked humbled at his words, and he liked how that made him feel.

'It's not all about Dean,' she blustered. 'It's bigger than that.'

Joe didn't say a word, instead waiting for her to continue.

'Do you remember when you asked if I had any brothers or sisters?'

Joe nodded. He remembered that conversation clearly. It was one of the first times he felt as if he was really connecting with Clara.

'I said I didn't, but that's not strictly true.' She blew on her hot chocolate, her eyes focused on the remainder of the cream. 'I've got a half-brother.'

Joe's heart pounded at the surprise revelation. Clara was always so upfront about everything that it didn't seem possible that she could keep something as enormous as a sibling secret.

'I don't see him,' she continued, avoiding eye contact. 'He lives in Carlisle with my dad and his new wife. Isaac – that's what he's called – is six months younger than me.'

Joe struggled to hide his shock as the penny dropped. Six months younger than Clara...

'Dad was leading a double life for years. He'd live with me and mum in the week, then spend the weekends with them, under the pretence that he was working away on a long-haul job. He was a lorry driver, you see.'

'That's awful. No wonder you find it hard to trust people.'

'Exactly. When my mum found out she was devastated, obviously, and although she loved him completely, she threw him out and filed for divorce, but it didn't faze him. He already had a replacement family waiting in the wings.'

'It's like something from one of Deirdre's soaps,' Joe said, trying to lighten the mood. He could see the tears welling in Clara's eyes.

'Dad seemed to forget I even existed,' she said sadly, wiping her nose on the sleeve of her misshapen cardigan. 'I sent him a card every year on Father's Day, but he never got in touch – not even a phone call.'

'That's harsh.'

'Then a couple of years ago Isaac turned up at my door. He looked so like my dad. It freaked me out.'

'And that was the first time you'd met him?'

'The only time. Some of the things he told me ...' Clara sniffed. 'Well, they upset me. Things about how my dad never even spoke about me.' Her voice faded to almost nothing as she added, 'And how he tore up the cards I sent.'

He didn't speak – he didn't know what he could say to make the story any less tragic – but as tears spilled from Clara's eyes Joe drew his hand over his own cheeks. He was surprised to find that they, too, were damp.

Clara

Friday, December 22nd 2017

Clara pulled the neck of her chunky navy jumper over the bottom half of her face and blew into the fabric in a desperate attempt to warm up. The office felt colder than usual today. Goose pimples prickled her arms, making it increasingly hard for her to concentrate on the rows of figures on the spreadsheet in front of her.

'You look like you've lost a pound and found a penny.'

Clara turned to face her boss and waved the figures at her. 'You're not far off the mark,' she said with a vague smile. 'I'd hoped by some miracle the bank balance might have increased.'

'If it comes to it, I'll get my begging bowl out again,' Deirdre said. 'But I'm still hoping we might get chosen as the charity of the year at church.'

Clara's stomach flipped. Two days to go.

'I wonder if Joe knows anything about who's been selected for charity of the year,' Deirdre pondered out loud. 'And if not, maybe we could wheedle it out of his dad somehow.'

'I'm sure it'll be top secret,' Clara replied, although she'd been wondering the same thing. The suspense was unbearable. If they hadn't been selected it would be nice to be forewarned, and if they had been chosen she wanted to perfect her 'gracious and grateful, but not overbearing' look. Was it wrong to serious consider bribing a man of the cloth? Probably.

'There was an email about a fund we could apply for too,' Deirdre continued, waving her hand dismissively, as though she couldn't remember the details. She probably couldn't. Retaining facts wasn't Deirdre's strong point, which was why she'd handed so much of the day-to-day running of the club over to Clara. 'The one that gave us money for sports equipment in the summer. The deadline's in a few weeks' time, I think.'

Clara remembered the fund. The form had been ten pages long and mind-numbingly repetitive, and when the lady had finally phoned to say their claim had been successful, she'd spoken with such a strong lisp that Clara had had to strain to understand. It had taken a full five minutes for her to realise they were being given the money.

Clara closed down the spreadsheet she'd been scrutinising and pulled up the club's email account, scrolling through the list of emails. Most of them were advertising excruciatingly expensive resources that would be way out of The Club on the Corner's price range even if they weren't in their current predicament.

Clara saw a name she recognised alongside an email headed FUNDING DEADLINE and clicked through to the main body of the email. Scanning the text for details she caught a few key words and most importantly a date – December 23rd.

Her heart sank.

'Deirdre' she said, unable to keep the snappiness out of her tone. 'The deadline's tomorrow. I can't believe you didn't mention this sooner!'

'The emails are a shared responsibility,' Deirdre pointed out. 'You are supposed to read them too.'

'I know, I know,' Clara mumbled, sending the downloaded form to the printer. She had a feeling she'd be up until the early hours filling in all the necessary details. 'I've had a lot on my mind lately.'

'I know,' Deirdre replied. 'Joe, for starters.'

Clara turned sharply to face her boss. 'What do you mean?'

'You can't hide it from me, Clara. I might be falling

apart at the seams but I have eyes in my head and a working brain. It's obvious there's something between the two of you. The presents, for one thing, and a little dicky bird tells me you've been going on dates too.' She peered over the rims of her glasses. 'I'm disappointed you kept it to yourself after I as good as set the pair of you up,' she said, with a critical cluck of her tongue.

'A little dicky bird? Or a spy?'

Clara wondered who'd ratted on them. Manchester was a big city and although her and Joe hadn't been hiding, they hadn't been advertising it either. Most of their dates – or rather, non-dates – had been in the centre of town, well away from the prying eyes and wagging tongues of the kids who'd have a field day if they thought Joe and Clara were anything more than friends.

'Who is it that's been gossiping behind my back? Is it Shannon?'

She was the kid most likely to spread rumours, who loved having a juicy story to share. When nothing exciting happened locally, she'd resort to reiterating whatever scandal was plastered in the magazines, which-ever actress had been sleeping with their co-star or who'd been to Beverly Hills for a boob job. But she much preferred it when she could spread gossip about someone she knew. The more Clara thought about it, the more she was convinced it was her.

'It wasn't Shannon.'

'Well, if it wasn't her, then who? I've got a right to know if someone's spreading rumours about me behind my back. That's slander.' Clara folded her arms across her chest. 'I'm not moving a muscle until you tell me who you've been talking to.'

Deirdre took off her glasses and rubbed the lenses between the cotton folds of her top before squinting as she replaced them. 'Are you sure you want to know?'

Clara nodded. There was a sudden tension in the room.

'It wasn't Shannon who told me you two had been going out together.' The glint in her eyes as they connected with Clara's told her what she needed to know even before Deirdre confirmed it. 'It was Joe.'

Joe?' Clara could hardly believe it. 'What did he say?'

Deirdre revealed how Joe had given her all the details, from how Clara had taken a mince pie home for her mum after their night at the café to their tearful recent heart-to-hearts.

'So, now you see why I've not believed you when you say there's nothing going on. Why didn't you tell me? I'm happy for you both.'

'We're friends,' Clara responded, batting away the fluttering in her core. 'Neither of us is on the lookout for love.'

'But you're attracted to each other! So what's the problem?'

'Has he told you he likes me?' Clara asked, her reply coming a fraction too fast.

'He doesn't have to, it's obvious. He spoke to you about Michelle. He told me how you'd opened up to him, too. You'd never have spoken to him about your dad if you didn't trust him.'

Clara's heart plummeted. She couldn't deny it any more, not to Deirdre or to herself. She had developed feelings for Joe over the past month.

'You were right. He's a good guy.'

'At last!' Deirdre said, throwing her hands up in the air. 'Now can you tell him that, and put us all out of our misery? I was disappointed when the two of you hadn't got together when I locked you in.'

'I knew you did that on purpose!'

'You needed coaxing. I thought a night alone together would push things along. Although I wasn't keen the idea of you getting jiggy on the couch.'

'Deirdre ...' Clara warned.

'Oh, he told me nothing happened, although I think he'd have liked it to. That's why you've got to tell him how you feel. When love comes around, you've got to grab it with both hands.'

'Love? You're getting ahead of yourself, Deirdre.'

'Don't spoil my fun. I was planning on going to the Arndale to buy a hat for the wedding first thing tomorrow,' Deirdre replied, her voice dripping in sarcasm.

'He's taking me ice skating tomorrow,' Clara said. 'You know I don't like anything like that. I'm much happier with my feet firmly on the ground. I don't even like climbing on step-ladders, for crying out loud, so sliding about over some death trap masquerading as entertainment isn't really my idea of fun. I'm petrified.'

Deirdre stifled a laugh, badly.

Clara blinked. 'I don't know why you're laughing. I don't see you ice skating.'

Deirdre tutted. 'Can't these days, can I? Not with my dodgy knee. Back in the day I used to be pretty good at it. Even had my own skates. They were white as snow with silver laces. I was the envy of every girl at school.'

Clara rolled her eyes, not in the mood for one of her boss's tall tales.

'Ice skating's so romantic.'

'Not to me, it isn't. I'm going to make an idiot of myself in front of him, aren't I?' Clara sighed, defeatist.

'You know what, Clara? From seeing the two of you together, I really don't think that's possible. He told me he cried when you told him about your past. That's a huge deal, Clara. Joe never cries.'

'I never planned for this to happen. When we started the countdown he wanted to help me trust again and I wanted to bring the magic of Christmas back into his life. At first I didn't even realise why he hated December so much.'

Deirdre nodded knowingly. 'Michelle. Yes, that was horrendous. Knocked him sideways, unsurprisingly, and totally changed him. When he came here as a teenager he was really involved in the church. It was expected of him, of course, what with his dad being the minister and everything. But it was obvious that he had faith. He was radiant with it. Not in a preachy way, like some people are, but as though he had a quiet peace.' Her face fell. 'Then when he came back from university he was a different person altogether. He'd lost his sparkle. But since meeting you, it's like the old Joe's back. That's how I know you're meant to be. He's had a rough ride, but that doesn't stop him from being one of the nicest people I'm blessed to know. He's got a heart of gold, genuinely cares for everyone. Did he tell you about the food bank?'

'I've not spoken to him today,' Clara replied, realising how much she missed his company. She hoped he'd turn up soon. She had a hat and scarf set in her bag ready to give him as today's gift. She'd thought he could wear it tomorrow for their skating session.

'They told him that thanks to the donations from the club they've been able to give a Christmas food hamper to everyone on their list.' Deirdre beamed. 'Isn't that fantastic? Think of what a difference that'll make to some of the poorest families around here.'

Clara didn't have to think. Clara knew. She remembered the joy of the cardboard box wrapped in brightly coloured paper being delivered by a rosy-cheeked man with a bushy white beard. She'd thought it had been Santa himself, until he laughed at the suggestion.

'Just a few presents for you and your mam,' he'd said, and her mum had cried as she'd taken in the tinned meats and box of cream crackers, the chocolate coins and a bottle of posh fizzy apple juice.

'That's amazing,' Clara whispered. 'I'll have to tell him how grateful I am for all his hard work on the project.'

'You do that. And there's no time like the present. Look, he's here now.'

Clara looked out of the window and just caught a glimpse of Joe's dark coat before he disappeared from view and she heard the loud bang of the front door of the club.

'Clara?' Deirdre said, as she made her way towards the door.

'Yes?'

Deirdre's eyes twinkled wickedly. 'Tell him how you feel, and if he tries to kiss you, for heaven's sake let him.'

Clara didn't need telling. She'd already made up her mind. If Joe didn't try to kiss her, she was going to use her own initiative. No more time for game-playing. She was falling in love with Joe, and she wasn't going to hide it any longer.

Clara ran down the stairs faster than she'd have ever believed possible, to be met by a startled Joe looking up at her.

'Where's the fire?'

'No fire,' she replied, catching her breath. 'But I wanted to speak to you.'

'Is everything okay? It's not Deirdre, is it?'

Clara shook her head. 'Everything's fine.'

His face loosened, visibly relaxing in response to her words and Clara inhaled as she prepared herself to continue her spiel. She could taste polish in her mouth, smell the bitter scent lingering in her nostrils. It made her feel woozy and as she made her way down the final three steps of the staircase she took extra care, in case her dizziness caused her to fall.

'Are you sure about that?' He placed his hand on her arm, his skin dark next to the luminescent pale of hers.

She jolted, his touch pulling her back into the entrance hallway and into the present.

'Deirdre told me that you'd spoken to her. About us.'

Joe opened his mouth, but Clara continued talking. She needed to say this now, before she chickened out.

'It's fine. I don't blame you. There were times I was desperate to talk about the countdown too.' She thought back to the night she'd almost told her mum, but had forced herself to stay quiet rather than try to explain. 'The presents and trips started out as something fun and a good way to get to know each other better. It worked too. You did help me believe that not all men are wankers and I think I helped you find some of the joys of Christmas wrapped up in the tacky gifts. But then things started to change between us. I found myself looking forward to seeing you, and I'd be counting down until the moment you were due to walk through that door. I don't know how it's taken me so long to realise that it wasn't only because I wanted to give you a bobble hat or a tacky jumper, it was because I wanted to see you. You've been the best bit of my day, every day.'

Clara paused, running her tongue quickly over her lips. Her mouth was dry, but she'd come this far, she might as well take the last step.

'I'm falling in love with you, Joe.' Her voice cracked as a hint of a smile crept onto Joe's face. 'And I think that maybe you might be falling in love with me too.'

She waited for him to speak, a painful moment of silence until he vehemently shook his head.

'I'm not falling in love with you,' Joe said with a nervous laugh. 'It's too late for that. I'm already head over heels.'

Relief swamped Clara, and she let out a moan she didn't realise she'd been holding in.

'Come here,' he said, arms wide open.

She willingly fell into his embrace, her face pressed against the contours of his chest. His heart pulsed against her cheek as life coursed through him. The moment in his arms felt like forever.

He stepped back and looked at her – really looked at her – before drawing the pad of his thumb along her cheekbone. It was the most sensuous thing she'd ever experienced.

And when their lips finally connected, Clara allowed herself to fall into the moment. It felt so natural, tasting the sweetness of him. It wasn't like it had been with Dean, or with anyone else. With Joe it was better. Easier. More real. There was nothing to hold them back any more.

'Merry Christmas, Joe,' she giggled as they finally came apart for air.

'Merry Christmas, Clara.'

And as she kissed him again, and again, and again, the hat and scarf set she'd planned to give him remained, forgotten, in her bag.

Joe

Saturday, December 23rd 2017

'I should have worn something more suitable.' Clara looked doubtfully at her mid-thigh- length skirt, and Joe knew she was thinking it wasn't going to offer much protection if she ended up laid flat-out on the cold, smooth surface of the ice rink. 'At least I'm wearing leggings, I suppose,' she added. 'I could have been in tights and that would have been a disaster.'

'You'll be fine,' he reassured her. 'Once you get out there you'll be so busy zipping about that you won't even feel the cold.'

'Zipping about? You've obviously never seen me on ice skates. My balance is abysmal.' Clara shivered – or maybe shuddered, Joe wasn't sure. 'I have a hard enough time staying upright on solid ground, let alone on a sheet of ice.'

'It's not real ice,' Joe said. 'This plasticky stuff is much easier to stay upright on, I promise. And you've got me to look after you. Come on, let's get these boots hired. You'll feel more confident when you're out there.'

Joe hoped he was right. Clara had made it clear she wasn't entirely comfortable on skates, but this was their first proper date – not a non-date, a real, honest-to-goodness date – and he wanted it to be romantic. Ice skating was supposed to be the ultimate in Christmas romance, wasn't it? It was in all the Christmas films. Anyway, it was a good excuse for hand-holding and clinging on to each other.

The temporary outdoor ice rink was heaving with skaters; some who could give Torvill and Dean a run for their money, but most of them novices like Joe and Clara. Onlookers gathered to watch around the edge of the rink, mesmerised by the smooth gliding motion of the more eloquent ice dancers (and amused by the disgruntled expressions of those landing with a bump on the ice as they clumsily fell).

Clara jiggled as she waited in the queue, hands buried deep in the pockets of her cherry-red coat.

'We don't have to do this if you don't want to,' Joe offered, noticing her apprehension. 'We can do something you're more comfortable with. Although, you can hold on to me if you're nervous. I've not skated in a while, but I used to be pretty decent, once upon a time.'

'I don't need a knight in shining armour.'

Joe smiled. 'I know you don't. And I'm hardly riding in on a trusty stead. I thought it might reassure you, that's all.'

'I trust you,' she said, taking her hand out of her pocket and sliding it around his waist. The contact sent a fizz up his spine. 'Just promise you'll look after me?'

'Always,' he answered, slipping his arm around her and pulling her close.

'Good,' she said. 'Because we're nearly at the front of the queue, and if we're doing this, we're going to need boots.'

As a nervous smile flickered across her face, Joe hoped Clara wasn't doing this entirely for his sake. He wanted their first date to be exactly what Clara deserved – nothing less than perfect.

* * *

'I don't know if I can do this.' Clara pulled her boot away from the ice and back to the safety of the green carpet that lined the rink edge.

A child behind groaned in annoyance. Clara had already made to head out onto the ice three times and changed her mind at the last moment.

'Of course you can,' he said, calmly but firmly, taking Clara's hand in his.

Clara tentatively put first one foot and then the other onto the ice. Joe could feel the tension ripple through her body, her arms locked stiff.

'We'll take it slow,' he assured her, as she reached across his body and clung to his forearm. 'I promise, I won't let you go unless you want me to.'

By the time they were on their third snail's-paced lap of the rink, there was a fiery intent in Clara's eyes. Her grip on Joe hadn't loosened, but her knees were more relaxed. Her movement was somewhere between a skate and a walk and could never be described as elegant, or speedy. Nevertheless, Joe was immensely proud of her, for both her effort and for facing her fear head-on, and he told her as much.

Clara looked embarrassed. 'It's not much fun for you, babysitting me when you could be whizzing around.'

'It's a good excuse to hold your hand,' he smiled. Her fingers were icy but her palm was warm in his, and wafts of her heady vanilla scent surrounded her. She smelt like a cupcake shop. Super-sweet and delicious.

'I can always sit out for a while so you can go faster,' she said hopefully, and Joe laughed.

'Not a chance. If you sit out, I sit out. I want to spend time with my girlfriend.'

Clara grinned. 'And I want to spend time with my boyfriend.'

Joe leant down and softly kissed her forehead, not letting go for a second.

'Aren't we the most sickening couple?' he said, still not quite able to process that that's exactly what they were now – a couple.

'Totally,' she said, squeezing his hand.

It was then that Joe's nose twitched. He tried to avoid the sensation of the sneeze building within him, clamping his mouth shut and wriggling his nose like a bunny in the hope that it'd go away, but he couldn't stop it. Not a chance. As the roar escaped him, Joe instinctively let go of Clara's hand to bring his own hand to cover his mouth. The surprise of the action sent Clara off balance and she wobbled, falling almost in slow motion.

Clara looked tiny sitting there on the ice, her hands clasped tightly together in front of her chest. He knew it was to ensure no one skated over her fingers. She'd told Joe that was a phobia of hers more than once as they'd made their way around the rink.

'I'm sorry. Honestly, Clara, I'm so, so sorry. I didn't mean to let go, I did it without thinking ...'

And then Clara threw her head back and laughed.

'I know you didn't mean it, you fool,' she said, shaking

her head. Her furry black earmuffs bobbed. She reminded Joe of Minnie Mouse, but without the annoying whiney voice. 'But you're not much of a gentleman leaving me sat here. I'm going to end up with piles.' She held her hand out to him and Joe pulled her up, relieved not to be in her bad books, even though she was rubbing her coccyx. 'I bet I look like I've wet myself, don't I?' she said, trying to peer over her shoulder.

Joe looked. The part of her skirt that covered her bottom was definitely a darker shade than the rest of the denim.

'And now you're looking at my butt.' Joe was unsure if her tone was teasing or genuine disapproval.

'I was only looking because you asked.'

'Yeah right,' she said, giving him the side eye. Joe bet Minnie never looked at Mickey like that.

'It's true!' he spluttered. 'I'm not one of those men who objectifies women.'

'I know you're not,' she assured him.

'Good.'

Clara linked her arm through his. They moved cautiously together as a brass band played 'Silent Night'. The sound was haunting and melancholy. Spellbinding, Joe thought. Much like Clara herself.

'I think you enjoyed it,' she said, as they sailed into the barrier at the side of the rink.

'The skating?'

She raised her eyebrows salaciously and her mouth curled at the corners. 'Looking at my arse.'

Joe could feel his face flush. The truth was, he'd been struggling to banish thoughts of the gentle curve of Clara's arse ever since her fall.

'Ta da,' Clara said, as she bravely let go of the side of the rink for a fraction of a second. Her face was filled with terror, but she was moving, albeit slowly. When she'd negotiated a wobbly turn, her jagged movements seemingly using every bit of strength and courage she had, she grabbed back on to the side.

'Bravo!' Joe cheered, clapping his hands together. 'I knew you could do it.'

'I genuinely didn't think I could,' Clara said with a nervous laugh. 'I surprised myself there.'

'You should be really proud. Skating scares you, but you still had a go. "Feel the fear and do it anyway".'

'I could barely move,' Clara admitted. 'But I did it, didn't I?'

She was still shaking. It could be because of the Manchester temperature – never warm, especially in the middle of December – but Joe had a sneaky suspicion it was more to do with her nerves than the chill in the air.

'You did it,' Joe said. 'You're incredible.'

And as he wrapped his arms around her waist and spun her around, he thought that right now he really must be the luckiest man on the planet.

Clara

Sunday, December 24th 2017

Joe and Clara stood in the grounds of St Michael's church, the winding pathway leading up to the arched entrance. It was enchantingly pretty as the light from inside the church radiated out through the stained-glass windows, the bright colours glowing with festive positivity through the darkness.

'My head's buzzing,' Clara admitted. 'I can't stop wondering whether The Club on the Corner will be the charity of the year. Do you think we've got a chance?'

'A great chance. But I'm preparing for a headache after this too,' Joe laughed, 'from the noise. The nativity service never goes to plan, but it's always good fun. The little kids get so into it.'

Two excitable girls ran past, their lacy white dresses flowing behind them as coronets of tinsel crowned their angel costumes.

Clara smiled. After her disastrous outing as a mooing sheep, she'd been an angel herself in numerous nativity plays. She'd hated the feeling of the tinsel scratching against her forehead. One year she'd itched so much that the headmistress had quietly approached her mum to ask if she'd checked for head lice recently. Her mum had been mortified. The year after that she'd been cast as a carol singer, which only required wearing her usual coat, scarf and hat. Far less irritating, but rather dull.

'They look cute.'

A boy Clara assumed was a king from his pointed crown (a band of cardboard covered with tin foil) was walking obediently alongside his parents, clutching the wrapped box he was holding as though it was a genuine treasure.

'That's Stanley,' Joe said, raising his hand to wave at the young boy. Stanley's face erupted into an enormous grin, but he didn't take his hands off the box, carefully protecting the block of gold he had to present to Baby Jesus. 'His dad is the choir master.'

'There are more people here than I expected,' Clara observed. They were milling around chatting, exchanging cards and presents and hugging each other, filled with the festive spirit. 'Are there always this many?'

'On Christmas Eve there are,' Joe replied, 'but most

Sundays it's noticeably quieter. There's a strong community, and the members of the congregation are really committed, but Dad wishes more of the people here tonight would come regularly.'

'I suppose people like the idea of being in a church for the big events. I wouldn't say I'm a Christian but churches are so calming. I can see why people choose to get married there, even if they don't believe in God.'

'I can't imagine getting married anywhere other than in a church,' Joe said.

'I can't imagine your dad would let you, anyway. He'd want to be the one to marry you, wouldn't he?'

'Yeah. I don't think he'd trust anyone else to run such an important ceremony. Apparently, when I was christened he was a nervous wreck letting someone else take the lead. And that was his best friend from college, my godfather! He likes things to go according to plan.'

Joe was interrupted by the first peal of church bells calling out into the early-evening dusk, their descending scales the very essence of a traditional Christmas.

'Is that our call to go in?'

Joe nodded. 'Brace yourself,' he grinned, linking his arm through Clara's. 'They don't say "you've not seen a nativity service until you've seen a St Michael's nativity service" for nothing.'

* * *

'Hark the herald angels sing, glory to the new-born king!'

The dulcet tones of Stanley's dad's choir might have been well-versed, but the rest of the congregation were far less tuneful. Clara had never heard so many out-of-pitch voices, at least, not since the audition rounds of this year's *X Factor*.

'They're doing well,' she whispered, nodding towards the group of angels gathered in front of the font. They resembled statues with their heads held high and still, hands pressed together in prayer. 'That one at the front can't even be at school yet.'

The tiny girl had tumbling blonde ringlets framing her chubby face. She was the image of a cherub in a Renaissance painting, unlike the older girl to her right, who had been shoehorned into an ice-blue satin dress that Clara recognised as being the signature outfit of Elsa from *Frozen*. Her face was hard and fierce, as though she'd rather be anywhere but up on that stage.

'They're doing fantastically,' Joe agreed, 'but the real fun starts when the animal parade gets going.'

Clara had heard about the live nativity, and although she'd never been to one before she had clear expectations. A donkey, definitely. Maybe a couple of sheep from the nearby city farm, too. After all, shepherds were a key feature of the Christmas story, as the number of children with tea towels tied around their head attested. She was looking forward to it.

Everyone shushed as a confident teenager stepped up to the lectern to tell the next chapter of the Christmas story. A wave of peace washed over Clara as she listened to the familiar verses, and although she wasn't religious she was glad she'd agreed to come to the service to represent the youth club.

The church was packed, just as Joe had predicted, with fold-out emergency chairs being brought in for latecomers to perch on. The flickering of the tall white candles that flanked the altar went some way to disguising the chill in the air of the old building.

The story played out before her, with 'Mary' whipping a baby Jesus (who looked remarkably similar to the Baby Annabel Clara had seen repeatedly advertised on TV in the weeks leading up to Christmas) from behind a strategically placed bale of hay to an enthusiastic round of applause from the congregation.

'And on that note, it's time to bring the animals to the stable to celebrate the arrival of Our Lord,' said Reverend Smith, a look of mild panic registering on his face. 'Let's hope our furry friends are better behaved than they were last year,' he added.

'What happened last year?' Clara whispered, as people craned their necks to get a better view.

'There was a bit of trouble between a Chihuahua and a Great Dane,' Joe said, biting down on his lip. 'There's Scooby over there, look,' he said, nodding in the direction of a frazzled-looking woman struggling to pull an enormous mutt towards the front of the church. Clara had never seen a Great Dane in real life before, but Scooby was bigger than she'd imagined, more like a Shetland pony than a dog.

Clara raised her hand to her mouth. 'Was the Chihuahua alright?' The lack of handbag-sized dogs at St Michael's tonight was mildly perturbing. Could Scooby have eaten the miniature canine in one mouthful?

'Was the Chihuahua alright?' Joe repeated with a chuckle. 'Oh yeah, Petal was fine. It was poor Scooby who came off worse, dopey thing that he is. He's blind in one eye, so wasn't ready when Petal decided to start biting his leg. She drew blood and everything. It caused quite a stir.'

'I can imagine.'

Clara scanned the animals on the stage. There was a dapple-grey donkey with a doleful expression on his face, probably wondering what all the fuss was about, but the majority of the animals were domestic pets.

Clara highly doubted there were four pugs present at the virgin birth, let alone the dirt-brown snake that Leon, a regular at youth club, had around his neck. It gave her the heebie-jeebies. She'd never like snakes.

Once all the animals were in the spotlight, Reverend Smith invited everyone to stand to sing the final carol of the night, 'Away in a Manger', and although the vocal abilities of the church-goers hadn't improved since their earlier efforts, Clara found it especially moving to see the children dressed up, as the familiar Christmas carol echoed around the 200-year-old church. The skin on the back of her neck rose into goose bumps beneath her scarf.

But it was when Joe laced his fingers through hers at the start of the third and final verse, Clara's goose bumps multiplied. It was as though every hair on her body stood to attention, and she was glad she hadn't removed her bobble hat. If she had she'd probably look as if she was being electrified. She was sure a million volts were surging through her body.

She squeezed tightly, marvelling at how right it felt to have his hand in hers. She took in the weave of their grip, their entwined hands reminding her of a piano keyboard as his black skin contrasted with the pale tone of her own.

*   *   *

Chaos ensued as a gaggle of proud parents scrambled forward to take photos of their offspring in their costumes, and dogs who'd had enough of being the centre of attention began yapping. The large ginger cat belonging to Joe's family had made himself comfortable, though, snuggling into the bed of hay where Baby Annabel had been earlier.

Joe's hand pulled away from Clara's as he bent down to pick up a hymn sheet, which had fallen to the floor. She was surprised by the overwhelming sense of longing that filled her, the desire to reach hurriedly out and take his warm hand back in her own. She hadn't been looking for love. She hadn't even wanted it, but somehow it seemed to have crept up on her, muddled in with tinsel and Gluhwehn and Christmas carols.

After everyone had got their pictures to preserve this moment in history (or more likely to be uploaded online and never looked at again once the 'likes' stopped coming in), Joe's father took his place at the pulpit and, with a look of quiet relief, sent the children back to their parents.

'I'm sure you'll all agree that the tradition of the St Michael's nativity service on Christmas Eve is a very special one. It's an opportunity for our community to come together and celebrate Jesus's birth, just as those present in the stable did over two thousand years ago. New life is worthy of the biggest celebration, and for many of us in the twenty-first century Christmas is the biggest annual celebration of them all. It's become a month-long party of rich foods, alcohol, lavish gifts and excess, and with so many modern distractions it can be easy to forget what it's all about. That's why we take this opportunity to share the charity we'll be supporting throughout the next year, as a timely reminder of the message Jesus taught us – to love one another. The charity St Michael's will be working with from January is one that is very dear to my heart. The committee voted unanimously in favour of supporting this safe, inspiring organisation, which has benefited many people in this church. It gives me great pleasure to announce our charity of the year for 2018 is The Club on the Corner youth group.'

Clara gasped.

Everyone was applauding, and the woman who worked at the post office patted Clara's back in congratulation.

'Did you know we'd been chosen?'

Joe's expression said it all, and the soft nod of his head confirmed to Clara what she already knew. 'I only knew for definite this morning. Dad says people were really enthusiastic about it. We've had a few parishioners express an interest in volunteering to help too, including the lady who runs the Sunday School. Everyone wants to help us, Clara. People didn't realise how desperate things had got.'

Clara cupped her hand over her mouth, unable to take it all in.

'So as well as the fundraising, people are going to give up their time?'

'They'll need to go through the necessary checks, obviously. But yes, so many people have offered their services. Stanley's dad even said he'd start up a rock choir, if there was enough interest. The choir at church is mainly made up of older members of the congregation, and I think he's hoping this might bring in a bit of new blood.'

'Rock choir? Singing "Bohemian Rhapsody" and that sort of thing?'

Joe laughed. 'Well, I think he was going to try and keep it as modern as possible to attract as many of the kids as he can, but yes. Popular songs that they all know, and then they can sing at events. It's another way to fundraise and keep the club in the public eye.'

'I can't believe it.'

'You'd better believe it,' Joe answered, 'because it's happening. And this is only the beginning. Next year is going to be a big one for The Club on the Corner.'

'I hope you're right,' Clara grinned, finally allowing herself to believe that maybe this was the glimmer of hope they'd been waiting for. 'I want us to give those kids what they deserve. You've seen them, Joe. They're a special bunch.'

'They are,' he agreed. 'I didn't realise how attached I'd get to them all, but I can't imagine not being part of the old place now.'

Clara swallowed. 'So you'll keep volunteering in the new year?' Her voice cracked as she spoke.

'I'm going nowhere. In fact, I'm thinking of going to college and training to be a youth worker. I'm the happiest I've ever been in my life, and that's thanks to that club. The kids, Deirdre, you ...' His voice tailed off and Clara noticed his Adam's apple bob as he mimicked her own gulp.

'Me?'

'Yes, you.'

'Come here,' she said, arms wide.

And as she enveloped Joe in a hug, the bells rang out their song. It was a song of peace, and joy, and love.

* * *

'Thank you. Thank you so, so much. You don't know

what a difference this is going to make to the club, and to all the children.' Clara knew she was rambling, but she was flooded with gratitude that just had to escape.

'I know first hand what a wonderful place The Club on the Corner is,' Reverend Smith said. He seemed mildly bemused by Clara's excitement. 'Joe's found friendships that have lasted into adulthood there, and now it's Simone's turn to benefit. It means a lot to us as parents to know that she's somewhere safe and warm.'

Clara almost laughed. The Club on the Corner could never be described as warm.

'You hear such horror stories about kids that have nowhere to go, and we at St Michael's believe that by supporting you and Deirdre and enabling you to have more children on site that there will be a noticeable drop in petty crime. It will have a positive impact on everyone, not just those that use the club. That said, it'll be great to see it full to bursting again. It's a crying shame, that enormous building going to waste because of staff ratios. That's why our first mission is to help find volunteers. Hopefully we'll be able to fund qualified staff to assist you and Deirdre too, in the long run.'

'I'm going to phone Deirdre and let her know,' Clara said in awe. 'It's everything we've been dreaming of. I'll go outside to do it. It's pretty noisy in here.'

People were in the festive mood as they gladly sipped

their Irish coffees, and as Clara glided through the crowd – floated, almost – she couldn't keep the dopey grin off her face.

Pulling her phone from her coat pocket, she found Deirdre's number and pressed the call button. It rang only twice before she heard the familiar voice at the end of the line.

'Hello?'

'Deirdre, its Clara.'

'Oh, hello love. Happy Christmas Eve!'

Clara wasn't sure when that had become a thing, but she repeated it anyway, 'Happy Christmas Eve. And it really is happy. I've got something amazing to tell you!'

'You don't need to tell me, Clara. It's brilliant, and I'm over the bloody moon for you, I really am.'

'Isn't it fantastic? It's not just me that you need to be over the moon for, though. Don't you mean you're over the moon for both of us?'

'Oh, I'm happy for Joe too, obviously. That poor boy's been through the mill and he deserves all the happiness he can get. You two were made for each other, you really were.'

It slowly dawned on Clara that Deirdre and her were talking at crossed purposes. Her boss didn't have a clue about The Club on the Corner being the charity of the year. She thought Clara had rung to talk about developments between her and Joe!

'No, no,' Clara interjected quickly, before Deirdre had her and Joe married off with two point four children, a house in the country and a Labradoodle for good measure. 'I didn't ring to talk about me. I rang to talk about the youth club. I've been at the church service at St Michael's, and Reverend Smith announced his charity of the year at the end of the service.'

She caught her breath.

'And?' Deirdre asked.

'And it's us, it's The Club on the Corner. They're going to help us find volunteers, and get new resources and hopefully fund some trained staff too.'

Deirdre gasped down the phone, and Clara felt a tingling around her eyes.

'Are you sure?' Deirdre said finally. 'You didn't mishear?'

'Of course I'm bloody sure!' Clara almost shouted, before feeling immediately guilty for swearing in the church grounds. 'He came to talk to me about it afterwards, and Joe said there are people at church keen to get involved. He said the choirmaster wants to start a rock choir. Can you imagine how much Shannon and her posse would love that?'

'I can't believe it. That's amazing.'

'I can't believe you thought I was ringing about me

and Joe,' she said, shaking her head despite there being no chance of Deirdre seeing it from the warmth of her front room.

'That's just as amazing as the news about being selected as the charity of the year,' Deirdre said.

'Stop it,' Clara said, embarrassed.

'No, I won't stop it. Admitting you've found someone you want to play a bigger part in your life isn't a weakness. Recognising that they make everything that bit brighter is a strength.'

'Thank you.' It was all that Clara could manage. She felt surprisingly choked up by her boss's honesty.

'Joe's not like Dean, and he's not like your dad. Don't let him get away, not if he makes you happy.'

'I won't,' Clara whispered.

'There's a good girl. Now, I might treat myself to a port and lemon to celebrate, so you get back to that young man of yours, alright?'

Clara smiled. 'I will. Night night, Deirdre. Enjoy your drink.'

'Night, love.'

Spinning on her heels, Clara turned to face the bright lights of the church.

And there, bold as brass in his ridiculous Michelin-man coat, was Dean Harford.

* * *

Clara's eyes closed as she exhaled in frustration. How typical that he'd be here to put a dampener on what was turning out to be the best Christmas Eve she'd experienced in her life. And wearing that shit coat, too. She wished Joe was out here with her, making her laugh by blasting out the chorus to 'Stay Another Day'.

'Clara.' Dean greeted her with a nod, his hands buried deep into his pockets and his eyes only just visible through the tufts of grey fur that trimmed his hood. 'I'm glad I caught you. I've been wanting to speak to you. I tried to when I saw you at the Trafford Centre, but you ran off.'

'Dean,' she replied, offering a courtesy she didn't feel he deserved.

'I got your letter. The one asking about tickets for a match for that football fan at the youth club. Jordan, did you say his name was?'

'Oh,' she stumbled. 'I'd forgotten about that.'

'It was in with a sack of fan mail,' Dean said, with a shrug of the shoulders that Clara knew was meant to look nonchalant. He was anything but, and Clara highly doubted he had a sack full of letters from his adoring public. Two appearances for the Man United reserves back in the day and now part time in the lower leagues.

He was hardly a superstar. 'I recognised your writing straight away. Thought it might be a love letter at first.'

'Cut to the chase, Dean.' She fought off the impulse to roll her eyes. He was so big-headed. Love letter. As if. He'd have loved that, having her scurry back to him. Well, if he'd come here to ask for her back because things had gone tits-up with Bella, then he could think again. Joe was ten times the man Dean ever was. More than ten times the man. Twenty times. A *million* times.

'I've sorted it.'

Clara's spine set rigid as she cocked her head. 'Pardon?'

'I've sorted it. The tickets for the big match.'

He looked delighted with himself and if he didn't have something Clara so desperately wanted she'd have swung for him. He looked so smug. So *punchable*.

'You'd better be telling the truth, Dean,' she warned. 'You've messed me around for so long that it's what I expect of you. But Jordan? He doesn't deserve to be dragged into your little games.'

'It's no game,' he said defensively, producing an envelope from his pocket. 'Pulled a few strings, didn't I? Got in touch with a few contacts from back in the day who put in a good word with the guy in charge of the community scheme. Got VIP tickets for the kids, and a tour of the ground. They might get to meet some of the squad too, if they're lucky, but he couldn't promise that. They've got a strict match-day routine. Anyway, it's all in the letter.'

Clara took the envelope he was offering and pulled out the letter. It was on thick paper, she noted, good quality. As she unfolded it she noticed it was headed too, the famous red and yellow crest emblazoned at the top of the page like the badge of honour it was for so many supporters the world over. She held the letter close to her face in order to read it in the darkness of the winter evening. Everything he'd said was true.

'I can't believe it,' she said, folding the precious letter and putting it carefully into her pocket. 'You really did sort it.'

She couldn't wait to tell Jordan, to see the joy on his face when he realised he'd be going to a game at Old Trafford. The Stretford End might only be a few miles down the road, but it was a world away from Jordan's reality.

'Thanks, Dean.'

'I'm not all bad. I know things got messy towards the end, when I was seeing both you and Bella ...'

Clara held her hand up to cut him off. 'I don't want to hear it, Dean. I'm very grateful for the tickets, but I don't want to hear your excuses. Our relationship is in the past. Ancient history. You've moved on, and so have I.'

Dean's mouth gaped open. 'You're seeing someone? The guy you were with the other night?'

Clara almost laughed. He'd hate that she wasn't moping over him. Poor Dean and his over-inflated ego.

'That's right,' she said, with a perky smile.

'Oh.' His shoulders visibly sank, even though they were smothered by the padding of his coat. 'That's nice.'

'It is, isn't it?' Clara replied, almost skipping back towards the church. 'Thanks for the tickets, Dean.'

The more she thought about it, the more grateful she was that Dean was the past and Joe was her future. Not only for Christmas, but for good.

* * *

The crowds had thinned out considerably. Two girls were playing chase in the aisles. Their gauzy costumes flowing behind them made her heart race with nerves, especially when they neared the candles. One flyaway spark and the whole place would be alight – there was that much acrylic in the pure-white angel costumes they were wearing. Deirdre would have gone nuts, with her health-and-safety hat on.

Clara was surprised to see it was almost seven o'clock. No wonder people had all dashed off. The kids would be desperate to get home, keen to leave a mince pie for

Santa and a carrot for his red-nosed helper, and the parents were probably geeing themselves up for a late night, regretting that they didn't start wrapping earlier in the month.

Joe was collecting the now-crumpled hymn sheets from the shelves on the back of the pews. Clara felt a warm rush at the sight of him.

'Joe!' she called, her voice echoing around the almost-empty space.

'You're back,' he said. 'I thought you'd been ravished by a bear, you were gone that long.'

'There aren't many bears roaming the streets of suburban Manchester.' Clara slipped into the row behind Joe, scooping up the flyaway papers. 'I got through to Deirdre, though. In the nick of time too, I think. She was about to start on a bottle of port.'

Joe grinned. 'Good for her. I might join her in raising a glass myself when I've finished up here. Although Billy's with his family tonight, understandably, and I've never been one for drinking alone ...'

'Is that an invite?'

'If you want it to be.'

Clara locked eyes with Joe.

'I want it to be.'

Joe smiled shyly at the floor.

'Then let's get this place tidied up. There's a brand-new bottle of vodka at home waiting to be cracked open and it's got our name on it.'

Clara moved faster at the thought.

*   *   *

Clara hadn't seen his flat before and was curious about what it would be like. He wasn't the sort to hoard, but he didn't strike her as a minimalist either. He wasn't bothered about big name brands, at least not if his clothes were anything to go by. Not because he was scruffy – if anything, he was leaning towards smart – but he didn't swan around in expensive designer labels. He wasn't like Dean, thankfully.

Dean! She hadn't told Joe about the tickets.

'I almost forgot to tell you,' she began. 'I saw Dean at the church.'

Joe snorted. 'Me too. He was hard to miss in that coat. He took up half a pew.'

Clara wondered if Joe might just be a teensy bit jealous.

'Don't be too hard on him. He's used his contacts to get the kids from the club tickets for the match at Old Trafford.'

'Don't be too hard on him? After the way he treated you? You're obviously a better person than I am.'

Clara shook her head. 'I'm really not. He was a total twat when we were together, but I was too blind to see it at the time. I thought I loved him. Maybe I did. I'm not so sure these days.' Once she'd started scrutinising the relationship she'd remembered more and more things that he'd done which had annoyed her. The piles of dirty clothes in the corner of the bedroom. Picking the fluff out of his belly button as they watched TV. Using the last of the toilet roll without replacing it. And the milk. On their own they were irritating but harmless enough habits, but even so Clara was glad she didn't have to put up with that on a daily basis any more.

'Love's funny like that,' he said, pouring a generous slosh of vodka into a stubby glass. 'I often wonder how I'd have felt about Michelle if she'd lived. People say we were this golden couple, as though we were born to be together. The truth is, we were little more than kids, and it was a long time ago. I've changed a lot over the years. Would we have drifted apart over time?' He shrugged. 'I guess I'll never know.'

Clara gladly took the glass, knocking back the neat alcohol with one deft flick of the wrist. Her throat warmed as the liquid took hold, although she couldn't hold back the wince. It was alright when you were actually knocking it back, but the aftertaste? That was vile.

'She was lucky to have you, even if it wasn't for long,' she said.

Joe smiled. 'You think so?'

'Definitely. When you started helping at the club I was worried I'd feel like an outsider. You and Deirdre have known each other for so long. I felt like I wouldn't be needed any more.'

Clara's head was swimming, and not only from the potent vodka.

'You know that's not true,' Joe said gently, reaching out and placing his hand on hers. The contact was electrifying. 'That place would have closed down by now if it wasn't for all your efforts. Without your hard work and commitment, there'd be no club.'

'I'm sure Deirdre would have found a way to keep the place going,' Clara blushed, although deep down she knew what Joe was saying was right. Deirdre thought the world revolved around the club, but when it came to business and finances she was well out of her depth. 'That place is her life.'

'Yours too,' he said, swilling his drink around in the glass.

'The kids deserve it. That's why I'm so thrilled that Dean managed to sort out those tickets, because the memories from a day like that will last a lifetime. That's what they need, people to offer them opportunities to try new things. It's an important part of growing up.'

He nodded. 'And hopefully the church will be able to help with that, too. The people at St Michael's are really great, Clara, and they genuinely want to breathe new life into the club. Next year is going to be amazing.'

'Amazing for the club, yes. But what about you? What do you want next year? Any resolutions, or goals, or dreams?'

'Just the one,' he said, laying his glass to rest on a small, circular table before sitting down next to Clara on the settee.

'Oh?' she answered, looking up at him through her lashes.

'I want to spend as much time as possible kissing the woman who's brought me back to life.'

Clara's eyebrows rose so high they almost shot off her face altogether.

'That doesn't sound too difficult.' Her voice sounded husky to her ears. 'But why wait until next year?'

'That's a very good question.'

Clara inhaled as Joe pulled her close. As their lips met, she relaxed. Things were looking up, for her, for Joe and for The Club on the Corner.

Epilogue

Joe

Monday, December 24th 2018

Delicate flakes of pure-white snow swirled on the evening air like glitter in a decorative snow globe. Joe was thoroughly glad of his hat, scarf and gloves. Even as well-wrapped as he was his teeth were chattering.

'Isn't it beautiful!' Clara sang, holding her arms out and spinning, scrunching up her face as the icy flakes landed on her cheeks. 'It's really Christmas now.'

Her love of the season was catching, and Joe had to admit that this Christmas had been his best ever – and that was all down to throwing himself into it with abandon. Not that he'd had much choice. Clara had been begged to decorate the flat from the middle of November, and although he'd grumbled, he had to agree the flashing lights, swathes of tinsel and fragile coloured baubles brought a sense of cheer to the place. It was totally different to the flat he'd been renting a year ago. The place he and Clara had now was beautiful – high ceilings, large windows that flooded the room with light even in the winter, and fresh, neutrally painted walls, which were the perfect gallery space for the framed photos of the two of them together that Clara insisted on putting up on show. Selfies of the two of them enjoying walks in the Peak District, photos of their city break to Barcelona and one of the two of them proudly cutting the ribbon at the grand relaunch of The Club on the Corner one crisp September afternoon in pride of place next to three photos from last year's countdown – one from the newspaper, another from their trip to *The Nutcracker*, and the photo booth polaroid. The little record player Joe had given Clara last Christmas sat on the sideboard, an ever-growing collection of vinyl stacked haphazardly alongside it.

So much had changed for Joe this year. A new home, a newfound happiness, and even a new job as he'd given up working at the hardware shop and become a paid employee at The Club on the Corner.

'It really is. It's perfect.'

'I can't believe a year's passed since the last nativity service,' Clara replied wistfully. 'Who'd have thought we'd have made so many changes to the club?'

Joe smiled. It had more than changed; it was like a completely different place. The building was much the same from the outside, except for the freshly painted doors, no longer the moss-green they'd once been, but now a vivid, inviting red. Being grade-two listed they'd always known the changes they could make to the building's exterior were limited.

The interior was where the real magic had happened. The flaky paint in the main hall was no more, now replaced by a fresh, bright magnolia shade. New curtains hung in the windows, thick velvet material, which added an illustrious glamour to the beautiful old building. The slate-grey shade Clara had chosen perfectly complemented the lead-work. The pipework had been modernised too, making the heating much more energy efficient and in turn keeping the large rooms far warmer than Joe, Clara and Deirdre were used to. Deirdre had even been wearing a short-sleeved blouse last week, something that never happened even in the height of summer, so it was quite the topic of conversation for her to be baring her flesh in the depths of a Manchester winter. The games room had been revived to its former glory, no longer a store room, now a space to be used and enjoyed.

'One hundred members ...' Clara smiled. 'One hundred young people who're able to access the club and everything it's got to offer. We'd never have been able to do it without the help of your dad and the congregation.'

'You'd have found another way, I'm sure. You're innovative like that.'

Clara shook her head. 'I would have tried my best, but it's made such a difference. I'm feeling quite depressed about it being the end of our year as St Michael's chosen charity.'

'I hope they've voted for the food bank,' Joe answered, hands shoved firmly into the depths of his pockets. 'They work so hard and rely entirely on volunteers, and sadly it's many of the families of the kids at club who'll be benefitting from that, too.'

'Oh, I know,' Clara said. 'They deserve it. They're changing people's lives. Families shouldn't be scraping by in this day and age. That's why I'm proud we've established a link with them, even if it does mean I have to liaise with Miranda.'

'The community's really pulled together. Everyone looking out for each other, everyone willing to help each other out. It's made the whole area feel much more positive.'

Clara laced her arm though Joe's as they walked through the archway to the church grounds. 'You're right. Things seem so much brighter when you're with people who want the same as you do.'

Joe's heart raced with anticipation. There might be shepherds and angels and a riot of children dressed as farmyard animals in readiness for the service, but they were blending into the background. All he could see was Clara. His girlfriend. His partner in everything. The woman he loved.

Lowering himself to the ground, trying desperately not to gasp as his knee flattened the inch-high layer of snow that covered the winding pathway, Joe pulled the box he'd been so carefully guarding out of his pocket. Snapping it open with a loud click, he smiled as Clara brought her hand up to her mouth in realisation, her eyes brimming with tears, which he hoped were of the happy variety.

'Clara O'Connell,' he began, swallowing down the lump in his throat. 'I never believed I'd meet someone as wonderful as you. Someone so kind, so spirited, so funny ... you're the best thing in my world, and I never want to have a time where you're not in my life.' He paused, taking in the nervous smile on her face. Lit by the hazy brightness of the lamplight and framed by the falling flakes of white, she looked more beautiful to Joe than she ever had before. 'I want our future to be together, for us to tackle anything life throws at us head-on.' He beamed, not quite able to believe he was about to say the next eight words, words he'd practised in his mind many times over the last fortnight. 'I love you, Clara. Will you marry me?'

Her face crumpled as she nodded, and Joe instinctively pulled himself back to his feet before wrapping her tightly to his chest. He inhaled the snow-laden air, fresh and crisp, and delighted as she whispered in his ear. 'Yes. Yes, yes, yes.'

She squealed as he lifted her feet from the ground and twirled her around, much to the glee of the families making their way towards the church.

'Stop!' she giggled, 'You're making me dizzy!' Joe carefully brought his fiancée back down to earth and removed the thick woolly mitten from her left hand to place the diamond solitaire on her third finger. He felt like the luckiest man alive.

'It's flawless,' she said, bringing her hand closer to her face to examine the stone. 'So delicate.'

'I'm pleased you like it,' he grinned. 'I wasn't sure whether I was better to choose one or to pop the question first and then go and choose one together.'

'You did it the right way,' she said. 'And it's the perfect choice. The only trouble is, my hand's freezing now, but I can't put my mittens on because I want to be able to see it!'

'Then we'd better get inside quick,' Joe said, folding his hand around hers. The metal of the ring against his skin was unfamiliar, yet right.

They skipped through the snow, giggling like giddy schoolchildren, until they reached the shelter of the church. They saw some familiar faces, Jordan and Cally, who had recently started dating themselves, Billy, Emma and little Roman, dressed as a shepherd, and Deirdre – all watching on with interest at their uncontrollable giggles.

'Are we going to tell them we're engaged?' Clara asked quietly, once more admiring her new fingerwear.

'After the service?' Joe suggested. 'I want to enjoy it being between us for a little bit longer.'

'Me too. It's the best kind of secret, and the minute we tell people they'll be asking when the wedding is.'

'When is it?' Joe asked, a flirtatious glint in his eye.

'Soon,' she replied with a grin. 'Maybe in the spring, if your dad can fit us in?'

Joe couldn't keep the smile from his face. Spring sounded good. Really good. 'Family perk, surely.'

And as they walked down the central aisle of the church, Joe savoured the thought that this was the beginning of the next chapter, one where he and Clara would take on the world together. He couldn't wait to see what their future would bring, because he knew everything would be wonderful. It was bound to be, because they had each other.

Katey's Advent Calendar of Thanks

Sending enormous thanks and sparkly Christmas greetings to –

HarperCollins/HarperImpulse and other Brilliant Bookish Folk

1. My editor and friend Charlotte Ledger, for giving me the opportunity to write the Christmas novel I've always wanted to.
2. Publicist Samantha Gale, for tirelessly shouting about HarperImpulse.
3. Books Covered, for yet more beautiful art work to grace my covers. You're brilliant.
4. Mary Jayne Baker, Vivienne Dacosta, Emma Finlayson-Palmer, Jenni Nock, Emily Royal and Katy Wheatley for being Joe and Clara's first readers and offering suggestions and solutions. Katy is also responsible for the fortune-telling fish.

5. Phillipa Ashley, Alice Broadway, Rachel Burton, Brigid Coady, Eve Devon, Miranda Dickinson, Kat French, Carmel Harrington, Lynsey James, Debbie Johnson, Erin Lawless, Rachael Lucas, Cressida McLaughlin, Rebecca Pugh, Keris Stainton, Lorraine Wilson and too many other writers to name for the friendship and encouragement.

6. The Wordcount Warriors and Beta Buddies for holding me accountable and being genuinely lovely people.

7. NaNoWriMo. I wrote the first half of this book for the 2016 challenge.

8. My wonderful agent Julia Silk for believing in me and my writing. Let's take the world by storm!

9. The blogging community for being so supportive of my books. What you do for authors is nothing short of incredible.

10. Everyone who has bought this book – I hope you've enjoyed reading Joe and Clara's story as much as I enjoyed writing it. If you are able to make time to write a short review online, that would be greatly appreciated.

Family and Friends

11. Zachary, for being the best Christmas gift I've ever been given and for making me smile every day.

12. David, even though you never did bring me that vegan rocky road when I was editing.
13. Clarence, for being the best feline friend.
14. My amazing mum, for telling me I can do anything I put my mind to.
15. Donna Brown, for showing me residential Manchester.
16. Laura Dean, for keeping me company as I walked Manchester's backstreets in the name of research.
17. Pippa Jackson, Jenny King, Steve North, Wendy North, Lydia Peto, Holly Raistrick, Fran Rhodes and Rachael Woodcock for understanding that when I don't message back immediately it's not because I don't care, it's because I'm writing. Thank you for not giving up on me.
18. Anna Tomlinson for the signed Patrick Ness book.
19. The friends I made at Monmouth Methodist Church Youth Club back in my teens. The strawberry laces mention is for you.

Special Places and Influences
20. Everyone who shared a rubbish joke on Facebook or Twitter, especially Carolyn Ward for Clara's favourite about 'Boo-bees'.
21. The Night and Day Café on Oldham Street in Manchester, where I wrote some of this novel on my research trips.

22. Salford Lads' Club, for being the inspiration for The Club on the Corner.
23. Bastille, Johnny Marr, Man Made and Frank Turner for providing the music that was my backing track as I wrote this book.
24. Lotus Biscoff spread. Enough said.

Merry Christmas, everyone!

Katey Lovell, Sheffield, August 2017